JUDGEMENT DAY
AN EDDIE VIRGO THRILLER

STEVE SHEFFIELD

INKUBATOR
BOOKS

Published by Inkubator Books
www.inkubatorbooks.com

Copyright © 2025 by Steve Sheffield

Steve Sheffield has asserted his right to be identified as the author of this work.

ISBN (eBook): 978-1-83756-541-2
ISBN (Paperback): 978-1-83756-542-9
ISBN (Hardback): 978-1-83756-543-6

JUDGEMENT DAY is a work of fiction. People, places, events, and situations are the product of the author's imagination. Any resemblance to actual persons, living or dead is entirely coincidental.

No part of this book may be reproduced, stored in any retrieval system, or transmitted by any means without the prior written permission of the publisher.

CHAPTER 1

The woman was in a white jumpsuit. Deerskin. Flared cuffs and fringes. The full Elvis-in-Vegas shit apart from his big collar and rhinestone studs. Instead, she had a cross of crimson sequins on her chest, which she'd sewn on herself, and a single pocket on the hip fastened by a tasseled zipper for the Glock 19 with its serial numbers filed off and fifteen rounds in the mag. Dressed to kill in fuck-me, thigh-high leather boots. The King of Rock and Roll would have been proud.

Destroy the flesh to save the soul. It made perfect sense. The prophet was right, but it didn't stop the nerves from dancing around in her stomach and that weird chemical smell hitting the back of her throat like it always did when she was on the verge of panic. The same one she used to get in the changing room, waiting to go out onto the tennis court. It was never about winning. She didn't want to let down her parents and coach, and tonight the pressure was the same. It was just a different man she wanted to please. So bad it hurt.

Air-con maxed out, it was still hot as hell in the back of the van heading south on the Cabrillo Highway towards the City of Angels. At least she thought that was the direction of travel, but she couldn't be sure because of the blindfold. It was a silky, blackout sleep mask like the ones they give passengers flying first class. When she'd asked why she wasn't allowed to see where they were going, they'd simply shrugged and said *prophet's rules*, and she wasn't inclined to argue. This was all about faith, and no time to show anything but total commitment. Twenty-one years on the planet, she'd never felt so confident about anything. It was nearly time.

One sin so grave that it can never be atoned for without the spilling of blood. The words of the prophet rang in her ears. He'd given her a private ceremony and sprinkled her forehead with water. To purify and initiate. She'd been naked and initially felt awkward, but the strength of his presence had swept away all self-conscious thought. He was the chosen one who had rescued her from the blackness of despair and brought light back into her life. Now was the time to prove her devotion.

She heard the indicator tick, and then the van slowed, turned right and cruised downhill. Was this the place? Who was the target? They'd shown her a photograph of him so she didn't take out the wrong guy, but she didn't know his name or what had happened to make him lose his faith. Some kind of mental aberration? An illness? Never mind, she had the cure for the virus of apostasy. A lead injection. Salvation was hers to bestow, and she smiled at the honor.

The van made six more turns, then stopped. It was time. One of the apostles known as Andrew removed the mask and opened the sliding cargo door of the van. Then the one known as James, the son of Alpheus, took her by the arm and guided her down onto the sidewalk. They were on a residential street. Before them was a split-level house in brick and stone, with a double garage and big, manicured lawn. The all-American suburban dream. Lights shone from the windows, and on the drive was a new-looking Mercedes convertible with the top down.

She looked at the apostles for confirmation that it was the right place, and they nodded. This was the point where, throughout the preceding days, she'd imagined her courage might desert her, but it did not. She strode along the drive with a bounce in her step, leaving the two men in her wake and noticing that the radiator fan of the Mercedes was still running. Someone had just got home. Lucky fortune or divine working, it mattered not; the timing was perfect. Everything was unfolding as the prophet said it would, and soon she would gain access to the next level in the hierarchy. With a mixture of reverence and excitement, she unzipped her pocket and pulled out the Glock.

The front door was black with a polished brass knocker, but she pressed the doorbell, as she'd been instructed to do. Inside, a chime rang out. Almost in an instant the door opened, and he stood there. The speed threw her off guard. She'd been expecting a few seconds to steel herself and say a prayer. Now here he was already in front of her, the man from the photograph with a strange benevolent look on his face, even though he was staring down the barrel of a gun held by a stranger in a white jumpsuit.

Before she could make her finger squeeze the trigger, the sound of a voice came down the stairway in the hall. 'Who is it, honey?' It was a woman's voice. There was something else. The playful screams of young children. Bath time? She couldn't hear water splashing, but it didn't matter. This was not right. She'd been told the target lived on his own and did not have a family.

The man in front of her still stood, now with a look of mild puzzlement on his face, as though he suspected he was the victim of some kind of prank. Maybe it was the knee-length boots or the sequined cross. Why didn't he slam the door? She had a split second to decide. Execute the target or turn around and double-check that this was the correct address. Her muscles tensed.

The man's demeanor changed again. Fear widened his eyes, and his hands shot up in a defensive reflex. CRACK. The sound of a gunshot seemed to fill the quiet street. There was a small, dark hole in the man's forehead, and the paintwork down one side of the hall was streaked with blood and brain matter. Little ribbons of half-cooked egg. *Shit, what just happened?* She'd done it, hadn't she? But she hadn't pulled the trigger of her gun. Not deliberately.

The only other explanation was that one of the apostles had sensed her hesitation and shot the target. She sensed a presence behind her and turned. James, the son of Alpheus, stood two yards back with something raised in his hand. It wasn't a firearm. He was filming with his smartphone. She'd done it. She'd shot another human in cold blood, and it had all been captured on video. Her baptism was complete.

CHAPTER 2

A wedge of fog squatted on the Santa Barbara shoreline like a giant gray toad, going nowhere fast.

Eddie Virgo peeled a dozen more rashers of back bacon onto the grill and glanced down the line to check how many hungry mouths still waited. He could see three, but beyond that who knew. The mist was real dense. He'd already cooked breakfast for six of the regulars. A mix of rough-sleepers, longtime drifters and the mentally fragile unable to cope with societal stress.

An average morning saw a dozen. Today looked like being less. Two or three sometimes went on stealing sprees to support their addiction, and maybe they were sat in a police cell, going cold turkey. Either that or any moment they'd emerge from the fog, off their tits on meth. That was always a possibility. Virgo was ex-FBI, but he didn't judge. People need to eat, and he could afford to be charitable. Of course, it also helped him feel better about himself and what he'd done in his not-too-distant past, but he didn't like to dwell on that. Sleeping dogs.

A voice called out, 'Hey, Mr. Virgo. Any chance of more eggs? Some bastard ate mine.'

Virgo ignored the paper plate that was thrust in his face. 'It was you, Jerry. I saw you.'

'Come on, man. I need more rations.'

'Give me ten minutes, Jerry. Let's see who else shows up.' Virgo looked down the line to check for new arrivals and was surprised to see a woman bringing up the rear. That was a first. He carried on cooking, and as she got closer, he realized she wasn't here for the free breakfast. She had Barbie-pink highlights in short but well-styled hair, and wore a striped business suit. Virgo flipped some bacon and tipped another scoop of eggs onto Jerry's plate.

Two final customers served, the lady now stood in front of the grill plate. She backed off a little, as if the smell of burnt fat offended her nostrils or she didn't want it seeping into the material of her suit. 'You're a hard man to find. Do you know that?'

Virgo turned off the gas and said nothing while he tried to make an assessment of who this woman was and what she wanted. Another lawyer or probation officer? No. Too unconventional. A journalist after a story? Maybe. Whoever she was, she had big chestnut eyes and Debbie Harry cheekbones. A dangerous combination.

She held out her hand. 'My name's Jessica Bender, and I'm here to hire your services as a negotiator.'

Virgo wiped the grease off his hand on some industrial blue towel and shook hers. 'Pleased to meet you, but I'm afraid you've made a wasted journey.'

Jessica Bender patted a leather bag that hung from her shoulder. 'Two thousand dollars cash for a few hours of your time.'

'Keep your voice down, ma'am.' Virgo pointed his spatula towards the Pacific Ocean, where somewhere in the fog his assorted rabble ate in silence. 'That's a lot of money 'round here.'

'Don't worry, I can look after myself.'

Something in her eyes told Virgo that wasn't an empty boast. He pulled his best sympathetic smile. 'Look, I'm sorry. I don't do that sort of thing anymore. I kind of took an early, or rather enforced, retirement.'

'Please. They've got my sister.'

'Then go to the police.'

'I did. They're not interested.'

'I'm sorry. I can't help you.'

'Come on, please. You're my last hope. Don't make me get down on my knees and beg, or is that what you really want?'

'Goodbye, lady. I hope you find your sister safe and well.' Virgo started to wash down the hot plate. He was conscious of her watching him. She had a magnetic presence that he could feel pulling him in, but he ignored it and carried on working.

Jessica Bender didn't move. She stood hands on hips. 'What exactly are you running away from?'

'Nothing. This is how I live my life.'

'Come on. Hiding away in an RV on your own? There must be a reason whether you admit it or not.'

Virgo was niggled. He stopped wiping. 'How did you know where to find me?'

'You were recommended by a mutual friend.'

'I don't have friends.'

'Yeah, I can believe that.' Jessica Bender shut down an embryonic smirk. 'Let's call them a colleague. They said you were the best.'

Virgo sensed he was being played. Had he really been one of the Bureau's top negotiators? Maybe at one time. He'd done okay for an ex-Army grunt who'd been blown up in Syria and stumbled into it as a second career, but there were always parts of the job he'd never been comfortable with, like the times when he had to talk nice to shitbags or agree to a compromise. Ends justified the means, but still rankled.

He said, 'I don't know who suggested me, but I'm not interested. Now if you'll excuse me, I've got work to do.' Then he picked up a wire brush and began to scrub the grill.

Jessica Bender stood motionless for a few seconds, made a loud huffing noise down her nose and marched off into the fog.

Virgo carried on cleaning. A small part of him was sad to see her go, because it was a long time since someone had made such an instant impression on him, and his curiosity was piqued, but it was for the best. This was not the time to dive back into the maelstrom of other people's problems.

After a while his customers drifted back in ones and twos to deposit paper plates and plastic cutlery on his trestle table, and he tore a black garbage sack off a roll, ready to fill. It was then that he heard a loud rasping noise coming from somewhere near the dunes. At first, he thought it was one of the California sea lions that often came up onto the beach, but the sound wasn't as harsh as their bark. Then he realized it was someone crying. Big sobs, punctuated by loud rasps as the diaphragm contracted. A few of the homeless guys stared at him and shook their heads, as though it was his fault the lady was upset. Maybe they thought she was an old flame whom he'd treated badly, and he wanted to shout out that he'd never seen the woman before in his life. Jerry even tutted.

Okay, okay. Virgo dropped the trash bag and set off into the fog. He found Jessica Bender sat doubled over on a bench, and held out a sheet of blue paper roll. 'I give in. Come and tell me what's happened to your sister.'

She stopped convulsing. 'Really?'

'I'm not saying I'll get personally involved, but I'll give you ten minutes to explain the problem.'

'Thank…you…thank…you…'

Virgo led her back to the RV, and a couple of the guys gave him knowing smiles. He made some coffee. Jessica Bender's chest still heaved, and her face was a battlefield of snot and mascara. It took a few minutes for her to regain her composure, and then she was struck dumb, as though the pressure of having to recount her story was too great, and she didn't know how to begin. Finally, she blew her nose on some more blue roll, closed her eyes, took a deep breath, and *whoosh*, the floodgates opened.

Casey was her younger sister. Always the favorite. Good looking, funny, top grades at school, and an all-round good person. Everyone liked her. But the one thing that made her truly exceptional was her performance on the tennis court. She had some natural ability, but the majority of her excellence came from a passionate and relentless devotion to practice. She could spend hour after hour working on perfecting just one stroke. The game became all consuming. Tournaments, club matches, coaching sessions, even tennis vacations. Parents became chauffeurs, cheerleaders and financial backers.

Naturally, Casey got a full scholarship to her college of choice, which was Berkeley. Straight into the first team. Flying up the individual rankings and still making sure that the academic work didn't drop off. Then out of the blue came the day everything changed. Their father died.

Jessica Bender stopped and blew her nose. Took some more blue roll and blew it again. The sobs that came this time were sad and affectionate, not distraught and deep-rooted, but showed no signs of stopping.

'Don't fight it.' Virgo refilled her coffee. 'Loss takes time to heal.' It was two years since the death of his wife, and every day still hurt just as much as the last.

Jessica tried a smile of acknowledgment, but her bottom

lip crumpled. Virgo was pulling out more blue roll, but she held her hand up to signal that she was all right to carry on. Casey took their father's death badly. She had a breakdown. Dropped out of college. Went off the radar, and then resurfaced last month in the commune of a religious sect in central California, where she was presently being held against her will.

Virgo had listened patiently, but the story was not entirely an unfamiliar one. In times of vulnerability, some people take refuge in a surrogate family. Blood relatives can neither understand nor accept it, but it doesn't mean their loved one has been abducted. He tried to sound sympathetic. 'Maybe your sister is there because she finds solace for her grief in the holy scriptures.'

'WHAT?' she exploded. 'We're talking about a bunch of charlatans masquerading under the banner of Christianity. They wouldn't know God if he grabbed them by the balls and sang don't stop fucking believin'.'

Virgo was a little taken aback by the reaction. He said, 'If she really is being imprisoned, the police will deal with it.'

'They say she isn't.'

'They've spoken to her in person?'

'If you believe them.'

'Are you saying they're lying?'

'Dirty or just lazy, I don't know. That's why we want you to go and see her.'

'We?'

'Me and Casey's mom. We thought you could buy her out. Grifters like that are only interested in money, and that used to be your job, didn't it? The negotiator?'

Virgo put his palms up in apology. 'I don't think it's something I can help you with.'

There was a piercing scream, and Jessica Bender collapsed onto the floor. The seal-bark sobs made a reappearance. Her body shook. Virgo was unsure how much was being overdramatized for his benefit, but the distress was undoubtedly genuine.

A seed sprouted in the back of his mind and quickly grew into an idea. It was three months now that he'd been residing on the Santa Barbara shoreline. The point of buying the RV was to travel, and he'd always intended to visit the wine valleys of central California. This was the opportunity. It would be hard to drag himself away from the sound of the ocean, thanks to an IED in Syria, which had damaged his inner ear and left him with severe tinnitus. The timeless noise of the waves made the night-times bearable. Good days were when the Santa Ana blew strong and whitecaps foamed and crashed. Bad days were the quiet ones.

Virgo still had reservations, but he opted to take a leap of faith. 'Okay, no promises. I'll go and speak to your sister.'

Jessica Bender got to her feet. 'You've saved my life.'

'I said no promises.'

'You'll do a good job. I know.' She unzipped her bag and pulled out a wallet. Calm and businesslike all of a sudden.

Virgo saw her start to count out hundred-dollar bills. 'I don't need two thousand, just two hundred. Enough to buy my guys breakfast for a few days while I'm away.'

'Please yourself.' Jessica Bender didn't argue. She slapped two bills down on the table and stashed the rest quickly back in the wallet. 'Is there a bathroom in this place? I need to fix my face.'

Virgo pointed to the other end of his living quarters and watched her strut off, one hand tousling the pink pixie cut, the other with a tight grip on the money bag, and wondered what he'd just let himself get suckered into. Why had he agreed to get involved when the sensible half of his brain had kept telling him to politely decline? Was it really because he was stuck in a rut and wanted to tour the valleys of central

California, or was it because he found himself inexplicably and powerfully attracted to this woman who'd just appeared from nowhere out of the fog?

He went back outside and got busy scrubbing the grill with a wire brush, because somewhere in his mind he knew the answer and didn't want to give his conscience time to acknowledge it. Sometimes it's best to leave precise motives hidden in their own mist.

CHAPTER 3

Halfway between LA and San Francisco, the city of La Esperanza was the eleventh biggest in San Luis Obispo County. Its community website announced without any apparent embarrassment, *We Live in Hope: a community of cowboys, wine and passion.* Interesting mix. Virgo parked the RV under a line of oak trees in the main square and stretched his legs. Thirty miles inland, the place seemed to have its own microclimate. Hotter. Still. Clear azure skies and a dryness in the air that caught on the back of your throat.

It looked like an upmarket town. Michelin-starred restaurants, vintners and old stores that someone had gentrified the shit out of and turned into boutiques and artisan craft stalls. Even so, when he passed a group of kids huddled in the shade of a bandstand, the stench of weed made his eyes water. He grabbed a coffee in the imaginatively named La Esperanza Grill, and set off to say *hi* to Casey Bender at the People's Order of Gabriel.

He liked to approach every situation without prejudice. Maybe this troubled girl really was being forcibly held captive on the outskirts of a quaint tourist destination, but at the back of his mind, he suspected that after a brief chat, he'd be in one of La Esperanza's bijou eateries, enjoying a filet mignon lunch washed down by a vintage cabernet. All he needed to do was find an overnight place for the RV.

A mile out of town, on a single-track highway heading up to the hills, Virgo found Casey Bender's alleged prison. It was a collection of pastel-colored buildings partly hidden from view by pines and desert willow, but the place wasn't trying to remain secret. There was a pair of huge iron gates emblazoned by a red cross on a white shield and an inscription that said *People's Order of Gabriel – Templar Sanctorum*, and the gates were wide open. No machine-gun posts. No razor wire. There was a sentry booth, but it was empty, and an automatic barrier, but that was up.

The place had its own parking lot and a small fleet of purple-liveried minibuses branded with the POG logo. Brand new and gleaming. Business must be good in the soul-saving sector. Virgo walked into the compound unchallenged and unsure where to go. He'd not reconned the lair of a religious sect before, and there were no signs saying *reception* or *general enquiries*. Ideally, there would have been an arrow marked *complaints department* or *kidnapped relatives pickup point*, but no. Some days things are never easy.

Once through the outer tree-lined cordon, the vista opened up. In front of him were what looked like accommodation blocks. Two story. Spartan, with small windows and no balconies. They were surrounded by lawned areas and benches, but nobody sat around enjoying themselves. To his right was what appeared to be the main building in the Templar Sanctorum. It was clearly based on the architecture of the old Californian missions. A blend of Spanish, Moor and Mexican. It had a three-domed bell tower, tiled roof and stucco walls. Beautiful and imposing.

Virgo saw movement through another gateway and stepped through. He found himself in a quadrangle with arched, terraced walkways around three sides. On the fourth wall was the church. Young people walked around the quad in pairs, carrying books. It could have been Harvard or Yale, but they were all wearing the same uniform of light gray slacks and button-up collarless shirts. Nobody was shouting or laughing. More North Korea than Ivy League.

He stopped a couple walking past. 'Excuse me. Who's in charge here?'

They looked at him as though he'd just offered to sell them a stamp bag of heroin, and scuttled off. He carried on in the shaded corridor towards the church. Halfway along, two guys appeared from a side alley and intercepted him. Jock types. Young like the rest, except these were wearing a different uniform. Baggy black cotton pants and black, short-sleeved tunics with a white sash. No collars. Seemed nobody liked collars in the People's Order of Gabriel.

'Can I help you, sir?' The first guy stood directly in front of Virgo with his arms folded so that he could squeeze out his biceps and make them look bigger. The unspoken message was clear: *this is a meaningless offer of assistance, and you are not welcome.*

Virgo pulled a wide smile. He could do meaningless gestures too. 'That's very kind of you. I'd like to speak to Casey Bender, please.' He also crossed his arms. Not that he needed to make his biceps look bigger than they actually were. Just a mirroring tactic to unsettle the man opposite.

'Have you got an appointment?'

'Have I got an appointment?' More mirroring. This time verbal.

'That's what I just said. Have you got an appointment?' The first crease of irritation appeared on the guy's brow.

One of the first things Virgo learnt as an FBI negotiator

was to put the other party under pressure, and the best way to do that was to keep asking questions. 'Did you say I needed an appointment?'

'No. I asked if you had an appointment.'

'So I don't need an appointment?'

'No, I mean yes, you do need an appointment.' Jock number one started to clench his jaw.

Virgo kept the smile going. 'Great. Can I have an appointment now?'

Jock number two had seen enough. He was a wide kid, with acne scars and a low forehead. He put a hand on Virgo's shoulder. 'That's enough, mister. Time to leave.'

Virgo took a deep breath and counted to five. Now was not the time to break bones and cause a scene. Cops might get called, and they might get twitchy when they found out he'd served time for killing someone. Even though he'd done it to save more lives. He took a step backwards, to give himself space if he needed to defend himself. 'That's a nice uniform you two guys are wearing. When I was in the 501 Parachute Battalion, I had a nice uniform too, but then, when I got selected for the special forces, I changed into a different set of combat gear altogether. The reason I'm telling you this is because I want you to understand that if you lay a hand on me again, it will be you who needs an appointment – with a surgeon to sew your arms back on. Now, if you'll excuse me, I'm going to find Casey Bender.'

The two guys looked at each other, then stepped aside. A parting of the jock waves. Virgo walked between them and continued towards the church. En route, he admired some ornate stone carvings in the recesses of the corridor, and the marble statues of saints and martyrs around the central lawn. Everything was new, but manufactured to look old. Even so, the materials and craftsmanship were top quality and must have cost a fortune. What else within the

People's Order of Gabriel was fake? Money can't buy authenticity.

As soon as he pulled open one of the giant wooden doors to the church, he heard the voice of a preacher. Strident, passionate, beating out a rhythm designed to inspire and invoke in human beings their primordial desire to believe and belong. In the pews, gray-clad figures hunched over notebooks, but the pulpit was empty. At the front was a twenty-foot-high cross, and mounted on it was a giant TV screen.

The man on the screen was smart and good looking. Early forties. More movie star than parish priest. He had it. The *it* thing that great orators have: confidence, poise, projection, timing, the gift of making every person in a crowd feel that he is addressing them personally. In a word, charisma. The video ended with a fitting blood and thunder exultation, and the screen went blank. Then it fired up again, and the title read *Dr. Daniel Nelson, Leader of the POG: Prophesy Number Nine, The Rise and Fall of Western Civilization,* and off he went in full flow again. It was like his greatest hits on repeat. The gray figures turned over to a fresh page in their notebooks, lapping it up.

Virgo made his way down a side aisle towards the front of the church. Still no sign of any figures of authority. It was as if all the pupils in this school were so well behaved and resourceful that they didn't need supervision or in-person support. The perfect set of students, except there was something dehumanizing about their uniformity and unquestioning absorption of what they were being told by the figure on the big screen.

He'd got as far as the altar when a door at the back of the sanctuary opened, and Dr. Daniel Nelson himself emerged, flanked by two red-clad wingmen. There was a collective gasp, and the congregation dropped as one to their knees. The prophet signaled to his followers to resume their education by raising his hands and pointing to the giant TV on the cross. For a moment he stood and stared at himself on the screen, as though he was captivated by his own stellar performance.

Then he sashayed over in Louis Vuitton sneakers and a designer suit, with a tanned hand outstretched way in advance. 'I'm Dr. Dan, welcome to the POG, our modest stairway to love and eternal life. I understand you want to see one of our flock?'

Virgo shook Dr. Dan's hand and wondered how news travelled so fast in the People's Order of Gabriel. He also wondered why a holy man of the Lord had a badly concealed handgun holstered under his right armpit. Maybe he really was a prophet and knew he was going to need it.

CHAPTER 4

Dr. Daniel Nelson was not tall. Maybe five seven. It was hard to say because he wore Cuban heels, and he never stood still. His body swayed, and his feet continually shuffled, like he was dancing to a soundtrack only he could hear. Probably some kind of hyperactivity issue. He bestowed a beatific smile on Virgo and said, 'May I ask why you want to see Sister Casey?'

'Her family are worried about her.'

'She's never been better.'

'They want her back home.'

'I'm sure you are aware Casey is an adult.'

'Adults can be vulnerable.'

'That's why God's protection is important.'

'Is there a problem with me seeing her?'

Dr. Dan laughed. 'You think we're monsters who kidnap people's children? Is that it?' More laughing. A little jig thrown in for good measure and a glance at the two red-uniformed wingmen to give them permission to join in with some chuckles of their own. 'Please be assured, Mr. Virgo, that our beloved member presently known as Casey Bender is safe and well and free to leave the Templar Sanctorum whenever she pleases.'

The humor had gone. Dr. Dan stared with piercing blue eyes. Unnatural. Metallic turquoise or teal. Either contact lenses or those risky implants done by backstreet clinics. Virgo returned the stare and resisted the urge to ask him how he knew his name. It was clearly a ploy. A device designed to demonstrate that he, Dr. Daniel Nelson, had the upper hand in the encounter, and it would be futile to argue or resist. Maybe it worked with some people. Virgo shrugged. 'I want to see her.'

'Look, she doesn't want anything to do with her family. You have my word as a man of God.'

'Not good enough.'

'Then I'm afraid our conversation is finished.'

'Okay. Catch you later.' Virgo walked off. He doubled around the far side of the pews and marched back to the front of the church, where he reached up and yanked the power cable out of the TV. Then he jumped up into the pulpit. 'Excuse me, listen up, guys. I need your help. Can everyone hear me?' He looked out across the gray-clad figures. Some nodded in acknowledgment; some gaped with open mouths. 'I'm looking for a girl called Casey Bender. Her family are very worried about her, and they believe she's being held in this place against her will. All I want for you to do is—'

Virgo stopped. The two red wingmen stood in front of the pulpit, and both had Springfield pistols pointed at his chest. One of them said, 'Please follow us, sir. Dr. Dan says you can speak with Sister Casey.'

They left the church and exited the quad courtyard. Passed through an arboretum, and skirted what looked like a dining hall and a kitchen garden. Then took a bridge over a crescent lake, replete with swans, and approached a gate in a tall, fastidiously manicured privet hedge. Virgo started to wonder where they were going. What if the Bender girl really had been kidnapped and one of these red-clad bodyguards was about to put a slug in the back of his head to shut him up? Somehow, he didn't think so.

He was right. On the other side of the gate was a grand mansion. They took him straight through the front door and ushered him into a downstairs room. He was expecting to see Casey Bender waiting inside, but the only person was Dr. Dan, sat behind an expansive leather-topped desk, with his funeral face on. He tutted, 'You made an unfortunate scene back there. I'd be grateful if you did not pull any of those childish stunts again.'

'Cut the bullshit.' Virgo had heard enough. 'Your two little helpers just pointed their guns at me in the church. What sort of fucking place is this? Either you allow me access to this girl, or I come back with the cops.'

'She didn't tell you?'

Virgo waited. The faint glow of smugness on Dr. Dan's face told him there was more to come.

'Casey's mother didn't tell you? I'm afraid that's typical of some families who feel rejected when their offspring choose to devote their life to something other than them. You see, the police have already been here at Mrs. Bender's request and interviewed Casey. By all means, verify this with Sergeant Chambers at the local police department if you so wish.'

Virgo prickled. This was the scenario he'd suspected when he'd succumbed to Jessica's histrionics and agreed to pay a visit to the People's Order of Gabriel, but now he was here, he didn't buy it. Something was wrong, and it wasn't just quasi-religious nutjobs feeling the need to carry concealed guns. Plenty of organizations need properly trained firearms staff to protect their personnel and property. It was him. The doctor. There was another character hiding behind the sanctimonious preacher.

'I don't care if the attorney general herself came and took a sworn deposition from Casey Bender.' Virgo sat himself down on an overstuffed, green-leather Chesterfield and crossed his legs. 'I ain't going anywhere 'til I see her.'

Dr. Dan checked the time on his iPhone. 'She's working on the farm. Will be for another five hours.'

'You've got a farm?'

'Farm, college, gardeners, physicians, chefs. We're a self-sufficient commune here.'

'I'm pleased for you. Why don't you give Casey a call and tell her she's got a visitor?'

Dr. Dan pursed his lips. 'We don't have cell phones, the internet or any other sources of superficiality and corruption. Temptation is best avoided.'

Virgo had encountered plenty of hypocrites, but this guy was in a league of his own. His subjects lived and worked incommunicado while he pontificated in a palatial office with a MacBook on his desk, and what looked like a mahogany drinks cabinet behind him carved in a replica of Noah's Ark. Maybe all the contents were doubles. On another day, Virgo might have lost his temper, but right now he was focused on making certain Casey Bender was in this fucked-up place of her own volition, and the easiest way to accomplish this was to play it cool. He reverted to type. The negotiator. Put the ball in their court.

'Tell me, Dr. Nelson, I need to speak to Casey, so how do you suggest we resolve this situation and resume with the remainder of our day?'

Dr. Dan hesitated. 'Come back at seven.'

Virgo sensed an advantage. 'I'd like to meet her on neutral territory. Not here, where she might feel pressured.'

'Neutral territory? We're not enemies engaged in a war.'

'Do you really want me to come back here?'

A shadow crossed Dr. Dan's face. Maybe he was remembering Virgo's storming of his pulpit. 'Agreed. I'll ensure that Casey is available for you to converse with in La Esperanza at seven o'clock. You're going to feel mighty embarrassed after all this fuss.'

'Thank you, but the days when I worried what people thought about me are gone.' Virgo stood up to leave.

Dr. Dan got to his feet and instantly started moving. A shake and shimmy and he was round the other side of the desk. He fixed Virgo with his electric-aqua eyes. 'God gave me the gift of seeing into souls. I look into yours and see grief. The loss of a loved one. A partner or wife? Give me your hands, and we can pray together.'

Virgo stormed out. A lucky guess. Guy was a fraud.

CHAPTER 5

La Esperanza Bar and Grill boasted a model steam locomotive pulling three carriages around a miniature wall-mounted track on a continuous loop. There were stations, signals, bridges, tunnels and numerous geographical features such as canyons, harbors and hills. Virgo watched it chug by his booth for the millionth time and racked his brain as to what he was actually doing here. He'd been a fool to fall for Jessica Bender's sob story. Even so, it should have been a quick in-and-out job, followed by a filet and cab sav. Now, here he was drinking Coke Zero, pissed because it appeared Dr. Blue Eyes had shafted him. No sign of Casey, half past the hour. Peeep, peeep, peeep: all aboard the Suckerville express.

What made it worse was the con artist had been right about his loss. Two years since he'd lost Crystal, and the guilt weighed just as heavy. He'd given her the pepper spray that was supposed to keep her safe. She had been a nurse just finished an evening shift at a south Washington hospital when someone tried to rob her in the street. She'd fought back. It was easy now to say that was a mistake, but at the time you don't think of the risks. He had been a senior FBI agent. You can't just give in to the bad guys. If only you could get a time machine and go back to change some of your attitudes and decisions, life would be less painful.

More customers arrived. This time a young couple. Virgo didn't pay them much attention, but they hovered by the doorway, scanning the room, then came over. The woman said, 'You must be my mother's latest waste of money. You're more persistent than the last one, I'll give you that.'

'Tenacious. It's my middle name.' Virgo smiled. Casey Bender had an attitude. He liked that. She looked nothing like her older sister. She was fresh-faced, athletic, with long black hair in a ponytail and lips that didn't need collagen or color. 'I thought you were going to meet me on your own.'

'It's okay; this is Jake. He's my new friend.'

'Does he have to stay?' Virgo scowled, left eye half shut.

Didn't seem Jake wanted to stay. He couldn't look Virgo in the one eye that remained fully open, and he chewed on a fingernail. Nervy and skittish.

Casey sat down in the booth. 'We have a *friend* system in the POG, like a buddy or mentoring scheme, where we take care of each other, and it's against the rules to be away from the Templar Sanctorum without your designated friend.'

'Dr. Dan not trust you on your own? Does he think you might get your head turned by the trappings of consumerism like the rest of us?'

'No, it's about looking out for one another.'

'It's called spying on your peers. The communists started it.'

'You don't have the faith, so you can't understand.' Casey nodded to Jake, indicating that he should sit. He did. It appeared she was the senior partner in the friendship. 'Now, how many times do you want me to swear that I'm in the POG of my own free will? Or has my mother tried telling you

I'm suffering from temporary insanity and unable to make informed decisions?'

Virgo looked into her young eyes and saw nothing to suggest vulnerability or mental aberration. She seemed strong, confident and awash with the enthusiasm of youth. He wanted to shout that Daniel Nelson was nothing but a scam merchant, living the high life, while his followers sacrificed worldly goods and toiled in the fields, but he knew it would be a diatribe that cut no ice. Belief is a powerful force. It can't be nullified by words alone. Instead, he passed Casey and Jake menus and told them to order what they wanted. To his surprise, they both went for steak and eggs. The waitress wrote the order on a slip of paper she tucked into one of the steam train's carriages, and off it puffed on the miniature tracks to the kitchen.

For over an hour, Virgo listened to Casey explain what a wonderful organization the POG was. It had saved her when she was at her lowest ebb. Brought love into her life where before there had only ever been stifling pressure. Now she had stability, comradeship and a sense of purpose in life. Only occasionally did she eulogize in such a way that Virgo sensed the true subject of her devotion was not God, but Dr. Dan himself. The POG was less a sect, more a cult. Whatever it was, there was no doubting the genuine desire she had to remain at the Templar Santorum.

Throughout this feast of adulation, Jake did not utter a word. He fidgeted and looked more sullen than ablaze with religious zeal. Occasionally, his eyes would dart around the room, as though he were casing the joint for a robbery, not dining in it. One time, he scratched his arms, and a sleeve rode up to reveal a red ink tattoo. An angel drawn in the form of a stick, like a cartoon. Then he pulled the sleeve down and wiped his nose on it. Virgo guessed drugs had featured in

Jake's life at some point, until good ole Dr. Dan had saved his soul. What a man that guy was.

Virgo asked for the check. Not only had he wasted his time, he was out of pocket. Tomorrow he'd head back to Santa Barbara. There was something he didn't like about La Esperanza, and he couldn't figure out what it was, but he was done. Casey Bender thanked him for the meal and went to the restroom.

No sooner had she gone than itchy Jake leaned across the table, eyes desperate, and said through clenched teeth, 'You got to do something, man.'

'She seems to know her own mind,' said Virgo.

'Not about Casey. She's one of them.' Jake's eyes kept flicking to the bathroom door. 'No, you've got to do something about the whole fucking POG. Dismantle it. Decapitate the fucking monster, or we'll never be free to leave.'

Virgo was confused. He'd been working on the assumption Jake was there to report back to Dr. Dan if Casey said anything out of turn. Not the other way round. 'What's stopping you packing a bag and walking out?'

Jake leaned further across the table and dropped his voice into a conspiratorial whisper. 'They own my soul. It's theirs.'

'Are you saying the POG has a psychological hold on you?'

'No, what—' Jake froze. His demeanor changed. He stood up, pushed Virgo in the chest and shouted, 'Why don't you just leave her alone, you fucking creep?'

Virgo guessed he was putting on a show for someone. He glanced around to see who it might be. Casey was still in the bathroom. The other booths were all full, and everybody was staring at him to see what the commotion was.

Jake hadn't finished. He stood with his arms wide. 'Come on outside, big guy. I'm going to teach you a lesson.'

Virgo didn't move. 'Sit down, Jake.'

'Fucking creep.' Jake punched Virgo on the shoulder.

Virgo shrugged. 'Are you finished?'

Casey came back the same time as the model steam train puffed round to their booth and stopped with the check. 'Is everything okay?'

'Everything's cool.' Virgo pulled out his wallet. 'Look after yourself and think about giving your family a call one day soon. That's all they want. And I'll give your sister a call and tell her you're just fine and maybe she should give you some space.'

Casey laughed. 'I haven't got a sister.'

Virgo wanted to say *are you sure*, but people generally know if they have a sibling. It was a shit end to a shit day and the last time he took pity on someone and tried to do them a favor. Everyone in the diner was still looking at him and talking behind their hands, as if he were both an evil maniac and expert lip-reader. Except two guys on stools at the counter, who were trying to look uninterested and making a bad job of it. No doubt a couple of POG stooges there to keep an eye on the meeting and the ones whom Jake had been trying to impress when they caught him talking out of turn. Virgo didn't care. He was finished with the place.

CHAPTER 6

Virgo was tired. He drove his RV to the edge of town, where there was a twenty-four-hour gas station with a truck stop tucked round the back. It was just a dirt area, but secure, and there were only a handful of rigs parked up. He had no inclination to find a campground, because first thing tomorrow he was heading straight back south on the Pacific Coast Highway. He bought a six-pack of Fat Tire from an old guy with a face like a walnut serving at the gas station, who said he was the owner and charged him ten bucks for overnight parking.

All settled down, he put a Dylan playlist on and his feet up. As a boy in the Lower East Side of Manhattan, he'd been surrounded by music and therefore took it for granted. Both parents had scraped a living playing in pit orchestras up and down the island. Mother on piano, father on bass or six string. Not a great line of work if you want to see much of your kids because there were shows six nights a week and matinees on a Saturday. No doubt a contributory factor as to why Virgo got into trouble and joined the Army. But he remembered the music from the few times they were at home:

Dylan, Joni Mitchell, Neil Young, but also Blondie and Talking Heads. When he needed to unwind, one of these classics was still his default.

The woman who had pretended to be Jessica Bender had given him her number. He tried it now, but it rang out. Who was she? Did she really have concerns about Casey's welfare, or was she a psycho who got her kicks from starring in her own imagined dramas? Intrigued as he was to know her true identity and what her game was, he really didn't want to get involved.

Dipping his toe back into the pool of what could be loosely described as work had been a mistake. He wasn't ready for it. Nor was he ready to start any kind of relationship with another woman, and he felt embarrassed that he'd been dazzled into making a bad decision. Thinking with his dick? No, it wasn't like that, although the attraction was undeniable. He didn't know what he'd been hoping for, but maybe he just wanted to feel alive again for a short space of time instead of filling his days with distraction activity. Maybe he just hankered after a little genteel company for a change instead of the homeless guys. Whatever it was, he'd been beguiled and taken the bait. You live and learn, even when you think you know it all.

Four Fat Tires down, he hit the sack. The ambience was good. Plenty of background noise to ameliorate the dog whistle that blew in his ear nonstop since the explosion in Syria. A couple of trucks with their engines on. Someone running a generator. Hissing air brakes. It all helped, and it wasn't long before he was asleep.

Loud knocks woke him. Someone hammering on the RV window with an implement rather than knuckles. He checked the bedside clock and saw it blinked 05:37. Maybe the parking lot had filled up overnight and a truck driver was pissed at a tourist parking an RV in one of their precious spaces. He rolled out of bed into his pants and opened the door to find two uniform cops brandishing flashlights and service pistols.

One was an old-timer, grossly out of shape, the other a kid whose face hadn't yet needed a razor. Maybe they were a father and son duo. Virgo had come across stranger things in out-of-the-way places where nepotism and family tradition dictated career paths.

The young one looked pumped. He said, 'Edward McKinley Virgo, I am arresting you for the murder of Jake Dearman. Step out of the vehicle and keep your hands where I can see them.'

Arguing or asking for more information at this particular juncture in proceedings was a waste of time. Virgo showed La Esperanza's finest his palms and joined them on the dirt of the lot. The kid Mirandized him while Pops snapped on the cuffs. Then a black-and-white taxi straight to jail. Do not pass Go. Do not collect $200. Strip-searched and in a cell that stank of bleach and body odor. It felt like old times. He made himself comfortable because he knew the game, and nobody would be speaking to him any time soon.

It was a surprise, therefore, when a couple of hours later, he was escorted to an interview room, where Sergeant Milton Chambers and Detective Ben Malone introduced themselves and gave him a coffee and mini bagels. The good cop, good cop routine. Different.

Chambers said, 'Do you want to tell us about it?'

Virgo said, 'I met a kid called Jake last night, and I'm assuming he's now dead and that's why I'm here. That's all I know.'

Malone had a report in front of him. He said, 'Jake Dearman's body was found at the side of the road in town just after midnight. The autopsy is scheduled for later this morning, but it looks like he was beaten to death.'

Virgo said, 'I'm not your man.'

Malone kept his eyes on the report. 'Witnesses in La Esperanza Bar and Grill claim they saw the two of you arguing yesterday evening and at one point coming to blows. Would you like to explain what this fight was about?'

Virgo said, 'There was no fight. He shared some concerns with me about the POG and then flipped when he saw someone in the diner. It was like he had to make a scene to show that we weren't friends and he had not just been confiding in me. Like he was scared.'

'Let me run another scenario by you.' Chambers stood up and planted his hands on the table. 'You buy a pretty, young lady a meal, and when it's over, you hit on her. Jake Dearman takes exception to this and forcibly remonstrates with you in front of the entire restaurant in a manner that causes you acute embarrassment and leads you to fatally assault him in the street.'

Virgo said, 'I prefer my scenario, on account of the fact it's true.'

'Witnesses heard him tell you, *leave her alone, you fucking creep*.' Chambers began to pace around the table. 'And of course, you're a man with a history of violence. A convicted felon.'

'That's bullshit, with respect.' Virgo tried not to overreact.

'You think blowing the back of a kid's head off with a nine-mil slug isn't a violent act?' Chambers laughed. 'Even in Mexico?'

'He kidnapped women for a living and cut their fingers off, and then when he got the ransom, he killed them anyway. Some might say I did the world a favor, but it was a mistake, and I wish it hadn't happened.'

'As a cop I come across a lot of bad people, but it's my job to bring them to justice, not designate myself judge and jury.' Chambers jabbed a finger. 'You're a disgrace to the Bureau.'

'I value your opinion, thanks.' Virgo flashed a smile, brittle and sarcastic. 'Why don't you try doing your job as a cop and start by finding out who from the POG was in the diner keeping an eye on Jake. Chances are they had something to do with him ending up dead at the side of the road.'

'Why would peace-loving followers of the Lord kick the shit out of their own brother?'

'Jake wanted to leave.'

'Just like Casey wanted to leave?' Chambers began finger-jabbing again. 'I know that's why you're here, tough guy. Her mother sent you because the rich bitch doesn't believe stupid county cops like us know what we're doing. We interviewed Casey Bender a month ago, and she made it perfectly clear nobody was pressuring her to stay.'

'Maybe she's got Stockholm syndrome.'

'What?' Chambers stopped pacing and jabbing. Silence. Then the eruption. 'Don't come here spouting your highfalutin FBI fucking bullshit. You wanted to do squat thrusts in the cucumber patch, and she told you to shove it up your ass.'

Virgo raised an eyebrow at the imagery, but remained calm. He said, 'Can I have more coffee and mini bagels, please?'

'No, you fucking can't.' Chambers bull-frogged his eyes and palm-slammed the table. 'You're going to tell us what you did to Jake Dearman, shitbag.'

The urge to laugh in the face of the crass overacting was strong, but Virgo deadpanned. He gave Detective Malone a glance as if to say *what's happening here*, but the junior officer looked sheepish and uncomfortable and couldn't meet his eye.

'What you got to say, shitbag?' Chambers had spittle on his chin and jacket lapel.

Virgo said, 'Check the security cameras at the truck stop, which will show I never left. Then you can apologize.'

A little bit of bluster drained from Chambers's face, but he kept the charade going. 'You're going back to federal prison, and this time you ain't getting out again.'

Detective Malone escorted Virgo back to his cell. He was quiet and serious, with a habit of sticking his chin forward to stretch his neck muscles, like a rooster. The custody office was busy with overnight releases and other prisoners being prepared for appearance at court. They had to wait for the jailer in a secure anteroom. Virgo took advantage of the air-conditioned environment to do some light exercise: burpees, planks and sit-ups.

After a while watching, Malone stretched his neck and said, 'What did Jake Dearman say about the POG?'

Virgo stopped mid sit-up. 'This still an interview?'

'No, I have a personal interest.'

'Then I guess he said it was a pretty weird setup that needed dismantling.'

'Anything else?'

'No.'

'You sure?'

'That's when he started hitting me.'

'That's a shame.'

Virgo was going to ask why, when a magnetic lock clanked and the door to the custody area opened. Ten seconds later he was back in a cell.

CHAPTER 7

Casey sat at the desk in her room and stopped writing. She glanced out the window. Still no sign of the apostles. How long was she supposed to wait? Every minute sat there wasting time was one that she could have spent out in the field earning credits for her work. It was her prime motivation in life. The thing she leapt out of bed for on a morning. The spring in her step and joy in her heart. Forty-five more credits to her name on the virtue log and she was eligible for elevation to the next level in the Order.

It had been 7:30 a.m. when a messenger from the prophet had knocked on her door and told her not to report for work. She must remain confined to quarters until one of the apostles came and spoke to her. Casey had asked what it was about, but the messenger didn't know or wouldn't say. No matter. Casey knew it was something to do with what had gone off last night in town at the diner. Why had her mother sent another overpaid, intellectually challenged stooge to try to persuade her to go home? Even from so far away, the awful woman managed to exert a negative impact, just when things were going so well. Did she really hate her so much?

Casey sucked on the end of her ballpoint and tried to concentrate on the entry in her journal. She preferred to call it a journal because it sounded less personal than a diary, and she was careful not to write anything in there that might cause shame or embarrassment if anyone else read it. There were rumors that the apostles conducted room searches when the general members of the Order were out at work. Writing was one of the things that helped her focus on the present and promoted mindfulness. Made her appreciate how her life had improved.

Meditation was the other thing that complemented her well-being, but that was something she reserved for later in the day. Evenings could seem long in the Templar Sanctorum. There were night classes, but that wasn't her scene. They were mainly an excuse to socialize and were primarily scripture classes, which were wasted on her. She'd already applied the same relentless obsession to learning scripture as she'd applied to tennis, and now knew more than the tutors.

Evening classes might be the best way to strike up a relationship with a member of the opposite sex, but Casey wasn't interested. Not that she lacked confidence, although she'd always felt awkward in some social situations. Maybe she was a late developer. The fact was, there was only one man she wanted to give her mind and soul to, and that was the prophet himself. Dr. Daniel Nelson. That was another reason she didn't go to evening classes. She couldn't stand to listen to some of the other women talking about him. The way they schemed and dreamed up ways to attract his attention. Casey didn't want to be part of some tawdry beauty contest. She put her faith in God.

She looked down, and the blank page of the journal stared back. The problem was, she didn't want to put last night's events on record. Something had happened between Jake and the Virgo character in the diner, but she didn't know what. Jake said it was nothing, but then he seemed more nervous than usual on the way back to the Templar Sanctorum. He was scratching and sweating. If she didn't know better, she'd have guessed that he'd fallen off the wagon and started using again, but that wasn't possible, even though some members of the Order swore that others in there were regularly taking drugs. It was just malicious gossip. Human nature can sometimes be cruel, even within close-knit religious communities.

She had put her bedside lamp out at eleven and gone straight to sleep. Something had woken her a little after midnight. Raised voices from Jake's room next door. An argument. The sound of a scuffle and a door slamming shut. When she slid out of bed and peeked through a gap in her curtains, she saw Jake being marched away from the accommodation block towards the main compound by four apostles. There was no mistaking their red uniforms. Was Jake still in detention? She'd heard nothing this morning through the adjoining wall. She could usually hear him coughing. Maybe he was being put in another re-education program.

It was no use. Casey couldn't concentrate on the journal entry. The frustration at having to forego work and miss out on credits was eating her up. It wasn't fair. She'd done nothing wrong. It wasn't her fault she had a mother who symbolized everything that was wrong with the modern world – materialistic, lazy, selfish, weak, ignorant and devoid of faith. Wealth was her only god, but *All who make idols are nothing, and the things they treasure are worthless.* Corinthians 10:28.

She stood to replace her pen on the bookcase and saw movement outside on the lawn. It was one of the apostles. When he got nearer, she recognized him as the one known as Matthew. Two minutes later there was a knock on her door, and she let him in. She knew something was wrong from the look on his face. He was haggard and stern. He couldn't look her in the eye.

He closed the door behind him. 'I've been sent to see you by the prophet himself, Dr. Nelson.'

The mention of his very name caused an adrenaline kick in her chest. She took a deep breath. 'What's happened? Is it Jake?'

'I'm afraid I am the bearer of bad news. Brother Jake has been taken from us.'

'What do you mean?' Casey knew. A rod of ice ran down her back.

'He's at peace now. The prophet says you must pray for Brother Jake and stay strong.'

'What happened? Was he ill?'

Matthew raised his hands shoulder high, palms out. Like he was denying personal involvement or indicating she should stop asking questions. 'We're not sure. The police found his body in town and think he might have been assaulted.'

Casey had a bad feeling. 'Someone beat him to death?'

'That's a matter for the police. They'll want to talk to you about what happened last night in the diner.'

'Nothing happened. We had a meal with the guy my mother hired, and I convinced him that I was very happy in the People's Order of Gabriel.'

'He's called Virgo,' said Matthew. 'You didn't see the fight between him and Jake?'

'No. I sensed an atmosphere when I came back from the restroom, but there was no fight.' Casey wasn't sure how the apostle knew what had taken place in the diner.

'That's a shame.'

'I heard an argument and some kind of altercation in Jake's room just after midnight.'

'You did?' Matthew seemed disappointed. 'Don't mention that to the police officer who comes to interview you.'

'I don't feel comfortable telling lies.'

'Just don't mention it. The officer won't push it.'

'How do you know he won't push it?'

'Have faith in our leader, the prophet. He is the chosen one.' Matthew opened the door to leave. 'And report immediately to the admin block. You are to be assigned a new friend.'

The door closed, and he was gone. That was it. A fellow member of the Order had lost their life, but their small world carried on as though nothing had happened. Casey liked rules and routine. It was one of the main things that had helped her recover from the mess of anxiety and depression that she'd once been in, but now, for the first time, she thought there ought to be space for some unstructured human emotion. A recognition of loss. Instead, she had to go and become mentor to another newcomer to the fold and ignore the feeling of guilt that was starting to well up inside.

Gardeners were tending the rose beds as she left the accommodation block and cut across the manicured lawns. It was a beautiful day. The air was still morning-fresh, but the sun already hot. No clouds. She took a footbridge across the lake towards the building that housed the Order's admin department, and that was when she noticed Dr. Daniel Nelson in the parking lot outside his residence. There he was in the flesh. The prophet himself.

Casey carried on walking, but then stopped, aware that she felt different. Something had changed. She didn't feel the urge to work in the field. Wasn't desperate to gain another credit. Couldn't care less if she never made it to the next level within the order or not. What had changed? It was him. She'd only ever wanted to do those things for one reason, and now when she turned and looked at that one reason as he stood outside his residence, there was no adrenaline kick to the chest. Nothing. Just a bitter taste of disillusionment on her tongue and a question that sat heavy on her shoulders. What did he know about Jake Dearman's death? Had he ordered it, or was he just covering it up?

CHAPTER 8

Pushing 2 p.m., Virgo sat in the RV, scrolling his contacts. It had taken the detectives three hours to establish he couldn't have killed Jake Dearman. Casey had gone back to the Templar Sanctorum with her friend and had last seen him there at 10 p.m. when he went into his room for the night. Security cameras at the truck stop showed Virgo arriving before that time and not leaving until the uniforms took him away. Looked like old walnut face at the gas station had saved his bacon with the video footage.

He found the number for Caleb Hawkins and hit *call*. The two of them had served together in The Activity, a unit in the US special forces so secret it doesn't have a permanent name. It's been Task Force Orange, Gray Fox, Centra Spike and even the Army of Northern Virginia. The current designated title is not public knowledge. These days Hawkins worked somewhere abroad for the CIA, where he could hack into IT systems on behalf of the US government, and they could deny all knowledge if necessary.

After exchanging personal insults, it only took Hawkins a few keystrokes to find the address of Casey Bender's mother.

The transaction cost Virgo ninety bucks because Hawkins never gave information for free. It was always a trade, and his currency was tickets for when he was on leave back in the States. It was the cheapest seat for Puccini's *Tosca* at New York Met. A bargain if you're into that kind of thing.

There'd been a change of plans. Virgo had abandoned the idea of heading south and forgetting about the POG. He had a feeling that someone had tried to set him up for the murder of Jake Dearman, and he wanted to know who and why. He'd been prepared to pretend the Jessica Bender deception had never happened, but being taken for a sucker twice in twenty-four hours was beyond the pale. Someone was going to find out it was a mistake to mess with a soldier from The Activity, even if it was twelve years since he'd left.

Mrs. Margaret Bender lived just off Highway 1 between Morro Bay and San Luis Obispo. Turned out it was a grand estate. Virgo left the RV in a limestone-chipped parking lot big enough for a fleet of Winnebagos and set off walking to the main residence. There must have been a dozen garages, stables, a paddock, dressage ring, indoor arena and two tennis courts, one clay, the other artificial grass. Everything immaculate. Virgo whistled under his breath: God must have some pulling power for Casey to turn her back on this, or that French guy was right when he said money can buy you everything apart from happiness.

Virgo stood in front of the mansion's ornate double doors that probably cost as much as his live-in vehicle, and hesitated. He felt naked without his gun and FBI badge. What if she told him to clear off or she'd call the cops. He had nothing to prove his bona fides, and explaining what he was doing there might be a challenge. Trying to help out a pink-haired stranger by driving a hundred miles up the coast sounded far-fetched. He rang the bell anyway.

Margaret Bender opened the door and said, 'Come in, Mr. Virgo. It's so good of you to call in person.'

'Pleasure,' said Virgo and walked in. *What the hell?* How come everyone knew who he was all of a sudden?

Mrs. Bender looked on the cusp of fifty, well presented with wavy chestnut hair and a generous layer of lipstick. She led the way into a kitchen the size of a basketball court and said, 'Tea or coffee?'

When Virgo looked, she was holding up a bottle of Jim Beam Bourbon in one hand and a bottle of Bombay Sapphire in the other, with a mischievous glint in her eye. He said, 'Water would be great, thanks.'

Margaret Bender went coy. 'I do apologize, Mr. Virgo. What must you think of me? I know it's too early to start, but since Casey left, it's the only way of getting through the day. You know Gerald passed last year?'

'I'm aware you're a widow, Mrs. Bender. I'm sorry for your loss.'

'Call me Maggie, please.'

'I went to La Esperanza and saw Casey.'

'Do you mind?' Mrs. Bender poured herself a generous gin on ice in a tall glass and showed it some tonic.

'Not at all.'

'Is she coming home, my daughter? I miss her terribly.'

'She's doing great, but I wouldn't expect to see her soon. Sometimes these things take a while to work themselves through.'

'Such a shame, but she was always a single-minded girl.'

Virgo wasn't sure exactly what he'd been expecting, but Maggie Bender didn't seem as distraught as he thought she might be. Maybe it was the drink. 'I liked Casey. She's not afraid to say what she thinks.'

'It's a Bender trait.'

'But she lost her father, and people cope with grief in different ways.'

'Believe me, I did everything I could for that girl.'

'I'm sure she'll appreciate it one day.'

'What else can I do, Mr. Virgo?'

'Pray to God that he keeps her safe and brings her home.'

'Fuck him and that useless son of his.'

'I understand you're angry.'

'And fuck the holy ghost. I never understood who that creep was anyway.'

'Calm down, Mrs. Bender.'

'Maggie.'

'Okay, Maggie. Can I ask you something?'

'You want to know why I'm trying to get Casey back when it was me who pushed her away?' She took on board half a tumbler of G and T. 'Guilt. It's killing me.'

'How did you know who I was just now when I rang your doorbell?'

Maggie Bender giggled. 'Is this a game?'

'No. I don't think we've met before.'

'Last year you couldn't switch on the TV around here without seeing your face. The senior FBI negotiator who had a mental breakdown and shot the kid in Mexico.'

'I wouldn't say *mental breakdown*.'

'That's what they said on NBC news. That you lost your wife and had a mental breakdown. Exact words.'

'I was there. I think I know better than NBC news.' Virgo realized he sounded defensive. He just didn't like the label. Didn't want anyone feeling sorry for him.

'That's why I hired you to negotiate on my behalf. Because I'd lost Gerald and knew you'd understand. Are you sure I can't fix you a drink?' Maggie's glass was empty apart from the ice.

'You hired me?'

'Well, I instructed the detective lady to locate you and secure your services. I trust the ten-thousand-dollar fee was more than sufficient?'

Virgo tried not to look shocked at the mention of ten grand. 'Have you got a name and contact address for the detective lady? I misplaced the details she gave me.'

'She's very good, isn't she? The best in the county.' Maggie Bender unpinned something from a corkboard and handed it to Virgo.

It was a business card.

Artemis Associates.
Your number one licensed Private Investigation Agency in San Luis Obispo.
Experienced, discreet, always honest and never beaten on price or results.

Virgo stared at it, and his cheeks burned. The pink-haired woman who'd pretended to be Casey's sister was a PI, and she'd lied to him about the size of the fee. Whatever her real name, she was a great actress and probably the best he'd come across. A fact that didn't make him feel any better. He stood up to leave. 'Take care of yourself.'

Maggie Bender looked sad. Probably at the prospect of losing company and having to drink on her own again. She mustered up the pretense of a smile. 'Thank you for trying to get Casey out of that place. I'm sure you did your best.'

Virgo said, 'I've not finished.'

CHAPTER 9

The offices of Artemis Associates were located on a corner above a Panda Express and shared a corridor with an acupuncturist and a debt-collection agent's, who promised *Can't Pay? We'll Take it Away.* Virgo knocked and walked straight in. The woman who had claimed to be Jessica Bender was doing a headstand on a yoga mat, dressed in leotard and leggings. A pile of work clothes lay on a small sofa.

He coughed. 'Busy day in the hectic world of private investigation?'

She rolled forward and sat up. 'Shit. It's you. I was going to call.'

Virgo looked around the modest-sized room. It was cluttered, and someone had taken the air-con unit to pieces and not put it back together. There were two client chairs, and on the desk was a plaque that said *Jessica McGann, PI. License No. 620912.*

He said, 'You told me half your real name. That's something.'

She blushed, or her face was scarlet from being upside down. 'Take a seat. I can explain.'

'Make it good.' Virgo didn't move. Arms folded.

'Mrs. Bender insisted I got you and nobody else to try to get Casey out of the sect. She'd seen you on TV.'

'You could have just asked me.'

'I did just ask, remember? You said *no*.' Jessica got up and wiped her forehead with a hand towel. 'But I had a backup plan in place.'

'The devastated-sister performance.'

'I did ten years in the LAPD but had to leave to look after my son after my husband, a fellow cop, left me for someone else on the force.'

'Is this another sob story? I'm not interested.'

'Shut up and listen, asshole. You wanted a good explanation, I'm giving it you.'

'Asshole? Add insult to injury, why don't you?'

'When I needed to find the great Virgo, I called some of my old friends in the Santa Monica detective division, and one of them said she knows you very well. She said it's pointless just offering you more money, because you don't want it or need it. She said appeal to his heart, because he's a prickly pear with a soft center, although I'm starting to have doubts.'

'How did you find me?'

'I'm a private detective. That's what I do. Detect.'

'Cell location?'

'No.'

'Probation officer?'

'I can neither confirm nor deny the source of my information, but I am aware that since your release from federal prison, you have to inform the probation service of any place you stay longer than seven days.'

Virgo didn't react. 'What happened to the money?'

'I offered it to you, and you refused it.' Jessica's eyes flicked down and back up.

'You offered me two grand. Mrs. Bender gave you ten.'

'So I took a commission. Do you know how many days and weeks I spent trying to track that girl down?'

'Eighty percent commission?' Virgo pulled the Artemis Associates business card out of his top pocket. 'Look here, what does it say? *Always honest. Never beaten on price or results.* Isn't there a law about false advertising?'

'What did I do wrong?'

'Always honest? You spun a web of deceit.'

'You weren't a client, so it doesn't count. I subcontracted you.'

'Under false pretenses, and you led Mrs. Bender to believe that you had paid me ten thousand dollars.'

Jessica McGann threw the towel on the floor and started to get undressed out of her gym gear. 'Okay, you want the money. I'll get you the fucking money.'

Virgo turned around and faced the door. 'Yes, please. I think that's the least you can do.'

'Give me a week.'

'A week?'

'I had bills to pay.'

'Okay, I'll wait.'

'What happened to Mr. Superior, I'm not bothered about money as long as the poor homeless guys don't starve? Just give me two hundred bucks so they can eat while I'm away? What happened to that guy?'

'It's the principle.'

There was a pause, and Jessica McGann said, 'It's safe to turn back now.'

Virgo swiveled and saw she had the striped business suit on and was fixing her face in the mirror. He said, 'Call me when you've got the money.'

She kept looking in the compact mirror. 'You never told me.'

'What?'

'How things panned out at La Esperanza when you went to rescue the damsel in distress.'

'Casey was good. She's happy at the Templar Sanctorum.'

Jessica McGann laughed. 'The great negotiator failed?'

'I never said I'd get her out.'

'Bombed, flunked, tanked, come up empty…worth every cent of ten grand.'

Virgo bristled. This woman had a gift for getting under his skin. 'Someone tried to set me up for the murder of a POG member. I could have gone back to prison because of you.'

'Flopped, floundered, found lacking, fell flat. The full goat rodeo.'

'Thanks. I hope your business picks up.'

'Bye.' She kissed her hand and blew it towards him. Then smiled. 'Say hello to the homeless guys for me.'

Virgo smiled back despite himself. 'I'm not going back to Santa Barbara.'

'What? Are you running off to hide away from the real world somewhere else?'

'I'm going back to La Esperanza. Someone tried to set me up for a homicide, and I take that kind of thing personally.' He marched out and cursed his way down the stairs, angry at how easily this woman teased and irritated him.

Midafternoon, the street below was quiet. Virgo sat in his RV, planning his next move, aided by a plate of chili reheated in the microwave. There seemed little point barging his way into the POG compound and hoping that someone would talk, because they were probably scared they'd end up like Jake Dearman. He was the last one to get caught gossiping off-script to an outsider. The chili was good. Plenty of bite without burning the lips, and the beans hadn't turned into little rocks like they did sometimes when he overheated them.

The other option was to go back to the local police department and offer to work with them, but that required a leap of faith on his behalf that he wasn't prepared to make. Detective Malone seemed approachable and possibly harbored his own suspicions about the People's Order of Gabriel, but Chambers was not to be trusted.

Virgo had been puzzling how Dr. Dan knew his name, and the only explanation he could come up with was that someone at the POG had called La Esperanza police department and run a check on the license plate of his RV. Virgo knew the police database would have links to his conviction and file. Maybe the POG and the local cops had some kind of symbiotic relationship going on, like the warthog and its back-scratching mongoose.

What the situation required was more intelligence-gathering to inform the decision-making process. Something he'd done many times in The Activity. Often the mission was surveillance undertaken behind enemy lines or in a hostile environment. Recon and report back, although sometimes a decision was taken to destroy assets there and then if the opportunity presented itself.

Virgo was scooping chili in a slice of flat bread when something through the RV window attracted his attention. A beat-up, tan Chevy careened up onto the sidewalk, spewing smoke, and two guys jumped out. They both had shaved heads on stubby necks, and sleeveless vests to show every inch of skin was inked. One of the guys carried a baseball bat, though he looked like he'd never been near a home plate. They ran straight into the doorway next to the Panda Express, where stairs led up to Artemis Associates.

Definitely not visiting the acupuncturist, thought Virgo, but maybe the debt-collection agency had annoyed them by sending threatening letters or repossessing their other car, the one that wasn't a crap-colored wreck. As much as he now hated the Jessica McGann he'd once found so alluring, he dropped the flat bread and went to check on her.

When he reached the top of the stairs, the door to Artemis Associates was ajar, and he could hear raised voices. He barged in. Jessica McGann sat behind her desk, a defiant look on her face. The two no-necks stood in a classic threatening stance: feet wide apart, chest out, gut sucked in, arms bowed and fists clenched.

Virgo said, 'Are these the guys who've come to fix the air-con?'

Jessica said, 'They're just leaving.'

The guy with the bat said, 'Not until you agree.' Then he turned to Virgo. 'Fuck off, shithead, and come back later.'

Outside the arena of war or similar combat situations, Virgo would never choose to strike a man from behind, so he tapped bat guy on the shoulder and said, 'You've ten seconds to walk away, or I'm going to break one of your arms.'

Bat guy looked at his shaven-headed twin and smiled. Bravado or maybe genuine puzzlement. 'Who do you think you are? Fucking Bruce Willis or Robocop?'

Virgo said, 'Five.'

'What?'

'Seconds.'

A moment's hesitation flickered in bat-guy's eyes; then he made the decision and went for it. Someone unused to fighting would have swung the baseball bat through an arc, which gave their opponent ample time to prepare and counter, but this guy was streetwise and had fought before. He used the wooden bat as an extension of his fist and rammed the end of it towards Virgo's face.

Virgo expected no less and was ready. Close-quarter combat is more about momentum and leverage than blows. It can take a lot of blows to permanently disable an opponent, but only one well-executed maneuver. He waited until the last possible moment and swayed backwards to let the end of the bat fly past his nose, and then when bat guy followed through, off balance, he grabbed his neck and twisted him to the floor. In one movement he had him in an elbow lock and used his own knee as a fulcrum to snap the joint with minimal pressure.

There was a scream of pain. Virgo was already primed for no-neck number two, but that guy didn't want to know. He had his hands half-raised. The one with the broken arm shouted, 'What the fuck did you do?' and 'You're gonna die.' With a lot of shouts, the two tattooed gangsters shuffled down the stairs and out of the building, leaving behind the baseball bat as a souvenir on the floor of Artemis Associates.

Jessica McGann sat stony-faced and motionless behind the desk.

Virgo said, 'Are you all right?'

She said, 'What do you think you're doing, moron?'

CHAPTER 10

Virgo negotiated an obstacle course of cardboard boxes, Ziploc bags and discarded gym wear, and peered out the window. The beat-up Chevy squealed its tires as it bumped back onto the highway and roared down the street, leaving behind a fog of burnt engine oil. He said, 'I thought you might appreciate some help.'

Jessica McGann clenched her jaw. 'I can fight my own battles.'

'Against two knuckleheads armed with a wooden club?'

'Yes, if necessary.' She brought her right hand up from under the desk, holding a Walther PDP. 'Bullets are a great leveler.'

'Okay, I apologize.'

'I was handling the situation, but now the next time they come back, they'll be better prepared.'

'What do they want?'

Jessica shrugged. 'They're just a couple of local thugs who've been hired to try to frighten me off a case I'm working on.'

'You've got a case?'

'Comedy doesn't suit you, Virgo. Stick to pointless violence.'

'I was trying to help.'

'What were you doing hanging around outside, anyway?' Jessica stuffed the Walther into a tattered Gucci bag. 'Are you stalking me?'

'No. Refueling with calories before I go back to La Esperanza and find out who killed Jake Dearman. Sorry to disappoint you.'

'Just let me divert the landline to my mobile.' Jessica McGann tapped some keys on the phone and replaced the handset. Then she slung the Gucci bag on her shoulder, slid her feet into a pair of slingbacks, and said, 'Come on. I'm going to buy you a drink.'

They went to a craft beer sports tavern around the corner called the Shakespeare, which was empty apart from a guy sat at the bar with a French bulldog on the next stool. When the guy saw them, he went around to the other side of the bar and said, 'Usual, Jessie?'

'No, just a water, thanks, Max.'

Virgo said, 'Make it two.'

'Sure.' Max sniffed. 'Push the boat out.'

When they'd taken seats at a table in the window, Jessica pulled a cell phone out and started texting. 'Sorry.'

Virgo waited until he saw her hit *send*. 'What's this about?'

'I've got an offer for you.'

'Really?'

'We work together on the Jake Dearman murder.'

'I don't need a partner.'

'Okay, I work for you. You're the boss.'

Virgo thought about it. Surveillance is a resource-hungry activity. Having another operative to put a shift in was attractive. She also had local knowledge and maybe law enforcement contacts that could prove useful. 'What's in it for you?

Are you after charming your way out of paying me the ten grand?'

Jessica's cell shimmied on the table. She read the message and tapped one back. 'I want to get Casey Bender out of that evil cult.'

'Are you trying to get more money out of Mrs. Bender?'

'What if I do? Maybe it'll go towards paying for repairs to my office after those goons you annoyed come back and trash the place when it's empty.'

'Is there only you who works in there?'

'Just me.'

Virgo pulled a slight frown. 'The name Artemis Associates suggests there's more than one person in the business.'

'I know. Genius, isn't it? Sounds so grand and impressive.' The cell buzzed and pirouetted on the table again. She unlocked it and started to tap.

'I don't know whether I could work with someone who doesn't consider it rude to be constantly texting during a conversation.'

'It's Joey, my kid. He's always after something.'

'How are you going to spend hours in the field as a single mother?'

'Sexist bullshit is so twentieth century.'

'Excuse me for highlighting an inconvenient fact.'

'Joey's sixteen, and La Esperanza is thirty miles up the road. I can be home in under half an hour.'

Virgo weighed up his options. She'd proved she was an effective investigator by locating Casey and then him. And he'd made a mistake busting the guy's arm in the Artemis Associates' office, because there could well be financial repercussions for her business. He felt responsible.

Jessica McGann seemed to sense his prevarication. 'Come on, get me on the team. I'm a resourceful investigator with outstanding initiative, and I've a CCW license, unlike you.'

Virgo chewed his bottom lip. As a convicted felon he was banned from having a gun, whereas the pink-haired PI had a Carry Concealed Weapon ticket. He was tempted. What worried him was that he was being tempted by the wrong reasons, because the initial gut attraction he'd felt when he first met her hadn't entirely melted away, and it was too soon to move on from Crystal. It would always be too soon.

The cell phone on the table buzzed once more. Jessica picked it up. 'And I've got a teenage son who eats more than an entire football team, so yes, I need the money. Are you happy now? Give me a break.'

'Meet me at eight in the morning at La Esperanza. Don't be late.' Virgo still wasn't sure it was the right thing, but if it didn't work out, he could always bail. It wasn't like it was a marriage.

CHAPTER 11

Dr. Daniel Nelson kissed Ruby on the forehead, eased himself out of bed, and padded into the bathroom to dispose of his prophylactic down the john. He hated the things, but impregnating one of his wives would be worse. Childbirth was against the rules in the People's Order of Gabriel, and it was he who'd made the rules. He flushed two hundred million potential followers down the pan and took a cold shower. Got dressed in a cream linen suit and spent some time in front of the dressing room mirror, applying cleanser, tinted moisturizer, a touch of contour stick to the cheekbones and a little eyeshadow. Being the leader of a new religious order is a blast, but it takes work.

Normally the kitchen staff would have a breakfast prepared and waiting for him in his private refectory, but today was the first of the month. This was the day of temporal judgment, the morning where he gathered the apostles and rewarded success and punished failure. It was a meeting where he reinforced the total control he exercised over the lives of those who had sworn allegiance to him, and was much more exciting and satisfying than the sex he had just had, which had been dispassionate and tepid. Ruby was the longest standing of his six wives, and maybe it was time for her to be replaced.

Before leaving his residence, there was one more job to do. He went into his downstairs office, took off his jacket and washed his hands again in the adjoining bathroom. Good hygiene was important. He took sterile water from the fridge, added the special powder and cooked the mixture in a deep bulbous spoon. The syringe and needle were one piece and shrink-wrapped, and he checked for air bubbles before rolling up a sleeve and injecting into the inner elbow of his left arm. Then he waited. *Whoosh*. The hit was instant, and now he was ready. The last vestiges of inhibition and restraint were vanquished, and he was the mighty Dr. Dan. All geared up to do what he needed to do to maintain his position as the leader of the People's Order of Gabriel.

When he bounced into the ceremonial chamber, like a prizefighter entering the ring, they were waiting for him. All twelve in a line stood to attention. All dressed in the red uniform that denoted their status as his apostles and the blood sacrifice necessary to achieve it. His apostles, nobody else's. He was the first true prophet of the new millennium, and soon the Christian world would tremble in awe at the power of his vision and teachings. Politicians would fawn. The school curriculum would be changed. Ordinary folk in every state in the Union would realize they were witnessing history being made in their own lifetime.

Nelson took his place behind the lectern. No simple wooden stand for him. This was a hi-tech console with more switches, knobs and faders than the bridge of the USS *Enterprise*. He pressed a button, and hidden speakers pumped out Part 1 of Handel's *Messiah* as background music, then he pressed another, and all four walls of the chamber filled floor to ceiling with a video of himself standing in front of a giant cross in a white suit, looking supernatural with his electric blue eyes.

In the future, obedience and worship would be his by right, and he would not need to continually prove himself to be the supreme leader, but right now he had to earn respect and compliance, and he knew how to do it. People want something to believe in. They like rules. When frightened, they'll do as they're told, even if what they're told to do is bizarre and illogical. The absurd becomes the norm.

Nelson slipped a headset microphone on, and his voice boomed over the music. 'Friends, I appear before you this morning in a state of profound disappointment.'

Concerned frowns glistened on the faces of some of the apostles. They were all perspiring. Some had dread shrouding their features, like dogs who know they have misbehaved and are expecting a beating.

'Jake Dearman, member of our congregation, lost his faith and thought he could be a solo agent.' Nelson dropped his voice an octave. Somber with a hint of menace. 'This should not have been allowed to happen, and I think you'll agree someone needs to be disciplined.'

Twelve heads nodded. Everyone agreed.

'Good.' Nelson smiled. 'Step forward the apostle who was responsible for Jake Dearman losing his faith.'

Nobody moved. Two or three exchanged furtive glances. More sweat beaded on twelve brows.

Then a sandy-haired guy on the left end on the line took a step forward, jaw clenched and eyes closed. He pushed his chest out and braced himself.

'Not you, Matthew,' said Nelson. 'Step back in line.'

Everyone apart from Matthew looked disappointed.

Nelson smiled again. This was the best part. Playing with people's minds and seeing how far you could go. Without warning, he hit a button on the console, and a piercing scream filled the room. A tall guy with a goatee, three in from the right end, face-planted on the floor, his body convulsing like a salmon high and dry on the riverbank. Nelson nudged the fader up beneath the switch, and the convulsions increased with muffled groans and the sound of flesh and limbs thrashing against terracotta tiles.

The history of torture within the Christian church was a subject that had long fascinated Nelson. He'd considered bringing back a whole range of medieval instruments for occasions such as this: the rack, the wheel, the iron maiden, the scavenger's daughter and the pear of anguish. The problem with them all was their rudimentary reliance on breaking bones or rupturing internal organs to cause permanent physical injury. Modern technology offered far more flexibility and control and could still provide the fatal option if required.

Each of the twelve apostles were wearing stun belts, which delivered seventy thousand volts to the kidney areas in ten-second bursts, with twenty pulses per second. The specification was above what was legally allowed in any law enforcement environment around the world, and had cost accordingly. Nelson had once asked an apostle how it felt and was told it was like having red-hot knives hammered into every muscle in the body and each nerve and sinew frazzled. Fucking kill-me-now pain. Of course, occasionally urination and defecation were unfortunate side effects, but such minor unpleasantness was a small price to pay.

The prostrate goatee guy had a cut above his left eye, which was dripping, and saliva-blood was seeping from the corner of his mouth thanks to his teeth's involuntary contraction on the tongue. Nelson waited until goatee was sufficiently recovered to get to his knees, and then said, 'Andrew, it's your responsibility to ensure that members of the Order are properly supervised when they leave the Templar Sanctorum.'

Andrew couldn't speak. He nodded his head in acceptance of his failure, and multiple spots of blood sprinkled on the terracotta tiles. The other eleven apostles stared ahead, trying not to glance down, and trying not to look relieved. Most of them were breathing more freely now. A few were still rigid with terror and starting to sway from the pressure of having to stand such a length of time in the spotlight.

'But somebody else is more culpable.' Nelson's voice thundered over the *Messiah*.

Eleven pairs of eyes instantly gravitated to the console to see if their switch was the next to be pushed. They knew the layout. Could tell if Dr. Dan's finger was hovering in their personal pain zone. He loved it. This was what it was all about. Keep them off balance, wary of each other and in thrall of his omnipotence.

Nelson lifted his hands high so they weren't near the console, then let them swoop down low over the buttons, scanning left to right. Come on. Who's next to get their kidneys fried?

He pressed a button, and eleven statues held their breath, but there were no screams. He'd just killed the background music. He hit another switch, and the video walls went white. Then he put on his angry preacher's voice. 'Jake Dearman was a weak member of the People's Order of Gabriel. He was sent on a re-education program to cure him of his weakness, but it transpires the cure was ineffective. The apostle responsible for re-education must be chastised.'

A rapid thrust of the hand. A heartrending cry of agony echoed around the chamber, and Nelson felt the hatred and lust for vengeance swell inside him as he pushed the fader up to maximum. Then he hit the override switch to nullify the ten-second cutoff. A red light flashed on the console, but he couldn't stop. The groans and grunts and involuntary spasms had stopped, which was a bad sign and an indication that something was wrong. Too late. He'd wanted to push the boundary, and maybe on this occasion he had gone too far. So what? Lessons had to be learnt. They were all replaceable.

The body lying on the floor was Matthew. The apostle who had initially taken a step forward and been sent back in line. One of Nelson's favorite ploys – make them think they're safe and then do their legs. Keep them off-kilter. Insecure. Complacency is a breeding ground for egotism and needs to be avoided. It can give people ideas above their station and sow the seeds of challenge to authority.

Nobody moved. Eyes strayed towards the floor. The silence was deafening, and then Matthew made a low wailing sound. Nelson spoke into his headset. 'Take him to the medical quarters. This council of temporal judgment is concluded.' Then he marched back to his mansion and straight into the bathroom, put his head in the toilet bowl and puked.

CHAPTER 12

Virgo stood at the RV point and checked the time on his cell again. 0819 hours and still no sign of the pink-haired PI. Maybe an opportunity to earn some easy cash had come up elsewhere, and she didn't fancy putting in the hours and legwork on a real investigative job. Ten minutes later, an old-school VW Beetle convertible pulled up at the curb with the top down, and she said, 'Get in.'

He dropped his rucksack in the back seat and climbed in. 'You're late.'

'Ever tried getting a sixteen-year-old out of bed and to school?'

'Not my problem.'

'You always this bad-tempered?'

'Probably. I don't know.'

They drove through La Esperanza and out of town towards the Templar Sanctorum. The sun had already started to crank up the heat, and a gentle breeze brought a sweet and sour mountain bouquet down into the valley: lavender, fennel and chaparral sage. Traffic was light. La Esperanza wasn't a commuter town or a hub that drew workers in. No call center or Amazon warehouse. Businesses were local, and tourists were still eating breakfast or sleeping off last night's vino tinto.

Virgo directed Jessica to pull off the highway just beyond the entrance to the POG estate and its private parking lot. TV shows always make surveillance look like a piece of cake, but the reality is it's a difficult task to remain covert for any length of time. Should the subject be alive to the possibility they might be being watched, then it's virtually impossible to perform without specialist resources. If Virgo had still been in the FBI, a tactical team would have deployed in the middle of the night and installed hidden, battery-powered cameras in the ground or shrubs opposite the entrance. The images would have then been microwave-linked or sent 5G to a remote office or technical surveillance van parked miles away. They could have watched monitors with their feet up, eating pretzels.

Without the resources, the secret was not to be greedy and get too close. Chances were all vehicles and pedestrians leaving the Templar Sanctorum would head towards town away from where the VW Beetle was parked. If someone did turn the other way and drive past them, then they had to act like a couple of city dwellers who'd driven out for a hike in the hills. Virgo took a pair of Nikon Monarch binoculars out of his rucksack and settled down to watch and wait.

He had no specific tactical objectives at this stage other than to get a picture of what he was dealing with. Numbers, command structure, equipment, routine movements, deliveries, signs of defensive personnel such as guards and any perceived areas of weakness. The type of recon he'd done in The Activity. Once he had the information, he could then plan the best way of tackling the POG and finding out who killed Jake Dearman.

Two hours later, no vehicle or pedestrian had left or

entered the estate. It was going to be a long day. Even so, Virgo kept his attention level high, because it only took one moment's lapse in concentration to miss the event that was key to unlocking the puzzle. He fished around in his rucksack without taking his eyes off the target property and pulled out a protein bar, tore the top off the wrapper with his teeth and bit in.

Jessica said, 'I'm good. Thanks for asking.'

Virgo finished the mouthful. 'Thought you'd have brought your own chow.'

'How long have you been on your own?'

'What?'

'You're a widower, right? I just wondered how long it had been, because you're kind of insular.'

'I'd rather not talk about it.' Virgo took a massive bite of caramel and peanuts to glue his mouth closed and emphasize the point.

Jessica harrumphed and was quiet for a while. Then she laughed in a sardonic way and said, 'After my husband left, I tried internet dating. What a frigging nightmare. If I could share one piece of advice with you on how to deal with being alone, it would be this – steer clear of dating websites.'

'Thanks.'

'Full of fucking clowns and psychos.'

'Wise words. I'll bear them in mind.'

'What you should do is go down to—'

'Shush.' Virgo pointed to the gates of the POG compound. Movement. He used the binoculars to view what was happening. Three minibuses painted purple in POG livery pulled out in convoy and headed towards town. There appeared to be six or seven passengers in each vehicle. Clean-cut and fresh-faced like the residents of the Templar Sanctorum, but dressed like regular young people, not in the weird communist uniforms. Maybe they were off to knock on doors like Mormon missionaries and recruit new members. It seemed strange for so many to be leaving when Dr. Dan had told him they were self-sufficient in the People's Order of Gabriel.

Jessica said, 'Did you see Casey?'

Virgo said, 'No, but she could have been in one of them.'

'So are we going to sit here all day on the off chance of seeing her?'

'It's not all about Casey.'

'Not to you, but I'm going to get that girl out of there.'

Virgo tipped his head. *Good for you.* He wasn't sure if Jessica McGann was expressing a noble motive or had dollar signs flashing in her eyes, but either way it wouldn't be easy. What had Jake Dearman said about Casey? *She's one of them.* Good luck trying to talk that young woman into rushing back to the bosom of the gin-soaked mother who'd pushed her away. Wait, what was he saying? Virgo chided himself for judging. Who knows what goes on within a family and the dynamics that can cause fractures without any one person being truly at fault. He should know.

A car approached from the opposite direction and slowed on approaching the gates to the Templar Sanctorum. Virgo raised the Nikon Monarchs. Dodge Charger. Single male occupant. Just before the car turned in to the gates, he got a good view. The round face of Sergeant Chambers from La Esperanza police department in what was no doubt an unmarked police vehicle. Maybe making follow-up enquiries on the Jake Dearman case, but single crewed? Maybe someone else's mother had made a complaint that their son or daughter had been kidnapped by this strange religious sect that nestled in the heart of wine country.

Jessica said, 'Take a walk.'

Virgo said, 'Sorry?'

'Take a walk. I need a pee.'

'I'm watching the target property.'

'Come on. It's easy for guys. You can piss in a bottle.'

'What are you going to do if I take a walk? Is there a bathroom in the back seat?'

'Do you think you're the only one with a go-bag?' Jessica pointed to a duffel. 'I have devices in there designed for the female body. Most of my work is marital break-ups, which means I spend a lot of hours in the parking lots of motels or out in the middle of nowhere at spots where illicit affairs take place. There's no restrooms. A girl's got to have mobile facilities.'

'Fascinating, but I'm trying to concentrate.'

'Can't wait any longer.' Jessica started to unbutton her pants.

Virgo stepped out of the car and took a walk.

When he stooped back into the Beetle three minutes later, he said, 'The two guys who were acting heavy at your office, was that an adultery case?'

'I said most of my cases are marital break-ups. I'm not a one-trick pony.' She turned her head and looked out the side window. 'A sixteen-year-old kid died from a fentanyl overdose. His father hired me to find who the supplier was, and I guess I'm getting close because that was the second time they've tried to warn me off.'

Virgo shook his head. 'Sixteen?'

'In the same class at high school as my Joey. It scares the shit out of me.'

Virgo couldn't think of what to say. When he worked as a negotiator, the training would have kicked in, and he would have been straight there with the empathy and the banter. Two hundred words a minute, fired out like a machine gun. Now it was a struggle. He was getting slow, and he was worried anything he said would sound like a platitude.

Jessica said, 'I'm afraid he's mixing with the wrong crowd,

and it's not easy without his father being around.' Still staring distracted out the side window.

Virgo said, 'Doesn't sound like he was much of a role model. Your boy's probably better off without him.'

'Thing is, I think he's already started. Weed mainly, you know how it is…Anyway, forget it. Not your problem.'

There was a cloud of dust outside the gates to the Templar Sanctorum, and Sergeant Chambers sped back towards town in his Dodge Charger. A flying visit.

Nothing happened during the next five hours. The hottest part of the day came and began to fade. The blacktop shimmered. No sign of the three minibuses returning, or anyone else leaving the compound. Gravity was weighing heavy on Virgo's eyelids, and he was about to pass the binoculars to Jessica and take the opportunity to recharge his brain battery with sleep when he saw a vehicle approaching.

A pickup. GMC Sierra in black with four on board. When they got closer, he saw they weren't POG types. These guys were all baseball caps, ratty hair, ripped denim and plenty of tattoos. Maybe they'd seen the light, hallelujah, and were about to sign up for a lifetime in service to the Lord, but it was unlikely. Virgo read out the license plate as it turned in through the gates, and Jessica jotted it down.

This was what they'd been waiting for, Virgo was sure. The one thing that didn't fit the pattern. Something at odds with what the normal situation should be. It was what they'd taught him in the Army, although every human has used it for self-preservation since prehistoric times. Sixth sense or astute observation of situational behavior, call it what you want.

He said, 'Any chance of running the plates through the police system? All good PIs have contacts on the force, don't they?'

Jessica put a neon pink fingernail to her lips and tilted her head. 'Is this why you wanted me on the team?'

'We're not a team. I'm in charge, and you're helping out.'

'Okay, I'll see what I can do, boss man.'

Virgo picked his rucksack up from the back seat and got out of the car. 'Same time tomorrow. Don't be late.'

'What are you doing?'

'You've got a kid to get home for. I'm going to dig in and find out what these shitbags are up to, even if it takes all night.'

Jessica said, 'You need to get a life, but thanks.' The old Beetle made its distinctive doof, doof, doof, doof, unique to the rear-mounted, air-cooled engine and stubby exhaust, and she shot off towards home and her son.

CHAPTER 13

Bang on 0800 hours next morning, Virgo arrived on foot at the RV point and saw that the convertible VW Beetle was already there. Roof up this time. He opened the passenger door and ducked in. 'You're early. Well done.'

Jessica put a hand to her mouth and made a sarcastic yawn. 'Anything happen last night?'

'Zero. I kept obs until midnight, and nobody came or went.'

'How did you get back to town?'

'How do you think? I used to run farther than that carrying a sixty-pound rucksack.'

'What about the minibuses?'

'No sign of them.'

'Strange.' Jessica drove through La Esperanza and out on the road past the Templar Sanctorum. Reversed up into the same spot as the day before and said, 'Want to know what else is funny? That GMC pickup is flagged on the police database as being used by John Rinker. Number one coke and opioid trafficking scumbag in these parts.'

Virgo knew there must be a connection with Dr. Dan or someone high up in the food chain of the People's Order of Gabriel, but couldn't imagine what it could be. Preppy Bible bashers and drug-running gangsters are chalk and cheese. Of course, it could be someone in the compound was using and what they'd witnessed yesterday was a low-level delivery of a few bags of dope, but he didn't think so. He had an idea. 'You still got any contacts in the LAPD who can run financial checks?'

'Why do I feel as though I'm being exploited again?'

'Specifically on both Dr. Daniel Nelson's personal accounts and the People's Order of Gabriel.'

'I'm running out of favors.'

'Do your best.'

'Why don't you ask your old colleagues in the Bureau?' She stroked her chin. 'Oh, yeah, I forgot. Nobody wants to talk to the agent who went to prison.'

They had been in position less than fifteen minutes when there was activity at the gates of the Templar Sanctorum. Virgo used the binoculars and watched four golf buggies pull out onto the highway and start heading in their direction. Four POG members perched on each, all dressed in the gray, characterless cotton uniforms, most carrying a spade or digging fork. The buggies kept coming in their direction, and Virgo ducked down just before they drew level. He came up and peered over the dashboard just in time to see the convoy turn off the highway into a field twenty yards down the road.

Jessica said, 'I think one of those was Casey. Third one, sat offside on the back.'

'Possibly.' Virgo got back properly into his seat. 'That time I called to see her, she was out working on the farm.'

'I'm going to try to speak to her.'

'No, I don't think—' Virgo stopped talking because she was already out of the car and halfway across the road.

He caught up with her at the entrance to the field, where the gate had been left open. A gravel track ran down the treeline towards some outbuildings, and the buggies were almost there. He said, 'At least wait until we can catch her alone; otherwise she might end up next to Jake Dearman in the morgue.'

'You really think these guys are that crazy?'

'I saw Dearman's face when he realized someone was watching him talk to me.'

They hung back in the shade of an oak tree by the gate and waited. Doors to the outbuildings opened, and a couple of John Deeres appeared. Short wheelbase and narrow like the kind of tractors that go between rows of vines or orchards. Then two Kawasaki quads pulling trailers, and some workers with wheelbarrows and tub buckets. One guy looked like he was in charge, delegating tasks and pointing a lot, and then they split up.

Jessica said, 'That's her. She still moves like an athlete.'

Virgo watched a young woman with a ponytail threaded through the back of a baseball cap walk away from the group. Then she turned to talk to a fellow worker, and he saw it was Casey. They disappeared around the back of a pile of logs, carrying forks and wicker baskets.

Jessica set off after them, but Virgo shot an arm out. 'Be patient.'

Ten minutes later, there were no workers in sight, and they moved forward down the gravel track to where the outbuildings stood. Once there, they had a view of the land. Dr. Dan had said the POG had its own farm, but it was four small fields, each one ten or twelve acres in size. Farm was too grand a description. More like an oversized vegetable patch. As with so many other things in the Templar Sanctorum, it was a pretentious imitation of the real thing. There was probably a Walmart van delivering groceries to the compound right now.

All the POG farmhands worked in pairs. Casey was with a slight-built woman harvesting some type of root vegetable that could have been beets or turnips on the edge of one field, before a boundary fence marked the point where the land turned into chaparral and rose up into the coastal mountain range.

Virgo said, 'You distract the other woman while I talk to Casey.'

'What?' Jessica screwed up her eyes. 'I'll speak to Casey. You make small talk with the unimportant third party.'

'I can't. She might recognize me if she was in the church when I stormed the pulpit.'

'Really?'

'Yes.'

'Okay, but this might be our best chance. Don't screw it up.'

Virgo hovered at the corner of a wooden barn and watched as Jessica made a beeline for the woman who was Casey's co-worker at the point in their routine they were furthest apart. He couldn't hear what Jessica said, but there were tears, heartrending sobs and much waving of the arms. After a while, the woman dropped her basket and followed Jessica to a gap in the boundary fence.

Virgo moved fast. Casey was knocking soil from a bunch of vegetables when he reached her and said, 'For your own sake, don't do anything to attract attention.'

Casey shot up. 'What are you doing here?'

Virgo thought she appeared different from the other evening in the diner. The verve and vim had gone. She looked weary and vulnerable. 'Someone beat your friend Jake Dearman to death and fingered me for it. I aim to find out who.'

Casey looked around. 'Where's Myra?'

'She's okay, but we've not got long. She'll be back soon.'

'Myra's my new friend.'

Virgo noticed that Casey had her sleeves rolled up, and that on the inside of her right forearm were two stick-angel tattoos. He nodded with his eyes to them. 'Why have you got two and Jake only had one?'

'He was in the first level of the Order. I'm in the second.'

'How many levels are there?'

'Three. That's the Trinity. I'm almost there, but…' She gave a weak smile.

Virgo could see there was something playing on her mind. 'Tell me what happened to Jake after I left you.'

Casey's bottom lip quivered, and a lump the size of a golf ball appeared in her throat. 'I think I might have made a mistake.'

'We all make mistakes. Tell me what happened to Jake.'

'I don't know.'

Virgo said nothing. Sometimes the power of silence is the best way of repeating a question.

Casey looked around to see if anyone was watching or within earshot. 'He had his problems, but he wasn't a bad person.'

Virgo said nothing again.

'I don't know what happened to Jake,' said Casey. 'I just heard someone shouting and maybe dragging from his room around midnight.'

'Who?'

'I don't know.'

Virgo sensed she was holding back. 'Did you tell the cops?'

Casey laughed without humor. 'There was only one. I didn't trust him.'

'We can go to the FBI.'

'I'm not allowed off the site since we saw you in the diner.'

'Okay, I'll get them to come here.'

Casey's eyes flashed with panic. 'No, please. Don't do that. Promise you will never do that.'

'Why?'

'Promise me. If you have any serious interest in my well-being…'

Virgo saw one of the quads with a trailer heading their way. He put his hands on Casey's shoulders and looked her in the eye. 'It's not too late to leave. When you're ready, I'll get you out of this place and make sure you're safe.'

Tears leaked from the corners of Casey's eyes. 'I've got to stay.'

The quad was getting close. Virgo couldn't risk being there any longer. He vaulted a fence on the boundary and rolled into the scrubland. Dusted himself off and set off on a circular loop back to the Beetle with a single thought preying on his mind: what hold exactly did Dr. Daniel Nelson have over Casey Bender?

CHAPTER 14

'What do you mean, you left her in there?' Jessica's cheeks were flush with anger and her eyes deadly harpoons.

Virgo said, 'How was I supposed to make her come with me?'

'Some fucking knight in shining armor you are.'

'Should I have clubbed her over the head and dragged her out?'

A scowl of disgust crumpled Jessica's face. 'Well, that would have been better than leaving her in a place she clearly doesn't feel safe and doesn't want to be anymore.'

'It wasn't like that.' Virgo heard himself sounding defensive and didn't like it. 'There's something we don't know about. She's in a virtual prison with no bars on the windows or fences on the perimeter.'

'All the more reason you should have whisked her away while we had the chance.'

'What if she'd screamed or shouted for help?'

'What if aliens turn us into flesh-eating zombies? What if

the world is made of mozzarella? *What if* is the coward's cop-out for doing jack shit.'

Virgo had been called a lot of things in his time. Coward was a new one. The temptation was to lash out and hit back with an equally below-the-belt verbal attack, such as suggesting the real reason Jessica was so furious was because getting Casey home to Mrs. Bender was a big payday. That would have been unfair because, although there might be a grain of truth in it, he was sure Jessica had a genuine concern for Casey's welfare. That was why he said nothing and took a chocolate bar out of his rucksack. Took a big bite and chomped. Big angry chomps.

They were back in the old Beetle. Jessica seethed in silence for the next couple of hours, and then she couldn't contain herself. 'What did I tell you? Don't screw up because this might be our best chance.'

Virgo said, 'Okay. Drop me in La Esperanza. I think it's best if this working arrangement is dissolved and we both go our separate ways.'

'Suit yourself.' She fired up the engine and drove back into town. Pulling into the square, her phone made pipping sounds, and she grabbed it. 'Fuck. Alarm activation at the office. Jump out here.'

'Keep going. I'm coming with you.'

'I don't need help.'

'Fine. I'll wait outside while you tackle the bad guys.'

Jessica gave him half a sideways smile and floored the gas pedal. Flat out the Beetle didn't do much above sixty, but the highway was jam-free, and in half an hour they pulled up outside the Panda Express.

Virgo was true to his word. He let Jessica go upstairs first and saw her unzip her shoulder bag and palm the Walther PDP. The door to Artemis Associates was open, and there were wood splinters on the floor caused by the wrecking bar that had been used to force it. They stopped and listened. No noise. Jessica balled in, Walther first, and used it to check all four corners. Clear. No intruders present. She sat down behind her desk and let out a big sigh. 'Bastards.'

The place looked like an explosion in a stationery factory, but then again, thought Virgo, it didn't seem much different to when he was there last time. The leotard and leggings were still piled up on the sofa. The intestines of the air-con were still ripped out and strewn in front of the window.

After a while, Jessica took a deep breath and stood up to check the single filing cabinet in the corner, which doubled as a table for a coffee machine and cups. The top drawer was hanging open, and when she peered inside, she said, 'They cleared out all my current cases.'

'Hard-copy files, but what about digital?'

'I'm an analogue girl.'

There wasn't a desktop in the office or a MacBook, and Virgo couldn't recall seeing one last time. 'Do you think it's the same guys?'

'Shit, Joey's home.' A bolt of panic lit Jessica's face. 'One of the files had all my bills showing my personal address.' She snatched the keys off the desk and hurried out of the office.

The Beetle was already moving before Virgo got the passenger door closed. Storefronts flashed by. Pedestrians took a step back from the curb. They ran a red light and narrowly missed being sideswiped by a ten-wheel truck. She horn-blasted an old guy on an electric scooter out of the way and screamed down a straight strip of highway before squealing into a left-hander with two wheels defying gravity. One more high-pitched blast of the engine and they were there.

It was a single-story wooden house painted lilac that looked like a kit-built World War II army barracks. Dirt yard with a couple of fruit trees. Under her breath, Jessica said,

'Please God, let him be okay,' and ran to the front door. Virgo followed. It was unlocked. They bowled through the hallway into a lounge, where a teenage boy lay on the couch with headphones on, eyes Gorilla-glued to a screen, thumbing the buttons on a gamepad. Their presence never even registered with him.

Jessica turned to Virgo, relief making her shoulders sag. 'False alarm. Thanks for the backup.'

'Why isn't he in school?'

'I couldn't face a battle this morning and didn't want to let you down by being late again.'

'Your kid's more important than keeping me happy.'

'I'll tell myself that when I can't afford to buy him new clothes or feed him. I need the work.'

Virgo glanced around the lounge and through into the kitchen diner. The place was clean and comfortable, but simple. No luxury furnishings or expensive gadgets. He felt bad about putting her under pressure to pay up the full ten grand from Mrs. Bender. She'd made him angry by deceiving him into going up to La Esperanza in the first place, but it wasn't as though he needed the money. That was just him making a point.

Jessica had read his mind. She said, 'Don't even think about giving me a free pass on the 10K. I'm good for it.'

'Let's take a rain check on that.'

'No, a deal's a deal.' Jessica went into the kitchen and put the coffee maker on. Tidied away breakfast plates that still had toast crusts and bits of egg on. Opened a pack of cookies and put them on the table. 'Help yourself while I freshen up.'

Virgo chewed on a chocolate chip and pecan cookie, and the nagging problem of Casey Bender came back into his head, like the hook of a song that won't go away. He'd been so focused on getting information about Jake Dearman's murder that he'd underplayed in his own mind the jeopardy

Casey was in. If she was scared and in danger, then she had to leave. The only thing stopping her was her own loss of capability for critical thought. She'd been brainwashed. The question was how to get her out if she refused to leave.

Jessica came back in and made coffee. 'I can almost hear the cogs in your brain.'

'It's because they're rusty.'

'I bet they used to whir and race like a Rolex.'

'Not really. I mainly used to rely on the training. If you're well trained, you don't need to think. Your actions are second nature.'

Jessica leant over the table and said, 'Okay, stop thinking, now.' She clicked her fingers in front of his face like a stage hypnotist. 'Right, what does your training tell you to do?'

'Go into the Templar Sanctorum and fetch Casey out by force if necessary. She's in danger, and the number one priority is her safety.'

'Well done. We got there in the end.' She clinked her cup against his.

Virgo swilled some coffee around his mouth. It was bitter. 'We need to act now, but not knowing where her apartment is in the complex, it could be days or weeks before we see her again.'

'Block 2, level 2. Room 15.'

'What?'

'Or it could be room 17.'

'Where did you…?'

'You know, the one thing I learnt when I stopped being a cop and became a PI is that as a civilian you have to sweet-talk people. When I had an LAPD badge, I could rely on it to threaten a person with arrest, strip-search them, seize their goods or raid their premises. I had powers. Now I have to be their best friend, which is why Myra Kim told me all about herself while she was helping me look for my fictitious lost dog. Hers is room 16, which is Jake Dearman's old room, and Casey's is next door, so that means she's 15 or 17. Possibly 14 or 18.'

Virgo nodded. 'I'm impressed.'

Jessica tossed her head as though it was nothing. 'What would be the best time to go in?'

'From what I saw last night, they have lights-out at ten thirty and one nightwatchman on the gates. I'd say between eleven and midnight.'

There was the squeak of sneakers on the vinyl floor, and Joey walked past them on his way to the fridge, Bluetooth headphones still wrapped around his head.

Jessica waved her arms and shouted, 'Take the frigging cans off.'

Joey got a Coke and fingered the ring-pull. Then he saw he wasn't alone and slid the headphones an inch off his ears. 'Hi.'

Jessica said, 'This is Mr. Virgo, a gentleman I'm currently working on a case with.'

Virgo said, 'Pleased to meet you, Joey.'

Joey was tall, with long, light brown hair that fell in ringlets, dimples and a shaving rash. He mumbled something that could have been *likewise*, and squeaked back into the lounge.

Jessica gave Virgo a wide smile and said, 'Thanks for coming back with me. It means a lot.'

CHAPTER 15

Virgo stashed his Winnebago a mile from the Templar Sanctorum, down a short track that led to a picnic area. He set off to cover the remaining distance on foot, hugging the shadows of the oaks that lined the highway. The sky loomed large. Clear as a limpid, indigo lake, and the moon was a candescent crescent tilted over the distant Santa Lucia mountains. Perfect night to mount a solo raid on a compound of psychotic crackpots.

Jessica had wanted to be the one who made it inside and got Casey out, but the threat from whoever had stolen her files had not gone away. She couldn't risk leaving Joey on his own. In the morning, she was going to beef up security or ship the two of them out to a hotel for a few days. The house was a rental, but they liked it and didn't want to move. If you have to make changes so significant that they reduce your quality of life, then the shitbags have won. The same with terrorism. Always carry on as normally as you can.

When Virgo reached the POG estate, the main wrought-iron gates were closed. This was what he'd been expecting from having kept the property under observation the previous night. Beyond the gates was an automatic barrier operated from a nearby booth, which appeared to be staffed by a single POG member. Other than that, there didn't appear to be regular patrols of the perimeter, although he had identified security cameras at strategic points, no doubt monitored from a central control station. Not a problem as long as he stuck to the route he'd researched and planned.

First job was breaching the outer cordon. In The Activity, this was the point that presented the highest level of threat, because however good the recon, there was always the potential for the unexpected: landmines, tripwires, dogs, infrared alarms, pressure pads, searchlights or just shitloads of concealed jihadis with AK-47s.

He picked his spot, thirty yards from the gates, took a pair of heavy-duty wire cutters from his belt and cut out a D section of the chain-link fence. Peeled it back and he was in. It had taken less than five seconds, and there had been no wailing sirens or salivating Doberman pinschers. Good start. He skirted the ornamental flowerbeds and cut through a tarmacked bay that had commercial dumpsters and recycling bins. Just as he was about to edge his way behind the inner-barrier control booth, there came the sound of a vehicle engine on the highway; then headlights swung round. The main gates opened, and one of the POG minibuses drove in and approached the inner control barrier.

The beams of light forced Virgo to jump back behind one of the bins. He dropped to his knees, the stench of rotting meat and vegetables clawing the back of his throat, and peered around the large, wheeled receptacle. A guy came out of the booth and cracked a joke with the driver of the minibus, then the barrier shot up, and the vehicle drove in and around to the parking lot.

Virgo watched eight or nine kids disembark, carrying bags and water bottles, looking tired but still buzzing and talking.

It was thirty-six hours since he'd watched three of the POG minibuses depart, and this appeared to be the first one back. Must have been a hell of a door-knocking session. Two vehicles were still out there somewhere, spreading the word of the self-proclaimed prophet Dr. Daniel Nelson.

He waited for the group from the minibus to disappear down the avenue into the main compound, and then followed at a safe distance. All the kids carried on to the accommodation blocks, apart from one who was carrying a fawn leather briefcase. He turned right through an arched walkway into the quadrangle. Virgo counted to ten and then moved swiftly and silently through the same arch. The inside of the courtyard was floodlit, and he could see the figure with the briefcase heading towards the far end, where the main bell tower domed up into the night sky. There was only one place he could be heading.

One of the doors to the church opened, and the figure disappeared inside. It was too early for midnight mass, and in any case, the People's Order of Gabriel didn't seem like the kind of outfit to observe Catholic traditions. It was odd that the one POG member with the briefcase went straight off the minibus to say his prayers and no one else did. Virgo made his way along the covered side walkway of the courtyard towards the church. He'd reached halfway when a guy wearing a black uniform stepped out of a recess and said, 'Hey, who are you?'

Virgo rocked on his heels. *Shit.* Decision time. He could try to talk his way out of the situation by claiming to be a lost guest or a troubled soul interested in joining the sect, or he could neutralize the threat. The problem with talking his way out was that it would mean abandoning tonight's smash and grab mission. That was it, decision made. Neutralize.

The guy was some kind of nightwatchman or guard, so presumably no mug. That said, he looked to be carrying a few extra pounds, and his movements were slow. Virgo walked towards him. There are a number of ways to render an opponent unconscious, including well-executed blows to the chin or solar plexus. However, the safest and most reliable method is to choke them out. Never fails. The problem is, they never willingly put their neck into your hands.

As soon as the guy realized a situation was developing, he reached into the top pocket of his tunic and pulled out a walkie-talkie. Virgo moved fast. He stepped in and softened him up with a straight jab to the bridge of the nose. Then, without pause, he continued through and locked his right arm around the neck. With the base of his left palm, he pushed on the back of the guy's head and constricted the windpipe into the crook of his elbow. Kept the pressure on until he felt the body go limp and the legs give way. Hands under armpits, he dragged the lump into one of the many recesses in the covered walkway.

Now the clock was ticking. He retraced his steps out of the quadrangle. Checked the coast was clear and ran across the lawns and flowerbeds to the accommodation blocks, rather than taking the circuitous paved footpaths. He guessed block 2 was second along and was relieved when he got there and saw a sign confirming it. The communal door was unlocked, and he took the stairs to the second floor. Nobody around. No noise. No frat parties drinking beer and singing 'Dancing Queen.'

He stopped outside room 16, which Myra Kim had said was hers. She'd also said Casey's room was next door, which Jessica had deduced to be 15 or 17, but the numbers alternated with the rooms on the opposite side of the corridor, so the ones either side of Myra Kim's were 14 and 18. Same difference. The chances of knocking on the wrong door were still fifty percent. Good odds unless someone's life depends on it.

No time to worry about it. If it was the wrong one, someone else would have to get choked out. He knocked gently on the door of room 14. Nothing. He knocked a little louder. Still nothing. He didn't want to risk waking the entire corridor by banging on the door any louder and was just about to tap again when it opened, and Casey Bender said, 'Shit, it's you.'

'In the flesh.' Virgo walked in and closed the door. 'Get your things together. We're leaving.'

'Meaning what?'

'I'm taking you out of this place. It's not safe.'

Casey laughed. 'You've got it wrong. I don't want to leave.'

'Were those tears of happiness this morning?'

'I was upset about Jake, but I'm okay now.'

'Bully for you, but Jake's not okay now. He's still dead.'

'Get out.' Anger flared in Casey's eyes, though she kept her voice down. 'Get out of my room now.'

'Not without you.' Virgo folded his arms and stood in front of the door. 'You've got sixty seconds to gather your essentials, or I'm going to drag you kicking and screaming out of this place.'

'Please leave.' The spark of anger in Casey had been doused. 'If you have a genuine concern for my well-being, please leave and don't come back again.'

'Sometimes people make bad choices. They need saving from themselves.'

'I'm begging you, please leave me be.'

Virgo checked his watch. 'That's twenty seconds you got left.'

Casey began to shake her head. 'You wouldn't...'

'I once carried a guy three miles after he lost both legs below the knee in an IED explosion. He wanted me to leave him be as well, but now he's married with kids and sends me a bottle of single malt every Christmas.'

'You wouldn't…'

'You don't need to bother with the single malt though. I'm not a big whiskey drinker.'

'I can't…' Casey was crying.

'Time to go.' Virgo took a step forward, about to grab an arm.

She stifled a scream. 'All right. I'll tell you.'

'What?'

'I'll tell you why I can't leave this place, but you have to promise not to tell anyone. I mean anyone.'

Virgo saw something behind her eyes that was dark, but still thought it must be a kind of joke or stalling tactic. 'Deal. I promise. It's our secret.'

'I killed someone.' She gave a little nervous laugh through the tears.

'Okay.'

'Shot them in cold blood on their doorstep.'

Virgo knew straight away she was serious. 'Let me take a wild guess. Dr. Dan told you this person was the devil incarnate.'

'No, this person had sinned and needed saving. The sacrifice of Jesus was not sufficient to atone for what he had done, so I had to be an avenging angel and shed his blood. That was the only way to keep his soul from eternal damnation.'

'Sounds like you were doing him a big favor.'

'Don't mock things you don't understand.'

'I'm sorry, but isn't Dr. Dan the savior of souls? Why didn't he go himself and blow away an unarmed guy in his own home?'

'It was my baptism.' Casey started crying again. 'This might sound stupid, but I think it was the happiest night of my life.'

Virgo shrugged. He wasn't entirely shocked. The chemicals in her brain would have been haywire after a cataclysmic event like that. 'When did this take place?'

'A few weeks ago on my birthday. Dr. Dan said it was the perfect time to make a commitment.'

The temptation to shout *what the fuck did you think you were doing* was strong, but Virgo kept it cool. 'What was his name, the guy you shot?'

'They said it was best I didn't know. It wasn't important.'

'That figures,' said Virgo. He'd killed in the past, and it was much easier to pull a trigger when the target was a depersonalized symbol of a hostile regime or some terrorist death cult. 'Where did he live, the guy who needing saving with a nine-mil slug?'

Casey looked cross and embarrassed. More tears. 'I was driven there with a blindfold on, so I don't know, but my guess is north LA. Beverly Hills or Santa Monica. What does it matter?'

'It doesn't matter.' He put his arm around her shoulders to comfort and guide her towards the door. 'Look, I'm not going to drive you straight to the police station, but I'm still going to get you out of this fucked-up place.'

'Stop.' She pushed his arm away. 'It's all recorded on video and stored in the loyalty library.'

Now Virgo was shocked. 'They filmed you killing a guy?'

Casey was already nodding. 'And if I ever leave, it gets posted online.'

Virgo was running through the implications of what he'd just been told when a deafening alarm started to blast throughout the accommodation block. He pulled back the blinds and looked out the window. Lights were flashing around the compound, and figures were running to take up prearranged posts. He'd spent too long talking to Casey, and the guy he'd choked out must have come round or been found.

For the second time that day, he put his hands on Casey's shoulders and looked into her eyes. 'I've got to go, but we'll figure out a way to get you out.'

She returned his stare without flinching. 'Go and don't come back. I'm okay here. It's my life now.'

CHAPTER 16

Virgo took the steps down to the ground floor four at a time and darted straight out of the door of the accommodation block. If he was quick, he might make it out before they got the perimeter sealed. What he hadn't factored into the equation was the guards already stationed outside the residential quarters. Two of them, dressed in the black ninja suits and carrying some kind of nightstick. He almost barged straight into them. Hard to say who was most surprised, him or the ninjas.

There was no time to turn and run. In any case, he didn't want to give them the opportunity to radio in for extra resources and get a huge posse chasing after him, so he stood his ground and fronted them up. Showtime. Immediately, he could tell the two guys had received no formal martial arts training. Like many other things in the Templar Sanctorum, their appearance was just for show. Neither adopted a balanced combat stance nor brandished their weapons in a way that suggested they had any idea how to use them. One of them grunted and swung the stick from above his head, like it was an axe being used to chop a massive log.

Virgo swayed to his left and raised his right hand, letting the stick roll down the outside of his right forearm, away from his head and body. The tip of the wooden baton hit the floor, and the guy on the other end stumbled forward with another grunt. Virgo's right hand was already coming down at maximum velocity. The bony outside edge struck his attacker's carotid sinus, and the guy's eyes went white as they rolled into the back of his head. He hit the floor, out cold.

Before his second opponent could react, Virgo pivoted and hit him with a roundhouse kick to the ribcage. The guy sucked air. Virgo moved in to finish him off, but ninja number two was made of sterner stuff. He snapped the nightstick round and caught Virgo on the thigh, then dropped his head and went to butt Virgo in the chest. Virgo shot a fist up, which landed flush on the ninja's mouth, but wasn't enough to halt the momentum. The guy was big and heavy. The top of his head struck Virgo in the sternum and knocked him onto his backside. Not a great position to fight from.

He needn't have worried. The two blows he'd already landed had done their job. The guy tried to bring a fist crashing down into Virgo's face, but his strength and co-ordination had gone. Virgo blocked it, then rolled. Rabbit-punched the guy at the base of his skull, and was back on his feet and away. Ninja number two never moved.

The quickest way out of a hostile raid is the way you came in, because you know the route and the perimeter is insecure, so that was his aim. However, as he was about to dash out from the shadow of the accommodation blocks, four more figures emerged from the quadrangle with flashlights and fanned out across the lawns, effectively blocking his path.

He cut down a gap between blocks one and two and found himself on a service road. It was marked on both sides by solar lights in the shape of mushrooms, positioned every ten yards, and looked like it snaked around to the main gates.

Virgo started to follow it when he heard the sound of a diesel engine and threw himself to the ground just as a Gator utility vehicle came flying round the bend. Single crewed. The driver had one hand on the wheel and another on a walkie-talkie clamped to his ear. Too absorbed to see a figure lying down in the ryegrass.

The Gator traveled down the track and came to a stop at a gap in the laurel hedge that lined the length of this side of the compound. Virgo commando-crawled in the opposite direction through the ryegrass until it was safe to stand up. Then he ran through the bends until he reached the avenue that led to the main gates. There was a group of people milling around the barrier, but he stooped unseen behind the commercial dumpsters and towards the location where he'd cut the D hole in the fence.

Shit. He stopped. There were four more guys with heavy-duty Maglites inspecting the damage and preventing any further incursion or escape. The alarm siren went quiet. Then a voice came over a Tannoy system. 'Sentinels and guardians, remain in position until further notice. The intruder is still within the compound.'

Not for much longer if I can help it. Virgo ran back the way he'd just come. Back to the service lane with its solar mushroom lights. He hugged the line of laurels until he could go no farther without being seen by the guy sat in the Gator parked up twenty yards away. This was the tricky part. If he jumped out and ran towards the vehicle, it would give the driver time to drive away or, worse, use the Gator as a weapon and floor it straight at him. Both bad outcomes.

In the theater of war, you should never trust a wounded enemy or one who surrenders, but Virgo was banking on the guy in the Gator never having fought for his country. He put his hands up and limped towards the vehicle. 'My leg's broken.'

The guy hesitated. 'Stay where you are, mister.'

Virgo kept coming. 'I need medical assistance.'

'Hey, I said stay there.'

'I can't hear you for the pain.'

'Back off.'

Virgo saw the walkie-talkie being raised lip-wards and powered the last few yards like an offensive tackle. He hit the guy with his shoulder and crunched him clean off the utility vehicle. Before he could get up, Virgo had clambered through to the other side and used three short, sharp punches to the jaw to put this sentinel out of action. Before he climbed onto the Gator, Virgo picked the walkie-talkie up from the gravel and clipped it on his belt. It was a VHF radio common in the military and law enforcement.

There was no way he could ram his way through wrought-iron gates in a Gator, but it was perfect for what he had in mind. A cross-country trip. He spun it round and shot through the gap in the laurel before bouncing and scraping across a field of corn stubble. The lights of the compound faded, but the moon took over. Across another rutted field and a small steel bridge that spanned a creek, and he was on a track that ran parallel to the main highway. After a while he reached an exit gate that was padlocked. Easy enough to climb over, but it meant leaving the vehicle behind.

He waited two minutes and monitored the traffic on the radio for any sign that his escape had been reported, but there was none. He slung the walkie-talkie into a drainage ditch, vaulted the gate and jogged back to the RV. Only when he had driven through La Esperanza and five miles out the other side did he pull over to the side of the road and think about what Casey Bender had just told him. Then he shook his head and said to himself, 'Holy shit.'

CHAPTER 17

Eleven apostles stood in front of Dr. Dan, each shrinking to varying degrees from the power of his cyan-lightning eyes. Matthew was still confined to medical quarters. What a disappointment that boy was. It was a little after eight in the morning, and none of them had been to bed. This was the first time there had been an extraordinary meeting of the council for temporal judgment, which meant that punishments were likely to be swift and severe.

Violins marked the opening bars of Handel's eighteenth-century oratorio, and Dr. Dan slipped on his headset microphone. He had slept but fitfully. The Tannoy announcements had gone on into the early hours and disrupted his routine, from which came much of his strength in body and mind. Post-sleep coitus had to be cancelled, which was displeasing because today's wife was Gina, one of his current favorites.

When he'd first heard there had been a break-in, he'd assumed the intruders were targeting the factory or the depository, but that appeared not to be the case. Both the goods and the money were safe. Whoever had entered the compound was interested in block 2 of the residential quarters, which was of concern, but not in the same league as someone trying to get in the factory. Never mind. Someone had to be made an example of, and more importantly, the others needed to watch the example being made.

Dr. Dan waited and let the pressure mount. He knew all the tricks. When he was a kid at school, called plain Brian Salt, he was not an academic student. It wasn't until his life was going nowhere as a sales assistant that he started to study. Psychology, religion, sociology and all that shit. There he came across a thing called the Stanford Experiment run by a guy called Zimbardo in the '70s, where a group of college undergrads were split into guards and prisoners to test whether cruelty was innate in human nature or could be caused by a situation. It concluded that good people could do evil things if social dynamics forced them into it. Dr. Dan wasn't interested in the whys and wherefores, he just wanted to be the guy running the experiment. He wanted to be Zimbardo.

He spoke softly. 'Who was in charge of compound security last night, Bartholomew?'

'Me, sir.' Bartholomew took a step forward. Eyes blinking, veins pulsing in his temples.

'Thank you.' Dr. Dan smiled. 'Simon and Thaddeus, restrain him, one arm each, and hold him tight.'

Two of the red-suited apostles positioned themselves on either side of Bartholomew, and each locked two arms around one of his. He did not resist.

Dr. Dan's face dropped. This was serious. 'John, take a step forward.'

At the end of the line, John pushed out a nervous foot and brought the other up to join it.

'It is time.' Dr. Dan closed his eyes as though drawing on a reservoir of moral strength. 'John, approach the prophet.'

John didn't move.

Dr. Dan slowly raised his lids and saw nobody stood in front of him. He bawled, 'John, approach the prophet, now.'

John took tentative steps and walked up to the console. Composed himself with a deep breath and tried to look earnest and confident.

'Behold.' Dr. Dan reached inside his jacket and pulled out a seven-inch hunting knife.

The confidence evaporated from John's face and left a mask of fear.

'Take this dagger from my hand.' Dr. Dan held it out like it was the bread and wine of Communion. The body and blood.

John took the knife. A visible shiver racked his spine.

'Do it, do it, do it.' Dr. Dan became animated. Feet pacing, head nodding and arms swinging wildly, as though he were possessed. 'Do it, do it, do it.'

John was frozen to the spot. Confusion mixed with fear.

Dr. Dan pointed to Bartholomew. 'Pull down his pants and cut his balls off.'

John didn't move.

'Do it…do it…do it…' Dr. Dan was strutting back and forth, whipping up the rest of the team with his hands, like he was conducting an orchestra.

In no time, the rest of the apostles were chanting in unison. 'Do it…do it…do it…do it…do it…'

John turned and walked towards Bartholomew, the knife hanging down by his side. He stopped in front of him, unable to look his fellow apostle in the eye.

Bartholomew started to gently struggle. Testing the effectiveness of his restraints. A natural reaction to the prospect of imminent testicle removal. The arm-locks were solid. He began to panic and upped the struggle. 'Touch me down there and I'll fucking kill you.'

The mantra grew louder. 'Do it…do it…do it…'

John bent down and yanked Bartholomew's pants down to the ankles, only to get a knee in the face that knocked him over and sent the knife skittering across the tiles.

Dr. Dan raised his hands to stop the chanting. 'Brother Bartholomew, cease your resistance. In ancient times the eunuch was the highest-ranked official in the palace.'

Bartholomew didn't look convinced, but he stopped thrashing about. The prophet had spoken. He stood with his genitalia on full view, and rivulets of sweat coursed down his face.

John stood and recovered the knife. Blood seeping from a split lip.

Of their own volition, two other apostles positioned themselves behind Bartholomew and locked themselves onto his legs. He began to try to free his limbs, face red and spit foaming in one corner of his mouth.

Dr. Dan pushed a fader up on the console, and the music grew louder. A bass voice sang about people living in darkness who saw a great light, and the chorus chimed in, *hallelujah, hallelujah, hallelujah, hallelujah.*

The apostles raised the volume of their mantra to match the Messiah. 'Do it…do it…do it…'

John dropped to his knees in front of Bartholomew and glanced back over his shoulder for any sign this was a test. A prank or parody.

Dr. Dan bared his teeth and made a slashing motion with his right hand.

Then it happened, and a visceral scream filled the council chamber.

CHAPTER 18

'You are kidding me, right?' Jessica shook her head and took a bite of toast topped with a mound of mashed avocado.

Virgo said nothing. It was the seventh or eighth time she'd asked the same question, and he was fed up of giving the same answer. That was what Casey had told him. Period.

They were perched on stools at a small breakfast bar in her kitchen. The sound of Joey getting ready for school, assisted by thumping drum and bass, came through the thin partition walls. At least he was out of bed. No one could sleep with that noise shaking the floorboards.

All the avo toast gone, she said, 'I managed to get hold of Barry yesterday afternoon. A guy I worked with on the force.'

Before Virgo could query who Barry was, there was the loud crash of a bedroom door slamming, and Joey trudged in like a teenage Neanderthal. Straight to the refrigerator, pulled out a slice of pizza and sloped back to his bedroom.

Jessica didn't bat an eye. 'He now works in the Commercial Crimes Division out of the new Parker Center, and the interesting thing is, he says the People's Order of Gabriel is classed as a charitable organization, so don't have to submit annual returns to the IRS. There's no way of knowing where all the cash came from to build the empire.'

'What about Dr. Dan?'

'Nothing.'

'He's got no money in his account?'

'There's no trace of a Daniel Nelson resident in La Esperanza in any financial system.'

Virgo took a drink of lukewarm canned coffee and nodded to himself. The POG was a perfect vehicle to launder money, but what was the scam? Were the missionaries he saw going out and returning on the minibus really spreading the word, or were they defrauding people into donating dollars, or worse still, burglarizing their homes? No surprise Nelson didn't have a bank account. Why would he need one when he could use the POG as his personal piggy bank?

There was a buzz, and Virgo's cell shuddered on the countertop. He snatched it up and saw it was a spam text. He'd put a call in to his old colleague Caleb Hawkins and was expecting a response. If anyone knew how to hack into Dr. Dan's loyalty library, it was him. The only alternative was to physically break into the compound again and try to steal the hard drive, but last night's narrow escape was fresh in his mind. There might come a point where he had to take the risks necessary to obtain physical possession of the files, but first he wanted to see what was in them. At the moment, he only had Casey's word.

A thought occurred to him. 'Any chance your pal Barry could check the LAPD homicide system and see who Casey shot? We know it was her birthday and probably north of the city.'

Jessica checked her appearance in a mirror on the back of the kitchen door and tweaked her fringe. 'Barry told me never to call him again.'

'Some pal.'

'It's okay. I've pumped him dry over the years.' More tweaking. A pluck of an eyebrow. 'The problem with the police-private investigator relationship is it's a one-way street. They have all the information, and we've got nothing to offer in return except blood, sweat and tears.'

'I guess we could check newspaper reports.'

'Did I say I'd run out of sources in the force?'

'Not exactly.'

'Then leave it with me.' Jessica grabbed her car keys. 'Help yourself to more coffee. I've got to do the school run. Back in ten.' She was gone.

The drum and bass stopped. Muffled shouts gave way to banging doors. The Beetle's engine went *doof, doof, doof* and disappeared down the street.

Virgo looked around the kitchen diner he'd been left alone in, feeling awkward. There was a corkboard on the wall with photographs pinned up of a smiling Jessica and Joey at different ages, and other mementoes: a ticket stub to a Dodgers game, stickers, badges, restaurant cards, certificates of achievement and a free repeat pass for a whale-watching trip. The tat and ephemera of life that have no monetary value but mean so much.

It brought it home. How tough it had been for this woman bringing up a boy on her own and trying to make a go of her own business. None of the pictures included Joey's father. It was as though he had been edited from the show, and although that made it easier for Jessica, how did it subconsciously impact on the boy? Virgo knew he wasn't an expert on the subject. He and Crystal had talked about starting a family, but events overtook them, and then she was gone.

He remembered the day they first met. He was recovering from the Syrian bomb blast in the Womack Medical Center, North Carolina, just starting a physio session, and she was a nurse on the next ward who called in to say hi to a friend. It was like they'd been as one in a previous life and fate had brought them back together, which was strange because he didn't believe in that crap. Within days, they were inseparable. Married inside a year. She was the part of him that had been missing since he became a man, and he liked to think that he made her whole too. They were a union in law but quintessentially in nature.

In the dark weeks that followed her death, people didn't know what to say to him, though that didn't stop them. Usually it was banal crap, but sometimes it was stupid stuff like *you're not too old to find love again*, or *at least you didn't have kids*. Was that supposed to make him feel better? Some days he wished that he had a son or daughter to give him motivation in his life and be the flesh and blood legacy of Crystal's time on earth. Instead, he had nothing but memories.

His cell rang. The screen illuminated, *Caleb Hawkins*. Virgo picked up and filled him in on Dr. Dan, the People's Order of Gabriel and his collection of snuff videos that he used to blackmail his followers into remaining faithful to the cause.

Hawkins belly-laughed. 'You shitting me?'

'Yeah, I like nothing better than wasting my time manufacturing nonsensical tales of murder, psychopaths and religious fruitcakes.'

'What do you want me to do about it?'

'Hack into the system and get me a copy.'

'How?' Hawkins laughed again. 'Is he going to click on the link if I message from Amazon to say he needs to reset his password?'

'You're the CIA expert.'

'I need an *in* to his network.'

'Uncle Sam's finest.'

'And you're ex-Activity, so why don't you mount a covert method-of-entry mission and shove a stick loaded with my malware in his USB port, or have you lost your nerve, wussy-boy?'

'Too risky. There's a girl in there who would pay the price if anything went wrong.'

Hawkins sighed. 'Okay, I'll try, but it's gonna cost you.'

'What's new?' Call ended.

Five minutes later, the Beetle doof-doofed back onto the drive, and Jessica came in through the kitchen door like a gust of wind and said, 'What that kid needs is a male role model in his life. Teach him respect and self-discipline.'

Virgo didn't like the way she was staring at him like he might be the potential paradigm of manly virtue Joey needed. He went for a rapid change of subject. 'What are you going to do about the threat to your security?'

Jessica took an opened tin of tuna out of the fridge. 'What threat?'

'The reason we nearly killed a dozen pedestrians driving here yesterday.'

'Oh, yeah. The shitbags who stole my household bills.' She spooned tuna onto a slice of bread and made a sandwich. 'Maybe they'll feel sorry for me when they read them and leave me alone.'

Virgo couldn't tell if Jessica was being serious. She liked to dramatize situations, and maybe the hundred-mile-an-hour race home to save Joey had been just another one of those theatrical rollercoaster rides. 'You're not moving out?'

She folded the sandwich in Saran Wrap. 'Do I look like I scare easy?'

'Or installing a personal-attack alarm system?'

'Who was it who said attack is the best form of defense?' She started to pile dirty breakfast pots into an already full dishwasher. 'George Washington?'

'It was Sun Tzu. The military strategist.'

'I think it was George Washington, and history was my best subject in high school.'

'I'm not arguing.'

'That's a smart move, because I'm right.'

'Okay. Do you want me to come with you?'

'Where?' She squeezed shut the straining door of the dishwasher.

'I'm guessing you know who it was who sent the goons to threaten you and break into your office, and you're going to pay them a visit. I thought you might want someone to have your back.'

Jessica pulled the Walther out of her shoulder bag and racked the slide to check there was a round in the chamber. 'Please yourself.'

CHAPTER 19

Daniel Nelson stared at the blank screen on his MacBook and waited for inspiration to course through his body and out onto the page through his fingertips. The great Romantic poets – Byron, Shelley, Keats and of course the biggest degenerate of them all, Coleridge – had all used the wily seductress opium as their muse, but these days writers such as himself did not need to rely on the fickle pods of the poppy plant. The stuff from a lab was more predictable and powerful. Good enough to stimulate the most dormant and recalcitrant of brains.

He'd already decided on the subject and skeleton of Sunday's sermon; it was the fleshy prose that required the artist's rhetorical touch. Social justice. It was why he'd named his movement the People's Order of Gabriel. To invoke the struggle of the oppressed masses against historical and societal inequalities and provide a framework for the future based on the redistribution of wealth, unilateral disarmament, protection of the climate and a new relationship with God, informed by the Nelson Prophesies.

Hitler had first posited the *big lie* theory in *Mein Kampf*:

repeat a falsehood so fantastic people can't believe anyone would have the audacity to make it up. Then he put it into practice by convincing a nation that everything wrong with Germany was the fault of one race and orchestrated the murder of six million Jews. Daniel Nelson thought his own deceit was modest by comparison, but the principle was the same.

The juices began to flow. His fingers danced on the keyboard.

> *When will capitalism finally collapse? It's not a question of if, because the signs are already there that the final downward, death spiral has begun, and we must decide what type of country we want to live in when the New Age arrives. Do we want government bureaucrats to run the economy while a state-sponsored black market thrives underneath, or do we want true transformation and a sharing and sustainable society?*

There was a deferential knock on the office door, and one of the secretariat stuck his head around. 'Mr. Rinker is here to see you, sir.'

Nelson stopped typing. 'We are not scheduled to meet today. Tell him I'm busy.'

'Mr. Rinker said it was important.'

'Mr. Rinker is a stupid asshole who wouldn't know the significance of something if it punched him in his pig-ugly face.'

'He seems agitated, sir.'

'Fuck it.' Nelson slapped two palms down on the desk. 'Show him in.'

Before he could save the document he'd just started, the door opened again, and Rinker marched in. Nelson bestowed one of his best ultra-white smiles on him. 'John, always a pleasure to see you. To what do I owe the honor?'

John Rinker didn't wait to be asked. He sank his denim backside onto an easy chair and put his cowboy boots up on the coffee table. 'Quit the act, dickhead. It's me.'

Nelson kept the ultra-white welcome going, but only as a mask to hide his growing anger. One day this business arrangement would be dissolved, and then the cretin would pay for his rudeness and arrogance. He would find out which of them had the most loyal, devoted and disciplined set of followers, willing to commit the most unthinkable acts at the behest of their master. In the meantime, he had to be humored. 'I thought we were due to meet next week.'

'I got some advice for you that won't wait 'til then.'

Nelson felt himself bridle. 'I don't tell you how to carry out your side of the agreement; therefore I'd appreciate it if you don't tell me how to conduct mine.'

'Fine.' Rinker was wearing a baseball cap with the hood of a black sweatshirt pulled up over the top of it. Below the brim, his sharp features pinched themselves into even more of a frown. 'As long as you want the cops crawling all over the operation.'

'Don't worry yourself about the police.'

'Yeah, like you own the goddamn force.'

'I have a healthy working relationship with La Esperanza police department.'

'I'm not talking local fuckwits.'

'All right.' Nelson skipped out from behind his desk and began to waltz around the office. 'Come on, enlighten me. I'm all ears. Cure me of my ignorance with your sage words of advice.'

'Another kid died south end of the county. Makes it six in a month.'

'Death's a bitch, but that's what happens when people misuse a product.'

'You make it sound like over-the-counter headache medicine.' Rinker scratched his cheek. It was covered in patchy stubble and old acne scars. 'That shit is fifty times stronger than pure smack.'

Nelson dispensed with the smile and stood still. 'What do you want me to do about it? Get the surgeon general to put a fucking health alert on every pack of pills? Or maybe the FDA will draft us a leaflet with a black box warning?'

'I want you to tell your guys not to take a dump on the doorstep. No sales within the county border.'

'Relax.' Nelson was back on the move. Step, side-step, step, side-step to a beat only he could hear. 'There was a problem with one of the distribution staff thinking he could do some freelance work. That problem has been taken care of.'

'For good?'

'Is eternity long enough for you?'

Rinker mumbled something under his breath and scratched at his face again.

Nelson laughed and nodded his head. He knew where the balance of power rested in this relationship. Not only did the POG cut and press the magic powder, they ran the distribution network and washed the money. What did Rinker's rag-tag bunch of roughnecks do apart from drive the occasional truck over the border from Mexico into Texas? It was time for a little more *quid pro quo*.

He bent down to stare Rinker in the face and said, 'I want you to get rid of a man called Virgo.'

'He a cop?'

'A nuisance who has breached the sanctity of the compound.' Nelson knew it had been Virgo last night. One of the guards had recognized him before being put to sleep. The ex-G-man shouldn't have been so stupid as to invade the holy pulpit and show his face to half of the Order. 'He's convinced one of our girls needs rescuing, and I'm afraid he might be the persistent type.'

Rinker sneered. 'Just get rid of the girl. Problem solved.'

'I can't do that. I have plans for her.'

'Do the plans involve your dick?'

Nelson waltzed back around his desk and pushed a button. 'Mr. Rinker is ready to leave. Will somebody show him out.'

Half an hour later, Daniel Nelson sat staring at the MacBook. He'd not written a word since his business associate had left, and could feel the tension building in his muscles. The moment had been lost.

There was a demure knock on the door, and a secretary's face appeared.

He closed his eyes. 'What is it now?'

'There's a woman in a wheelchair wants to see you, sir.'

'Tell her to fuck off.'

'Sorry, sir?'

'I'm clean out of miracles.'

'She's not after a cure, sir. She wants to become a member of the Order.'

'All right.' Nelson massaged his temples. 'Get admin to carry out the financial checks and bring her to me.'

CHAPTER 20

Vernon Fonseca resided in a four-story concrete box of apartments wedged down the side of an offramp to Highway 1. Fumes, noise, light pollution, vibration and discarded cigarette wrappers, it had the full set. One of the warts on Central California's beautiful visage that the tourists never see, but keep sprouting up. Jessica McGann parked the Beetle behind a dust-coated Buick stood on cinder blocks instead of wheels and climbed out with a handkerchief clamped over her nose. 'What a shithole.'

'You expect drug dealers to live in a palace?' The wind grazed Virgo's eyes and made them water.

'Maybe this is just for show and he has a condo in Bermuda.'

'More likely any profit goes up his nose or into a vein.'

'You don't know this guy,' said Jessica. 'He's smart.'

The outer security door was locked, and there was a steel pad to key in the number.

Virgo said, 'You don't know the access code.'

Jessica said, 'I don't know which apartment he lives in either, but I'm a detective.'

Two minutes later, the outer door opened, and a stout lady wearing thick horn-rimmed glasses and pulling a shopping trolley came out.

'Excuse me, ma'am.' Jessica produced an open wallet and flashed a badge. 'We're looking for Vernon Fonseca.'

The lady seemed to be sucking a hard candy. It circumnavigated her mouth as she considered what she'd just been told, swapping cheeks and making a brief appearance on her lips before getting sucked back inside. Three times. Then she said, 'Is he the dope pusher?'

'Yes, ma'am.'

'I thought so.' The candy swapped cheeks. 'Apartment number fifteen on the third floor.'

Virgo already had his foot in the security door. Old habits die hard. Only firefighters get master keys, and law enforcement has to seize opportunities as they present themselves. Inside, there were bait stations in the stairwell and a clammy smell of boiled cabbage. Garbage sacks piled up in one corner, and an abandoned TV with a cracked screen.

Outside the door of number fifteen, Jessica looped her bag strap over the handle and said, 'When I yank down, you kick.'

It took six blows of a size-eleven desert boot. Deadbolts. By the time they gained entry, Vernon Fonseca was sitting in a high-backed leather chair, just sliding a cell back into his top pocket. He said, 'My lawyer will be waiting for us at the station.'

Jessica said, 'They could be there a while,' and pulled out the Walther.

Fonseca was a fancy dude. Silk shirt, nice tan, gold chain thick enough to throttle an ox. A crease of confusion appeared between his well-groomed eyebrows. 'You're not cops.'

'You don't know who I am, do you?' Jessica's mouth hung

open. 'You send rent-a-thugs to smash up my business and you don't even fucking know who I am.'

A tiny smile of realization tweaked one corner of Fonseca's mouth, but he said nothing.

Virgo looked around the apartment. Clean, well-furnished with all high-end stuff. Bose audio system, Smeg coffee machine, Bang and Olufson flat-screen and a seafoam green Fender Stratocaster hung by a Y-bracket on the wall. He lifted it down.

Fonseca stood up and shouted, 'Hey, put that back. It's a Richie Sambora signature edition.'

Jessica pointed the barrel of the Walther between his eyes. 'Don't yell.'

Fonseca's suave demeanor had evaporated. There was a pronounced snarl on his top lip. 'What do you want?'

Jessica said, 'You supplied opioids to a schoolkid, and they killed him.'

'Ha, is that it?' Fonseca gave a dismissive laugh. 'If you had any evidence, you'd have gone straight to the cops, so I suggest you take that toy gun out of my face and go fuck yourself with it.'

Jessica's arm didn't waver. 'I promised the kid's father I'd find out who sold him the drugs.'

'Big man, is he, Pops? Why don't you send him round here, and I'll show him what happens to wannabe vigilantes.'

'He's not after revenge. He wants to try to stop any more kids dying because there's a bad batch out there.'

'Not my circus. Not my fucking monkeys.'

'That's why you're going to tell me who your supplier is so I can follow the flow upstream.'

'This is hilarious.' Fonseca sniggered and shook his head. 'Is it one of those prank TV shows? Have you got a hidden camera in your blouse?'

'Find the suffering of bereaved families amusing?'

'We're done here.' Fonseca sat back down and crossed his legs. 'Go back to your shit job of watching dirty husbands give their secretaries the hot beef injection.'

It looked like Jessica's trigger finger was itching, but she smiled and turned to Virgo. 'You're the negotiator. Why don't you see if you can reason with him?'

'Sure.' Virgo was still caressing the seafoam green guitar. He went as though to replace the headstock in the Y-bracket, but then grabbed hold of the neck with both hands and swung the body of the six-string crashing into the apartment window. Shards of glass rained down onto the interstate offramp. Some pieces still jagged up from the frame, and he began to knock these off in a jabbing motion.

'What the fuck have you just done, prick?' Fonseca was up and almost upon him.

With one last jab, Virgo let go of the guitar and sent it soaring out into the chemical haze that passed for air in this part of the world. Then he turned in one movement and caught Fonseca with a solid bolo punch to the left side of his jaw. The knees gave out. Virgo grabbed him by the armpits and spun him around. Gave him a piledriver into the guts for good measure.

Fonseca was doubled over, back to the square space where once there'd been a pane of glass. Virgo waited. Four seconds. Five. Time for the man to get oxygen back in his lungs and brain. More waiting. Seven seconds. Eight. As soon as he started to straighten up, Virgo picked him up by the thighs and tipped his upper body backwards out the window. Then before the whole of Fonseca hurtled into oblivion, he trapped the back of his knees against the frame. There was a dull thud as the back of Fonseca's head swung into the concrete wall below.

Virgo took a deep breath. For a moment he'd thought he'd lost him, but now he was in control. As long as he kept pressure on Fonseca's shins, which were hooked over the frame, the shitbag was going nowhere. He was just hung out to dry like a roosting bat in designer clothes.

Jessica said, 'Wow. Interesting technique.'

Virgo said, 'Ask him again.'

Jessica said, 'They didn't teach you that at Quantico.'

Virgo said, 'Ask him again.'

Jessica leaned out the window space. 'Who sold you the gear?'

Fonseca shouted back, 'I told you. Go fuck yourself.'

'Oops.' Virgo lifted his hands and released the pressure on Fonseca's shins. Gravity kicked in. Big time. There was a scream. For a split second it seemed like the roosting bat was dropping three stories, headfirst onto asphalt; then Virgo grabbed his ankles.

Cries came up from outside. 'All right, all right. Shit.'

Jessica called down, 'Last chance. Give me a name.'

Fonseca said something, but it was swallowed up by the cacophony of engines on the freeway.

She yelled out into the smog, 'Louder. I can't hear you.'

Fonseca was panicking. Garbling his words. Only fragments were intelligible. 'No…didn't call…not my usual supplier…last time…nothing…please, come on, please.'

Jessica yelled again, 'I need a name.'

Fonseca screamed back, 'Jake…I fucking told you…Jake.'

CHAPTER 21

Casey plucked another handful of strawberries and dropped them into the box. Then she straightened her spine and did the oofing groan that old folk make when they get up out of a comfortable recliner. It was back-breaking labor. Nothing like the U-pick farms down the coast that her mom and dad had taken her to as a kid. Midday and it was pushing ninety in the shade, because man-made climate change had extended summer temperatures into the fall.

She looked back to check on Myra. The new friend seemed to be coping okay, but the worst was yet to come. The POG farm was strictly organic; however the rest of the valley pumped pesticides on everything they grew, and by late afternoon the chemical miasma would drift around and around in the bowl of the valley, bringing its generous gifts: skin irritation, headaches, scratchy eyes, drowsiness and sometimes nausea. Masks helped, but they made you hotter, and you didn't want that. Heat was the biggest danger.

'Let's take a break.' Casey motioned to the shelter in the

corner of the field, where there was a water cooler and wooden benches.

Myra looked up. 'It's okay. I think we should carry on.'

Casey shrugged. *Please yourself.* She rearranged the scarf protecting the back of her neck and went back to work. Myra was new and trying to gain credits to take her to the next level. The field supervisor would never chivvy or scold them like migrant workers, but all activity was monitored, and productive behavior would be rewarded. The POG organization was layered like an onion, and everyone wanted to break through the next stratification and take a step closer to the center.

The two stick angels on Casey's arm were enough for her. Just a couple of days ago, she would have done anything to get a third, but Jake's death had burst the bubble of her ambition. She was deflated but phlegmatic. This was the lifestyle she had chosen, and there was no going back. It was repetitive and physically hard, but still better than the mental pressure of her previous life. Her devotion to the People's Order of Gabriel might have been shattered, but her faith in God was strong and unwavering as never before. He would look after her.

She bent her back. Kept plucking the berries. Ignored the sweat running down her neck and consoled herself with the fact that at least she wasn't in one of the polythene fruit tunnels today. They were ovens. There was nothing wrong with boring manual work. It helped foster a healthy mind, which was ironic because when she played nonstop tennis, all the physical exertion did was make her fatigued and mentally fragile.

Now her brain was like a well-ordered filing cabinet. She could compartmentalize or lock things away, such as that night of her birthday when she shot a man in cold blood. It was archived. She could open the drawer and check it was still there; then when the drawer closed, it was gone. Jake's death was still in the pending tray, but that too would soon get allocated its own folder in the secure system. Everything neat and tidy.

She sensed more than heard a noise behind her and turned to find Myra collapsed. Face in the dirt, knees up under her chin. 'Hey, over here,' she shouted and waved to the field supervisor, then eased Myra over and onto her side.

The guy came running over with a bottle of water and emptied half of it over Myra's head before trying to get her to take a sip. The liquid just ran down her face into the soil. They sat her up. Her eyes were open but not focused. Breathing shallow. Between them, Casey and the supervisor managed to stand Myra up and walk her to the shelter. It took a while. She was dizzy. Disoriented. Mumbling one word over and over again. *Sorry.*

It was clear Myra couldn't carry on. The guy used his walkie-talkie to call for a buggy to take her back to the compound.

Casey took the opportunity to rehydrate with some water from the cooler; then she beckoned the supervisor over from the bench where he sat with Myra.

He didn't look pleased to be summoned. 'Is there a problem?'

'No, everything's cool.' Casey manufactured the best smile she could. 'It's just I hope that you don't mark Myra's performance down. It wasn't her fault.'

'It's not about blame. The fruit doesn't pick itself.'

'She needs the credits.'

'We all want to attain the next merit level, but credits have to be earned.'

'I'll pick her share. Mark me down instead.'

'That would be subverting the system.' He pulled a purple

notebook out of his pocket. 'Only true achievements can be recorded in the virtue log.'

Casey knew there was no use in arguing, even though Jesus broke protocols to be kind to others: the acceptance of tax collector Zacchaeus whom everyone despised, the forgiveness he showed to the adulterous woman, the healing of the lepers, the feeding of the poor and hungry. The People's Order of Gabriel had a set of rules that transcended the basic precepts of Christianity, but then so had most iterations throughout history.

The golf cart arrived. Casey was expecting to see a medic accompanying the driver, but it was one of the apostles called James. He pointed to the back seat and said, 'Jump in.'

Casey didn't move. 'It's Myra you've come for. She's not well.'

'No, I've come for you,' said James. He glanced dismissively at the hunched-up figure on the bench. 'Another buggy will come and fetch her in due course.'

'Are you sure?' Casey still didn't move. 'Where am I going?'

'I said get in. Now.' James had a deranged glint in his eye. Getting off on the power thing. 'Dr. Dan wants to see you.'

Casey clambered onto the rear seat, a ten-ton weight now in the pit of her stomach. She'd been expecting some form of interrogation following last night's visit from the macho Mr. Virgo. The great rescuer. When nothing happened first thing, she'd assumed no one knew it was her he'd been to see and that he'd made it out unrecognized. What possessed him to think he could get away with it?

The cart bumped along the rutted track and out onto the highway, where a breeze dried the perspiration on her brow and lips. She tried not to think of what sanction awaited her. Physical punishment held no fear, but shame and embarrassment were things that would make her hurt. Whatever her fate, God would look after her. Through the gates, under the barrier, past the arboretum, across the lake and into the grounds of the leader's private residence. Deep breath. *Here we go.*

James jumped out and barked, 'Follow me.'

They went through the grand doors, down a corridor and into a room where half a dozen staff sat at IT workstations, some wearing telephone headsets. Casey was mildly surprised, as she'd been led to believe that computers were not allowed within the grounds of the POG.

James carried on and led her into an adjoining anteroom with a row of chairs and a coffee table, where he said, 'Wait here until you're shown in.' Then disappeared.

She took a seat. It was like a dentist's waiting room. There were magazines on the coffee table, and a couple of reproduction prints on the wall, but the carpet and drapes were purple and bore the People's Order of Gabriel crest and logo. The corporate face of the organization. Again, it seemed slightly at odds with the social justice ethos of the Order.

Time passed. It could have been an hour, but more likely less. Nobody offered her a drink. Nobody said *hi, how are you* or told her what was happening. Her bladder was full from the water cooler in the field, but she didn't like to move. She closed her eyes and thought about the privations that Jesus chose to suffer: the beatings, the betrayal, the public humiliation and pain, the abandonment by his father.

She heard a door open. A voice on an intercom; *show her in.* Another door opened, and a guy appeared to escort her into the presence of the leader.

Dr. Dan sat behind a big desk. He didn't move. He flashed a hundred-watt smile and said, 'Pull up a chair.'

Casey sat in the nearest seat. Shuffled it forward a little and tried not to look nervous.

'Relax.' He must have picked up on the tightness in her

chest. 'I've been impressed by the commitment and professionalism you've shown since joining the Order.'

'Thank you, sir.' She looked into the magnetic eyes, and an exciting bolt of panic shot down her spine. She'd forgotten what it felt like to be stared at by him. The little hairs on the back of her arms stood to attention, and she felt light-headed.

'You tried your best to shepherd and support Brother Jake, but he strayed because of false teachings. He sinned and could not be brought back into the flock.'

Casey said nothing. She didn't know where this was going.

'Your mother has sent devils incarnate to try to take you away from here.' Dr. Dan gave a cheeky smirk and shrug, as though he couldn't believe anyone would do such a thing. 'But you resisted and stayed true to me, the prophet, and your new family here in the Templar Sanctorum.'

'It wasn't difficult, sir. The outside world holds no temptation.'

'Which brings me to the reason why I asked you here today.' Dr. Daniel Nelson put on a serious face. 'I would like to reward you with the highest honor available to you within the People's Order of Gabriel.'

Casey was confused. She was forty-five merit levels away from being eligible for the next angel tattoo. Above that was just the apostles, and they had to be male. 'Sorry, sir?'

'To be a wife of the prophet.'

'Oh.' Casey went cold. It was something that had never entered her head. As a teenager, she'd fantasized about how one day someone might ask for her hand in marriage. On a beach. In bed. Over a glass of champagne maybe or at an iconic location such as the Eiffel Tower or the Taj Mahal. Not sat in an office busting for a pee. What could she say?

CHAPTER 22

Traffic was light on the 101. They cut across an intersection, then peeled off into downtown, with the roof of the Beetle cranked back horizontal and Tom Petty refusing to back down on the radio. A pleasant 73 degrees with just a few wisps of cotton in a perfect blue sky. One of those days that makes you want to pack a bag and take a road trip up the coast, with no fixed itinerary and nothing to trouble your mental faculties other than whether to have a cool beer or a glass of Zinfandel. Virgo sighed. *If only...*

He said, 'Why don't you just call or email this guy?'

Jessica shot him a sideways glint of her oversized Dolce and Gabbanas. 'Why do you think?'

'Because he won't pick up or return your messages?'

'Bingo. Prize for the genius in the passenger seat.'

'You've pumped him dry like poor Barry?'

'Oh, no. There's plenty of juice left in old Karl, but since he got promoted to captain, he's disappeared up his own ass.'

'So what are you going to do? Shoot your way into the police station and kidnap him?'

Jessica shook the pink pixie cut. 'He'll be fine when he sees me. It's just a little game we play.'

Four blocks later, she parked the Beetle on the street outside the Famous Larkins Family Delicatessen Restaurant and said, 'You can buy me lunch while we wait.'

Virgo was ready to refuel. He ordered a signature corned beef and pastrami and drank an iced coffee while he waited. Jessica chose the same. She said Captain Karl was a creature of habit and that within the next thirty minutes he'd walk through the door and order a takeout. Smoked turkey on rye with potato salad and a matzo ball soup. Always the same. He'd be wearing pinstripe pants held up by red suspenders, with a crisp white shirt and a matching red tie. Never anything else. *Groundhog Day.*

The deli was doing a brisk trade. They managed to bag a tufted booth, but most customers sat at plain wooden tables arranged in long rows, elbow to elbow with their neighbor, and a constant line of office workers waited for takeouts. Plenty of noise.

Jessica pushed the Dolce and Gabbanas up onto her forehead. 'Do you think Fonseca bought his gear from Jake Dearman?'

It was the question Virgo had been batting back and forwards in his head since leaving the concrete apartment block, and he still didn't know the answer. Dearman had certainly looked like he'd been mixed up in drugs once upon a time, but he was no Mr. Big. The other thing Fonseca had said was that the product that killed the schoolkid hadn't come from his usual supplier. Jake was a one-off.

He said, 'Jake's a pretty common name.'

'Yeah, but this one just got killed. A frequent occupational hazard among young men who traffic drugs.'

'But usually shot or stabbed,' said Virgo. 'I think Jake Dearman was beaten to death to make it look as though I had done it. Of course, it could have been that someone wanted him dead because he was dealing, and I just happened to be a convenient scapegoat, but—'

'Shuuuush…' Jessica knocked the sunglasses back down over her eyes and sank down a little in her seat. 'He's here.'

Virgo looked over to the counter and saw the guy, as described. Red suspenders. Red necktie. 'Okay. What are you waiting for?'

'I have to follow him back to the station across the street and tailgate him in.'

'It doesn't sound as though Karl is an altogether willing participant in this game.'

'Don't fret. It never fails.' She crept out of the booth and disappeared through the door onto the sidewalk.

Virgo had never heard of the Famous Larkins Family Delicatessen before, but he found their signature corned beef and pastrami truly excellent. The meat was well peppered and smoky with plenty of shavings, and nestled on a bed of slaw, between two slices of double-baked rye, Swiss cheese and Russian dressing. A pickle on the side. The lunch of champions.

Nearly all his life, food had been just carbs and protein. Something to give him energy and strength. Then he got sent to prison, and he realized that what you eat is one of the few joys that can be embraced by anyone during their time on earth and is something that should never be taken for granted. He only served eight months before the FBI sprang him early to do a job, but that was plenty long enough for him to learn to appreciate good food. Shame he was a lousy chef, but he was working on it. One day.

He'd cleared his plate and was eyeing up Jessica's when she ran back in. A strange look of agitation clouded her features, and he couldn't tell whether it signified confusion or a failed mission.

'You'll never guess who Casey shot,' she said before her backside had touched the banquette seat.

'The king of England? Governor of the Federal Reserve? That guy from the Old Spice commercials?'

'Nope.'

'You surprise me. I'm normally good at the random needle-in-a-haystack thing.'

'Nobody. She shot nobody.' Jessica scraped the dressing off her sandwich and took a big bite.

Virgo waited a while. 'Did he check all of the city? Casey thought she was in Santa Monica or Beverly Hills, but she was blindfolded and pumped up. She could have been miles out.'

'Karl checked the whole of California. In fact, he checked the whole of the country for that day, and there wasn't a single person shot dead on their own doorstep. What's the name of the fancy FBI database?'

'ViCAP.'

'That's it. Karl had one of his analysts run the query just now while I waited.' She took another giant mouthful and wiped a smear of slaw from her chin with a screwed-up napkin. 'There's roughly one hundred gun deaths every day across the US, but not many victims get blown away on their own doorstep. It's what they call an unusual modus operandi. Are you sure she got the right day?'

'It was her birthday.'

'Then maybe someone disposed of the body, and it never got reported to the cops.'

'That's a possibility, but why?'

'Some crazy fucking reason, I don't know.' Jessica threw open her arms in exclamation. 'One that's no crazier than pretending you're an angel and putting a slug in a guy you've never met before.'

'You might have a point.' Virgo tilted his head and gave a

nod of acknowledgment. There was something surreal and insane about everything connected to the People's Order of Gabriel, and he was determined to find out exactly what the driving force behind it was. The religious pomp and ostentation were just a façade. He was going to tear the veneer down and see what lay behind it in all its naked glory. But first, he was going to have another of the Famous Larkins Family Delicatessen's signature corned beef and pastrami on rye, with slaw, Swiss cheese and Russian sauce. Some things are so good that one is not enough.

VIRGO HAD LEFT the Winnebago in the parking lot of the Veterans Memorial Hall in La Esperanza. It was a big, well-cared for area, split into sections by manicured hedges with a water fountain and a full-size flagpole at the entrance flying the Stars and Stripes. One of the sections had huge diagonal bays reserved for RVs. Home sweet home for the next twenty-four hours.

Jessica spun the Beetle off the highway into the parking lot and turned the radio down. She'd not said much on the drive up the valley from the city. 'I've been thinking of jacking the business in.'

Virgo could tell she was serious. He said, 'What would you do?'

'Get a regular job with a more reliable income, but it might mean moving back to LA, which would devastate Joey.'

'It must be tough running a private investigation agency on your own.'

'Sure is.' Jessica pulled over and switched off the engine. Gave him the big eyes. 'That's why I need a partner.'

'A partner?'

'Purely in the business sense.'

'Me?' Virgo saw the plan written on her face. 'Whoa. I'm not on the market.'

'Equals. Fifty-fifty split. Can't say fairer than that.'

'You are joking?'

'Come on.' Jessica slapped his thigh. 'Look at what we did back at the Fonseca place. We make a good team. You and me.'

'I've finished with all that.'

'You can be one of the associates in Artemis Associates.'

'I'd rather not.'

'Come on, make me plural. Purely in the business sense, I mean.' She slapped his thigh again. 'I've been living a singular lie because it sounded better.'

'Look, you're smart, gutsy and talented. You don't need a burnt-out, convicted felon who's angry at the world and wants a quiet life.'

'Okay, you're not perfect, but we can work on the wanderlust issues. You can sell the motorhome and rent a proper house that doesn't move around so much. More space, less wheels.'

'I don't—'

'At least say you'll think about it.'

Virgo knew Jessica was in financial trouble and was unsure how much of this offer was born out of desperation. Possibly all of it. Go into partnership and halve your debts, was that what this was all about? He liked her. She was witty and attractive, as well as being a good detective, but maybe she lacked commercial acumen, and in any case, he didn't want to be anchored down by a regular job.

He was wondering whether to placate her with something vague and noncommittal when he noticed the police patrol vehicle on the far side of the parking lot. Two uniforms, windows down, elbows out. Staring in his direction, with one of the cops looking like he was talking on his UHF radio.

Were they waiting for him? What had he done now? There was one easy way to find out. He stepped out of the car and walked towards the Winnebago. His phone pinged, and he saw it was the message from Caleb Hawkins that he'd been waiting for.

No time to unlock the screen. The cops were out of the cruiser and striding towards him. He stopped and treated them to a friendly smile. 'Is there a problem, Officers?'

'Not if you wait here for five minutes.' The taller one scowled back. No sign of a reciprocal smile. 'Someone's on their way to see you.'

'Why don't I just wait in my RV?'

The other one was also Mr. Frown-face. 'We'd rather you didn't do that, sir.'

Virgo had no idea what was going on, but didn't want to give the local cops any excuse to get overexcited. He stood his ground and glanced back to Jessica, who was still behind the wheel of the Beetle. She raised her eyebrows and put her hands up in exclamation: *what's going on?* He shrugged his shoulders back: *I don't know.*

Five minutes later, a phlegm-green Honda Accord nosed into the parking lot, driven by Detective Malone. He pulled up alongside and said to the two uniform cops, 'Thanks. I'll take it from here.' Then he turned to Virgo. 'What are you still doing in La Esperanza?'

Virgo said, 'I didn't know there was a time limit on visits.'

'Get in.' Malone motioned to the empty passenger seat. 'Let's take a drive.'

'I'm sure my mother told me something about not getting into cars with strange men.'

'Come on. I'd like to swap information about the POG, and I'd prefer it if people didn't see me in your company.'

'My mother would also be heartbroken to know I've

become such a public embarrassment.' Virgo opened the door and climbed in.

Malone started to pull away when there was a hammering on the roof of the Honda. He stopped. A back door opened, and Jessica McGann jumped in. 'Is he under arrest? Where the hell do you think you're taking him?'

Malone turned to Virgo. 'This your mother?'

Before Virgo could answer, Jessica's pink head appeared between the front seats. 'Hey, how old do you think I am?'

'Calm down. I know who you are.' Malone drove the Honda back onto the highway, around the town's main square and out along the west route towards the coast. A mile down the road, he said, 'There was some kind of incident at the Templar Sanctorum last night. Don't suppose you know anything about it?'

Virgo creased his forehead. 'What kind of incident?'

'I don't know. They didn't report it, but I heard something went down that they weren't happy about.'

'The place seems to have a lot of security for a religious institution.'

'So it was you?'

'I didn't say that.' Virgo wasn't sure if Malone could be trusted. 'You said you wanted to swap information about the POG. Why don't you go first?'

'Okay.' Malone blinked and checked the rearview mirror. 'We've had ten drug deaths this year, and this place is not Compton or Watts. We never had a single opioid overdose until the weirdos arrived.'

Jessica said, 'They've been happening in the south of the county too.'

Virgo said, 'Then get a warrant for the Templar Sanctorum and search the shit out of the place.'

'And where's my probable cause?' Malone slowed down. Took a right turn. 'Coincidence doesn't count, and besides, everyone in La Esperanza loves the POG because they donate heavily to community projects.'

Virgo said, 'Does Sergeant Chambers love the POG?'

Malone shot a rapid sideways glance. 'No, not at all. What makes you say that?'

Virgo gesticulated out the window. 'Just wondered why we're doing this lovely, scenic tour of the vineyards without his fat, shouty face in the car.'

'He's busy.' Malone kept his eyes on the road.

Jessica leaned forward. 'When we were keeping the POG place under observation, we saw a pickup go in that's flagged on your intel system as being used by John Rinker. There's your probable cause.'

Malone's left eyebrow went into an arch. 'You get it on video?'

'I wrote the number down,' said Jessica. 'I'll give you a statement if that's what you need.'

Malone said nothing. Looked like he was weighing up his chances.

Virgo felt the cell vibrate again in his trouser pocket. Probably Caleb Hawkins wanting to know why he hadn't replied to his last message. The temptation to slide it out and take a peek was strong, but he daren't risk it. He still didn't know if he could trust the cop, and at this stage he certainly didn't want to break the promise he'd made to Casey. So he folded his arms tight and felt the phone burning like a branding iron on his right thigh.

Jessica said, 'I take it you've heard of John Rinker?'

Malone snorted and laughed. Flicked the indicator stalk and took another right. 'The nearest thing we've got to racketeer royalty. Thinks he's fucking Al Pacino in *Scarface*.'

'Then bust his ass,' said Virgo, 'or does he donate heavily to community projects as well?'

'Do you know what?' Malone slammed the wheel in frustration. 'For someone who served in law enforcement, you are staggeringly ignorant of how difficult it is to gather evidence against the leaders of organized-crime syndicates.'

'Maybe it's because I've come to realize most of the barriers are internal bullshit.'

'Yeah, you bypassed them and went to prison.' Malone nodded. 'Smart move. I'll remember that if I ever get tired of walking around as a free man.'

'Going to prison is probably the only way you're going to come across a criminal,' said Virgo, 'being as you never try to arrest any.'

Malone said, 'Fuck you.'

They drove in silence through rolling hills. Precisely planted vines. Green pastures punctuated by stone barns, tractors and rustic roadside inns that were flanked by rosemary bushes and old oak trees. Malone seemed to know all the twists and turns as though it were a regular run he made when he wanted to get away and be on his own. In the distance, a winery that resembled an ornate German Schloss reared up, then disappeared as they dropped between apple orchards and came out by a lake bordered by pine forests on three sides. A couple of red-tailed hawks circled the shoreline. It all seemed an incongruous setting for anyone to ply a trade based on addiction and misery.

After a while, Virgo cleared his throat and said, 'Any developments in the Jake Dearman case?'

Malone looked like he was going to say something, then changed his mind. 'Nothing significant.'

Jessica said, 'Come on, what was it?'

'Tox results came back.' Malone jinked his shoulders as though it were unimportant. 'Dearman had a controlled substance in his bloodstream.'

'Let me guess,' said Jessica. 'Fentanyl? The latest Frankenstein drug to come out of the lab?'

Malone said, 'Nitazene. Makes fentanyl look like Alka-Seltzer.'

It went quiet in the back of the Honda for a moment; then Jessica's pink pixie cut shot between the two front seats. 'Hey, tell me those overdoses weren't nitazene.'

Malone was suddenly interested in some bugs that had flattened themselves against the windshield. He sprayed them with two jets of water and got busy with the wipers. They smeared. He did it again and then again, even though the glass was now sparkling clean.

Virgo said, 'There's your probable cause for a warrant on the Templar Sanctorum, or are you waiting to witness with your own eyes someone carry in a sign-written duffel – *Caution. This bag contains illegal drugs.*'

'I'll see,' said Malone and checked the rearview. 'Are you still willing to give a statement on oath that you saw John Rinker's car enter the property?'

Virgo said, 'I'll email it you by twelve o'clock tonight.'

'Not you,' snapped Malone. 'I'd rather go in front of a judge with something in writing from a licensed private investigator. Not a convicted felon.'

Ten minutes later, they passed the gas station owned by the guy who looked like a walnut and were back in La Esperanza, where Malone dropped them back off in the parking lot of the Veterans Memorial Hall.

Virgo watched the Honda drive out of sight and then snatched the phone out of his pocket. There were three WhatsApps from Caleb Hawkins. The first just said:

Accessed loyalty library no problem. Sent you link to download.

He scrolled to the next message.

Just had a quick look. SHIT!

And the third one read:

I've seen some fucked-up things in my time, but this is on a whole new planet of fucked-uppery. Why you no reply?

He held out the cell screen to show Jessica.

Jessica said, 'Here's the deal. We start afresh. It's goodbye Artemis Associates, hello the McGann Virgo Agency.' She made a dramatic sweep of her arm across the sky, as though there were already a biplane up there towing an advertising banner with the brand name on it.

'I don't think so.' Virgo kept the phone held up.

'You drive a hard bargain, but then you were a negotiator. Okay, we'll call it the Virgo McGann Agency even though it's alphabetically illiterate and doesn't sound anywhere near as good. Final offer. What do you say?'

'Still no.'

CHAPTER 23

Casey put a pot of water on the stovetop to heat up for herbal tea. Myra said she was fully recovered, but she didn't look it. There was some kind of rash on her neck, and her eyes were baggy and swollen. The infusion Casey was preparing blended chamomile with lavender and mint and was one she'd used many times to reduce muscle spasms and anxiety when playing competitive tennis. Now she used it very rarely and just for period pains.

They were in the communal kitchenette that each floor in the POG accommodation blocks had. Nothing fancy. A cooker, coffee machine, small refrigerator and four plastic chairs round a plastic table. It could have been a shared space in a first-year residential hall on some low-ranked college campus, but the walls had framed prints of Dr. Dan's prophesies, not posters of pop stars or movies or that one of the tennis girl lifting half a skirt to scratch her butt cheek.

The good thing about Myra's bout of heat exhaustion was that she'd been oblivious to the world when the golf cart arrived and whisked Casey away for her audience with the prophet. So there'd been no awkward questions about what he'd looked like and why he'd wanted to see her. Why Casey, of all the women in the People's Order of Gabriel? What was so special about her that the great leader, Dr. Daniel Nelson, had sent one of his apostles out to personally fetch her?

Myra might have been completely unaware of the big occurrence, but it didn't stop Casey asking herself the same questions. She knew she was presentable if she scrubbed up, and her body was lean without being skinny. Some curves in the right places. But there were other, more classically beautiful or more conventionally attractive women in the POG who were desperate to get physically and emotionally close to the prophet. She'd heard them. Language that would shame a sailor.

Of course, there had been a time not very long ago when she herself had been mesmerized by his presence. The remnants of the fire had been stirred up that afternoon when she looked into his eyes and felt the hot tingle spread through her nerve ends. Now the feelings of awe and raw excitement were tempered by a sense of suspicion and unease. Maybe that was the reason he had chosen her. He somehow knew about her revulsion to Jake's death and wanted to keep her close. Could he know that she'd seen four apostles drag Jake away? Maybe he'd sensed it. Used his supernatural powers to see inside her mind.

She poured the tea and held out a mug. 'Drink this. It'll put hairs on your chest.'

Myra flinched. 'Pardon?'

'It's what my grandma used to say when I felt unwell and she made me a hot toddy: apple brandy, lemon and sugar.'

'Did it make you feel better?'

'Made me spew.'

'Great.' Myra reluctantly took the mug and sniffed the contents.

Casey took her own tea and sat at the table. The first sip

triggered the memories straight away, as it often did. Something about the fragrance of the herbs hitting the olfactory receptors and being fast-tracked to a special part of the brain. It was like flipping the switch on a time-travelling machine. Bang. She was back in a hotel room, the night before a big tournament. Repeat visits to the bathroom. Cold sweats. Nausea and panic. The fear of failure engulfing her in wave after wave of debilitating anxiety and her desperate hope that it would all stop.

She closed her eyes, thankful that those days were gone. Whatever lay ahead, nothing could be as bad as that phase of her life. Her future was here at the Templar Sanctorum. Even if she hadn't made the commitment by the act of blood sacrifice, she would never choose to go home. Her mother was self-obsessed. Uncaring. Unloving and resentful. It had taken her father's death for Casey to realize that the woman who had brought her into the world thought more about money than her own daughter. And what's the point of being wealthy unless you use it to do good things?

The only question was whether she remained in the People's Order of Gabriel as an ordinary member or as a wife of the great leader. That afternoon she had agreed to his unemotional proposal of marriage. Taken by surprise, what else could she do? Reject the will of the prophet? It was unheard of and tantamount to blasphemy. An outright refusal would only have served to strengthen any suspicions he had about her wavering devotion to him. But now what? Would she go through with it?

Time was short. He wanted to move fast, and an engagement announcement was imminent. There was a technical issue that he needed to address first, but he said it was a minor point and would soon be resolved. Then it would be full steam ahead, and there would be no going back. If she was going to change her mind, she reckoned that she had twenty-four hours, forty-eight at the most.

There was only one thing she could do. As soon as it was lights-out time and she was back in her own room, she was going to kneel down at the side of her bed and pray to God. Only He could guide her as she approached this monumental fork in the road, and show her which path to take.

CHAPTER 24

The image was blurry and jerked around. Then it steadied and came into focus, and there she was, Casey Bender, smiling into the camera with a look of turbo-charged zeal illuminating her features. Dressed all in white: one-piece leather suit, boots and a Stetson. Looked like an extra in a Dolly Parton biopic, apart from a red cross on her chest and the silver-gray pistol in her hand.

Virgo said, 'Check out the date. Definitely her birthday.'

'What a way to spend it.' Jessica used the mouse to hit *pause*. 'Why couldn't she just have gone out, got trashed on tequila and made a fool of herself on karaoke? Or is that just me?' She hit *play*.

Casey waved, and the screen went blank. When it came back on, she was heading down the driveway of a house, and whoever was holding the camera phone was walking behind her. It was dark, but there were courtesy lights down one side of the path and a car parked on the other. She stopped at a gleaming clean black door and pressed the bell. Almost immediately, it opened, and a figure appeared, partly obscured by Casey's back and oversized cowboy hat.

Whoever was holding the camera made a diagonal move so that the lens was angled over Casey's left shoulder and afforded a clear view. The guy looked to be in his thirties. Clean-shaven. Neat hair. Polo shirt and slacks. At first, he didn't seem perturbed to be looking down the barrel of a gun, and made no attempt to close the door. Then his face changed and became gripped by panic. He put his hands up in front of his face, as though flesh and metacarpals could stop a bullet with a muzzle velocity of a thousand feet per second. Pure instinct.

There was a dull crack. Like the sound of a hammer hitting a steel pan. A crimson line of blood appeared on the white wall behind the guy's head, and he went down, entry hole above his left eye and already dead.

Jessica said, 'She fucking did it.'

'Mad.' Virgo shook his head. 'There's none so dangerous as those who have total conviction that their beliefs are right.'

'I need a drink.' Jessica stopped the video and poured herself a Chardonnay from the fridge. Offered one to Virgo, who turned it down. They were back at her house because it was the only place with a computer. He'd thought about getting one for the RV, but it meant installing a mobile router, and the 4G signal was often patchy in the areas he liked to hang out. Way off-grid.

There were sixty-seven videos in total in the loyalty library, but it hadn't taken long to find Casey's. Sorted in chronological order, hers was the most recent. Virgo understood why Jessica had reached for a wine to compose herself. There's something profoundly shocking about watching the last moments of a human life under any circumstances, but when it's a calculated execution and the victim is stood in all innocence on the threshold of their own family home, the discomfiture hits the observer even more.

Who was the guy? Was there even the tiniest grain of truth

in what Casey had been led to believe? That he was a sinner whose only chance of avoiding eternal damnation was to be blown away by an avenging angel? If he was an average Joe, the death would have been reported straight away to the cops and the body left in situ for the authorities to launch a full investigation. But either the body had been moved or the incident not reported at all? Why?

The video was good quality, and the shots of the guy's face were not too far away, so it wouldn't be impossible to check his image against all the bodies that had been recovered with gunshot wounds to the head. Back in his Bureau days, it wouldn't have been a problem, but now it might take a little longer. Not too long, he hoped, because he was determined that the monster who called himself Dr. Dan wasn't going to brainwash anyone else into committing the ultimate crime. At some point in the future, Casey would need to stand before a federal court of the United States and face justice for what she had done, but first Virgo needed to make sure she was safe.

Jessica refilled her glass. 'Want to see some more killings on camera?'

'Not really,' said Virgo. 'But maybe one of them might have a particular feature that enables us to identify a location.'

'A sign over the door showing full name and address?'

'Something like that.'

'One of those tacky stickers folk put on their mailbox to tell the whole world who lives there.' Jessica began to scroll to the start of the file. 'They might as well add their date of birth, social security number and bank details.'

She clicked on the first video and settled back to watch, like it was series 1, episode 1 of a box set. The format was the same. This time it was a guy dressed all in white. No hat.

Around the same age as Casey with sandy hair. He looked terrified, even though he was the one holding a handgun. The quality of the footage wasn't great, but it showed him approach a door and press the bell. He had his arm already outstretched, visibly shaking, and then as soon as the door was opened, there was a muzzle flash, and a figure crumpled to the floor.

The next was similar. Another guy, but this one was cocky. He was laughing and did a pirouette for the camera in his white suit and Trilby, like a six-year-old kid showing off his dress-up outfit. Then he marched up to a wooden door, which was half-glazed, so that you could see the occupant of the house approach and open it. This time the person whose soul needed saving with a bullet was a woman. Early forties. Lipstick. Maybe she was just getting ready for a night out. Bang. Down she went. Trip to the cinema or fancy restaurant cancelled for good.

The following videos stuck to the same depressing template. Jessica's wineglass was empty, and she checked her phone and scowled. Then she tapped a message and said, 'Joey's ignoring my texts again, and I can't wait any longer. I need food.' She jumped up and boiled a large pan of water, poured in a packet of penne pasta, then microwaved some frozen meatballs, covered them in a jar of red sauce and shoved them back in the microwave. As she dropped some slices of garlic bread in the toaster, she said, 'Do you want a beer?'

'Sounds good.' Virgo wondered if it would be possible to link Dr. Daniel Nelson to all of these crimes and indict him as a principal in the first degree. Would that make him the most prolific serial killer in US history? Bundy and Dahmer are the ones that people think of, but they only racked up single figures. The name of Samuel Little is less well known, but he was responsible for sixty confirmed murders, making him well out in front. Until now.

Mass murderers, as opposed to serial killers, are a whole different ball game. Their intention is to inflict multiple casualties in one single event and are less concerned about their personal capture or death. Even so, Dr. Dan would be up there numerically. Virgo knew guys in the Bureau who could recite verbatim the exact times, locations and numbers. Give you a history of the perp's family background and list the psychological factors that were at play. Great analysis and fascinating for geeks interested in that sort of thing, but it never stopped the next one happening.

Jessica served up the food, and Virgo ate. He had dined on worse, but then most of the guys who worked in the kitchen of the Federal Correctional Institution, Eagle Valley, were bank robbers and conmen, not gourmet cooks. He smothered the meatballs in Texas Pete sauce and washed them down with a bottle of Bud. Then he cleared the dirty plates off the table and loaded the dishwasher while Jessica tried to ring Joey several times without success. Cursing each time he didn't answer.

When he'd dried his hands and sat back down, she said, 'Are you ready to binge-watch series 2?'

Virgo planted his elbows on the table and leant towards the screen. 'Let's get it over with.'

Jessica hit *play*, and a familiar routine unfolded before their eyes. Then another, and another. A white angel. Fifty-fifty split male and female. A residential door. Well illuminated. A doorbell. A victim who was predominantly a man aged between thirty and early forties, but occasionally a woman. All shocked and surprised to varying degrees, but too panicked or taken off guard to try to dive out of the way or slam the door. A single shot. Always to the head.

Virgo had lost count of what number they were up to. He was numb. Now he knew how those poor bastards working in the Bureau's Child Exploitation Unit felt, having to sit through hours and hours of obscene pornographic footage. No wonder they were given free counselling. He was thinking it was time to call it a day when a loud scream nearly pierced his one good eardrum.

Jessica stood up and pointed at the screen. 'It's him. It's fucking him. Look.'

Virgo shook himself. 'Who? What am I looking at?'

'The victim. Look.' She bent forward and pushed a neon pink fingernail up to where the paused video showed a figure in the doorway of a house. 'It's fucking him. The same guy Casey shot.'

Virgo screwed up his eyes. 'You sure?'

'Hundred percent. I'm good with faces.' She opened up another window on the computer and brought up Casey's video clip. 'Watch.'

She fast-forwarded to when the door opened, and hit *pause*. There he was. Hair a little shorter. Different shirt. Maybe he'd clapped a couple of pounds on, but it was the same guy. No doubt.

'Well, I never,' said Virgo. It was all he could muster. His mind was racing.

'Must be that guy Lazarus,' said Jessica. 'Brought back to life by the great prophet Dr. Daniel Nelson.'

'Do you believe in miracles?'

'What do you think?'

'Me neither.' Virgo poked a finger at the screen. 'Run it slow-motion until we figure out how they did it.'

They rewatched it six times and cross-referenced their initial personal hypotheses with several other of the alleged snuff videos before finally agreeing on how the scam operated. When the supposed victim raised their hands up in an apparent final act of instinctive defense, what they actually did was fix an adhesive bullet hole to their forehead. Joke shop or eBay special.

Simultaneously, a person hidden behind the door fired a fake stream of blood and snot onto the wall beyond the victim's head, who then performed an already-dead collapse worthy of an Oscar nomination. The avenging angel stood holding a pistol that had just fired a blank, thinking they'd just killed someone.

Once you knew the tricks, everything fell into place because of what all the videos had in common. The door always remained ajar. The lighting was good. All the victims put their hands up to their face. Every wall was painted white to show up the blood. None of the angels fired at the torso or discharged multiple rounds because they must have been ordered to go with a single head-shot.

It was getting late, and they'd only watched and rewatched just over half of the sixty-seven videos. The more they went back to the same ones, the more they noticed what they'd missed the first time round. The guy Casey had shot was the victim in at least five or six others, but had taken steps to change his appearance: a mustache, a goatee, little round John Lennon granny glasses. Then there was a woman who also got her brains blown out on multiple doorsteps only to keep popping up with her hair in a different style. Even a couple of the houses showed up more than once.

Jessica said, 'Look, I can't concentrate any longer.'

Virgo said, 'Take a break, or let's call it a day.'

'It's Joey. He's never normally this late.' She went and put the coffee machine on. 'I don't know what to do about him, and he won't talk to me.'

'Teenage boys aren't chatty.'

'He's like a giant, mute sloth.'

'Give him time. He'll grow out of it.'

'I'm worried he won't live long enough if he keeps hanging with the dopeheads he calls friends.'

'You can't be with him all the time. You have to trust your values have rubbed off on him, even if he makes out they haven't.'

Jessica was about to say something else when there was a loud crash of a door being slammed, and then *ta-da*, he ambled into the kitchen. The giant, mute sloth. Back in its natural habitat of hunting for food in the refrigerator.

Jessica folded her arms. 'Where the hell have you been?'

Joey said, 'Out,' and helped himself to cold pizza.

'What's so hard about letting me know what you're doing? One quick call, a text, that's all I ask.'

Joey's mouth was already full of deep-crust pepperoni. He gave a nonchalant shrug to indicate that he didn't know the answer to that particularly difficult question, and disappeared into the lounge.

Jessica marched after him and closed the door behind her. Shouts came through the thin wall. Virgo tried to zone out. He grabbed the mouse and clicked on the most recent video in Dr. Dan's loyalty library. Casey's baptism. The best day of her life, as she'd described it to him, though would she still say the same now if she knew the truth? She'd fired a big fat blank at an actor. A good actor, it had to be said, and one who'd certainly fooled Virgo. The role-players were probably professionals from down in LA. Maybe even from one of those companies that specializes in arranging stunts for the movie industry. Must have been expensive.

Casey's excited face appeared on the screen. Virgo froze it and said, 'You're free.' The discovery changed everything. There were no invisible chains holding her inside that pseudo-religious compound named the Templar Sanctorum with such pompous grandiloquence. Nothing to blackmail her with. Like everything else in that place, the whole convoluted and sacred ritual of the avenging angels was nothing more than a sham. A charade. A mock simulation designed to sucker the vulnerable into a form of modern slavery. It was time to get Casey out and then bring the whole phony edifice crashing down.

CHAPTER 25

Jessica came back into the kitchen and didn't say anything. She went straight to the countertop and played around with the coffee machine.

Virgo said, 'First thing tomorrow, I'm going to drag Casey out of that lunatic asylum and take her home.'

Jessica kept quiet. Began to polish some cups with a towel.

Virgo said, 'Do you want to come?'

When Jessica turned round, there were tears pooling in her eyes. She blinked, and they ran down her face. 'Could you speak to him for me?'

'Who, Joey?' Virgo chewed on his bottom lip. 'I'm not sure that's a good idea.'

'That's what you used to do for a living, isn't it? Talk to people in crisis situations?'

'I started off trying to talk jumpers down from tall buildings and graduated to kidnappers who were threatening to kill a hostage they'd already removed body parts from.' He made a chopping motion with his index finger. 'None of them were normal teenage kids.'

'Come on, you were a negotiator. It's all about communication.'

'It was a role. I had clear objectives.'

'I want you to convince my son not to do drugs. Is that objective not fucking clear enough for you?' Jessica used the towel to wipe her cheeks. 'I'm sorry.'

'The last job I did as a serving federal agent didn't end well.'

Jessica sat down and put her hand on his. 'It's all right. I shouldn't have asked. I don't know what's the matter with me.'

'Everyone worries about the people they love. Wouldn't be human otherwise.'

'Is that why you don't want any more relationships? In case you get hurt?'

'How do you know I don't?'

'I'm a mind reader.'

'It's only two years since my wife died. I'm just not ready. I might never be ready.'

'You will be one day.' Jessica smiled through the mascara that had run down her face. 'Acceptance that you've got an issue is the first step to resolving it.'

'Are you a psychoanalyst as well as a mind reader?'

'I'm a self-taught expert in the field. Got the scars and the T shirt.'

'Maybe I don't want to resolve my issues.'

'I've been on my own fourteen years. Don't make the same mistake as me and leave it too late, because we're only here once. If that sounds like a cliché, it's because it's true.'

Virgo smiled. He wasn't afraid of being lonely and didn't care what other people thought about him. Most guys who are unfaithful do it because they're weak and need to feed their ego. The thrill of the chase. The forbidden fruit. There's nothing new in any of that stuff. He didn't even have a partner to be faithful to, just a memory, but it meant the same to him. He was strong and self-reliant, yet when he looked at Jessica, he felt a pull. Had since the first time she appeared out of the fog.

He sensed that she felt the same about him, but it was hard to tell with the act she seemed to put on most of the time. Perhaps the act was a defense mechanism that she'd developed to survive in the theater of private investigation, which was still a tough and unforgiving world. Whatever it was, her priorities were her son and her livelihood, not throwing herself into a new relationship. That was clear.

They sat in silence for a while. Virgo recognized that familiar feeling start in his toes and work its way up into his chest. The one where he knows he's about to do something he's going to regret. He took a deep breath and said, 'Perhaps I could see if Joey wants to talk.'

Two minutes later, and with a little devil on his shoulder telling him he was a gullible idiot, he walked into the lounge with two bottles of Bud. Joey was recumbent on the sofa, playing a video game that seemed to be set in a post-apocalyptic world where disfigured humans tried to decapitate, dismember, crush, impale and disembowel each other. Perfect bedtime viewing.

Virgo sat down in the chair opposite and waited. Joey carried on playing until he'd finished the level, then took his earphones off and said, 'What?'

'Your mother wants me to talk to you about drugs, but I'm no good at that sort of thing, so I thought we could just have a beer instead and pretend that I had.' He twisted the cap off one of the bottles and held it out. 'Deal?'

'Please yourself.' Joey took the Bud.

Virgo said nothing. Silence is important. Sometimes it's a void that needs to be filled.

It took Joey seven or eight hits to finish the beer and

decide he wanted to throw something into the void. 'Mom said you killed a man.'

'When I was in the Army, I contributed to the deaths of multiple enemy personnel, but I think she's referring to another occasion.'

'Cool. What was it like?'

'It was nothing to be proud of.'

Joey stared into his empty beer bottle. 'Do you fancy giving me some more advice about drugs? Get me another Bud, and I'm happy to play along. Deal?'

Virgo hadn't started his own beer. He handed it over. 'Look, I'm not qualified to give advice. By the time I was your age, I was so far off the rails I'd forgotten where the tracks were supposed to be. I'd been kicked out of high school for busting a kid's head open, and the New York City cops were always rousting me off the street corner. Soon as I was seventeen, I joined up, but even at army training school I was always getting into fistfights until one day I picked an argument with the wrong guy and got put in the hospital. Fractured jaw. Two teeth gone. Ribs hurting like hell.'

Joey took a drink. Eyes like saucers.

'That was the day changed my life.' Virgo lifted his top lip at one side. 'Those two teeth there are dental implants. Titanium alloy.' He let the lip drop. 'Anyway, the sergeant comes to visit me on the ward and asks me what I thought I was doing with my life, and I gave him some bullshit about just wanting my peers to give me a bit of respect, and he explodes. Fuck that, he says. The only respect you need is from yourself. Weak people want you to be weak same as them. When they can't do something themselves, they don't want you to do it either. If they haven't got a purpose in life, they don't want you to have one either. So have some self-respect and take responsibility. Be a man, not a sheep.'

Joey said, 'It's not easy to be a man when you're treated like a kid all the time.'

'It's never easy, but your mother loves you and wants the best for you.'

'Have you seen this?' Joey reached over the side of the sofa and pulled up a small black canvas flight bag. 'For my sixteenth birthday she bought me a pack of emergency Durex in case I ever get unexpectedly lucky, a rape alarm and pepper spray should I get jumped on the way home by a gang of asshole bandits, an EpiPen in case I suddenly develop some kind of allergy, and of course, a Naloxone inhaler if I take an overdose of whatever opioid she thinks all my friends are taking. Heroin, fentanyl, oxy...' He opened the bag to display the contents. 'Then she makes me carry it around with me everywhere I go. Imagine if I ever went on a date and the girl saw all this shit. What would she think?'

Virgo thought any sensible girl would run a mile, but kept his opinion to himself.

Joey said, 'She calls it my Just-In-Case Bag.' He zipped it back up and threw it on the floor.

'Maybe she overcompensates a little because she's on her own. It's not easy for her.'

'What about me?'

'Okay, it's tough for you too, but you're reaching the age when you have to make a decision. Keep thinking about yourself, or start taking ownership.'

'Is this the man or sheep crap again?'

'See, you're smart.'

'Baa, baa, baa...' Joey laughed.

'And witty.'

'Hey.' Joey looked serious all of a sudden and a touch awkward. 'Are you and Mom, like, you know, dating?'

'No. We're just working on a case together.'

'Cool.' Joey necked the Bud and finished it. 'The last guy

was a real fucking creep. You're okay.' Then he put his earphones back on and started to massacre some more humanoids.

Virgo smiled, feeling good about himself. Not being *a real fucking creep* was the biggest compliment he'd received in a long time.

CHAPTER 26
LA ESPERANZA - THE VETERANS MEMORIAL HALL

A little after 9 a.m. Virgo reached the parking lot. Last night he'd bedded down on the McGann couch because Jessica had taken on board too much Chardonnay to chauffeur him back to his motorhome. This morning, she did the school run, and he hopped on an early bus that brought him up through Cal Poly, Santa Margarita and Atascadero before cutting inland to the green valley that housed the People's Order of Gabriel.

First thing he noticed on approaching the RV was a folded sheet of paper tucked under the wiper blade. A flyer for some local business? Free wine-tastings at Big Al's vineyard or ten percent off lobster fries at Sally's seafood bistro? He was about to consign it to trash-can history when he noticed that none of the other vehicles in the lot had anything on their windshield. Just the Virgo-mobile.

He unfolded the paper and saw it was a handwritten note from Detective Malone and a cell phone number.

Call me when you get this. It's important.

Maybe his new best friend wanted to take him on another one of his scenic drives around the backstreets of the countryside. Take in some of the beauty spots and quirky villages they'd missed on the last run out. Whatever he wanted, it couldn't be as important as making contact with Casey. That was his number one priority now that he knew the kill videos were fake and Nelson had no hold over her. He climbed in the driver's seat and set off to give her the good news that she wasn't a murderer after all.

Virgo realized there was something going down as soon as he maneuvered the Winnebago towards the exit. A black Ford Transit parked one row back with the engine ticking over and two hombres in the cab trying to look benign and anonymous. He knew they weren't plainclothes cops, because he'd worked with plenty of those guys for ten years and could pick one out in a crowd of a thousand, even while he was riding on a galloping steed with one eye closed. No, these were lowlifes. The genuine article.

As soon as he pulled out onto the highway, he checked the door mirror. What a surprise. The Transit was on the move. He drove around the town square, under the ancient oak trees, past the cutesy stores and artisan craft boutiques and out onto the road towards the Templar Sanctorum. Snap. The Transit followed suit. No point trying to lose a tail in a fifteen-thousand-pound recreational vehicle that tops out at sixty miles per hour on a good day. So Virgo maintained a steady speed. If he took them down one of the many dead-end tracks that led off to picnic areas, he could get them hemmed in and take his chances. Two on one. Not bad odds as long as they weren't carrying. The problem was, they looked like the kind of gangbangers who might be.

Once out of town, the two-lane road ran through the valley bottom before starting to climb into the eastern hills. Two more miles and the People's Order of Gabriel gates would appear on the left-hand side. The diesel engine of the RV began to complain about the incline and dropped a gear. Then they crested the brow of the hill, and Virgo slammed on the anchors.

There was a truck with a livestock trailer slewed across the blacktop. No way past. Drainage channels either side. As soon as the tires shrilled to a stop, two more guys appeared from behind the truck and ran over. Leather jackets, black denim, facial tattoos. One carrying a shotgun. Virgo felt the front bumper of the Transit nudge into the back of the RV, and before he could decide whether to dive for the passenger door, both barrels of the 12-bore were in his face.

He stepped out, hands half-mast. 'You need to know something. I react badly to being threatened.'

'Arms behind your head, asshole.' The guy with the shotgun seemed to be team captain. 'Get in the fucking van.'

The front passenger was out of the Transit and had the cargo door open.

Virgo didn't move. If he got in the van, he was confident he could inflict serious damage at close quarters, and it would take the 12-bore out of the equation, but he didn't know how many more gangbangers were in there. He could be overpowered. Outside in the open air, the space was both an opportunity and a disadvantage. He could defend himself and escape, but only if he neutralized the firearm. Decision time.

He took a step towards the van and saw movement. There were at least two more in the back. He took another step. Deliberately hesitant. Banking on one thing. That the guy with the shotgun wouldn't be able to resist ramming the two barrels in the middle of his back, and Virgo wanted him close.

'Move it, motherfucker.' Captain Gangbanger prodded.

Virgo felt the steel dig into his flesh, as expected. Okay, hold tight, here we go. He pretended to stumble forward, but swung his left arm up and around behind him and knocked away the barrel. Then he maintained the momentum and brought his right fist through a hundred and eighty degrees. The guy with the gun had been spun off balance. He was just whipping his head back round when his jaw met Virgo's knuckles in a moment of consummate precision. There was only ever going to be one winner. The powerful jolt of kinetic energy was the kind that causes the brainstem to twist inside the skull. Circuits break, and the brain shuts down to protect itself. Lights out.

The shotgun was heading for the tarmac when Virgo grabbed both barrels and swung the stock up into the groin of gangbanger number two. This guy was three hundred pounds of blubber with a shaved head and teardrop tattoos on both cheeks. His eyeballs almost popped onto the teardrops. Virgo rammed the butt end of the stock into the middle of his face and put him on his backside. Then spun the shotgun back into a conventional grip and pointed the barrels at the driver, who was now out of the van. Virgo said, 'Get back in the cab and back that piece of shit up.'

Movement inside the cargo area of the Transit. It flickered in Virgo's peripheral vision. He turned. A head appeared. More tattoos. A bandana. Then a gloved hand with a pistol. That was as far as this guy got. *Bang.* As his body became framed in the sliding doorway, an ounce of lead pellets blasted a hole in his chest. He flipped backwards into the van.

Virgo pointed the 12-bore at the driver and gangbanger number two, who was just getting off the ground with blood oozing from the bomb site where his nose had once been. 'I reckon I've got one cartridge left. Who wants it?'

No volunteers. They stood with their hands up, looking pissed. Virgo sidestepped to where the guy he'd shot had dropped his handgun on the road and picked it up. Glock 19. Nice. He checked the mag. Slung the shotgun into the shrubs and dirt on the far side of the drainage ditch, and darted into the sliding doorway of the van, both hands on the gun, ready to fire.

Apart from the casualty who was on his back bleeding out, there was one other guy in the cargo area. He was hunched up into a corner, palms in the air, looking like he might drown in the sweat that was pouring down from his hairline. There was a pack of heavy-duty cable ties on the plywood floor. A pillowcase. Rope. A Husqvarna chainsaw and a can of gas, and a T-handled spade.

Virgo gave a little whistle through his teeth. Whoever these shitbirds were, they hadn't been planning to take him on a luxury tour of the local wineries.

CHAPTER 27

Detective Malone's voice boomed out of the loudspeaker. 'You should have called me straight away.'

Virgo said, 'Wouldn't have made any difference. They were already waiting for me.'

'At least forewarned, you would have been ready.'

'I'm always ready.'

'Why am I not surprised?'

Virgo gingerly guided the RV off the highway onto a rough track, approximately half a mile from the Templar Sanctorum. He was hands-free on Bluetooth. 'How did you know this John Rinker was going to do a number on me?'

'Did one of the guys who ambushed you look like a rodent wearing a baseball cap, with a hoodie hood pulled up over the top?'

'Not that I saw.'

'Then it wasn't John Rinker himself. Just some of his crew.'

'You didn't answer my question.'

'You know how it is. Cops have to keep some sources of information confidential.'

'You got a guy on the inside?'

'No comment.'

'Is your CI one of the Rinker gang or a member of the People's Order of Gabriel?'

'I never said I had a confidential informant.'

'You didn't need to.' Virgo pulled up and turned the engine off. 'This CI, did they tell you why Rinker doesn't like me?'

'Maybe nobody likes you, Virgo. You're a pain in the ass, and if I were you, I'd get as far away from La Esperanza as possible and as quickly as you can.'

'I'm not scared of Dollar Tree dons like John Rinker.'

On the other end of the line, Malone made a heavy sigh. 'You just shot a man. Possibly fatal. Of course, these guys might not rock up at the station and file a complaint, but if they do...'

'What? It was self-defense.'

'Do you want me to remind you about your criminal history and how a prior homicide conviction might count against you if it comes to your one word against several others'?'

'My eleven years in the Army and nine as an FBI agent mean nothing, do they? Don't try to bullshit me.'

'Hey, I'm on your side.'

'That's what Brutus said to Caesar just before he daggered him.' Virgo ended the call.

The track ran down to a five-bar gate that looked like it hadn't been opened for half a century and was shielded from the highway by a strand of Coulter pines. He took a screwdriver and carefully removed a vinyl-covered interior panel from the wall in the RV kitchen area and buried the recently acquired Glock 19 in the white glass wool insulation before carefully replacing it and pressing plastic caps on the screw tops. The only thing missing was a sign to hang next to it: *In case of emergency break here.*

Then he hooked his rucksack over one shoulder and set off along a dirt path that ran parallel to the highway. Just another hiker taking a break from his boring office job in the city and heading for the hills, where the air was fresh and the views Insta-friendly. After a while, he could see the three-domed bell tower of the Templar Sanctorum rising up through the trees on the opposite side of the road, and then he passed the imposing wrought-iron gates with their People's Order of Gabriel shield and coat of arms. He kept his head down and carried on.

Another half a mile and he was adjacent to the fields where they grew the fruit and vegetables. He clambered over some rocks at the side of the path and up into the chaparral. Traversed a slope thick with coyote brush and needle-leafed chamise, and settled down on a shelf of granite that afforded a clear view of the pastures below. He took the Nikon binoculars out of his sack and began to scan for Casey. Split each field into quarters in his mind, and then gridded each quarter so he wouldn't miss any section or duplicate those he'd already checked. Methodical and efficient.

A problem became apparent. Casey wasn't there. He started again at the beginning and worked through the system. Maybe she'd been bent down behind a bush or temporarily blocked out by another POG worker. No. Still not there. Third time, Virgo spent longer scrutinizing each person, but it made no difference. Not one of them was Casey Bender.

Strange, because Casey's new buddy was there. The girl called Myra. She was on her own picking berries as though she were representing the US in an Olympic fruit-picking competition. Virgo watched. After a while he figured out the pattern. There was some kind of supervisor in the shade of a tin-roofed shelter, who from time to time took out a notebook and wrote things down. Occasionally, he'd take a walk between the rows of bushes, and whenever any of the workers saw him look in their direction, they doubled their efforts. As soon as the guy looked the other way, they relaxed. Virgo began to sing the old Sam Cooke chain-gang song. *Hooh, aah…*

An hour dragged by. No sign of Casey. It was getting too late in the morning for her to have overslept. Maybe she was ill or being held in detention because her faith in the great prophet Dr. Dan was on the wane. Stuck in a classroom subjected to some dystopian conversion therapy. He decided it was not time to panic and attempt another incursion behind enemy lines. He'd been lucky to make it out of the compound on the previous occasion, and the safest bet was to stick it out.

He was getting tired of sticking it out when his cell juddered and the screen lit up: *Jessica Bender*. He'd still not altered her name in his contacts since the first meeting where she'd taken him for a fool. He ought to still be angry, but now he smiled to himself and swiped. 'Hi, where are you?'

'You've gotta see this.' Jessica sounded agitated and hyped.

'Try and be a little more specific.'

'You're not gonna believe it.'

'I might surprise you.'

'I watched the rest of those fake kill videos, and there's something you need to see with your own eyes.'

'I haven't got any others.'

'They're not all fake.'

Virgo felt his skin crawl. 'What?'

'They're not all fake.' Jessica's tone was solemn. Not joking. 'There's a couple of genuine fatalities.'

'Are you sure?'

'They're like the deadest people I've seen. This is what I'm saying, you need to take a look.'

'Meet me at the Memorial Hall.' Virgo pocketed his cell and packed his rucksack before taking one final look at the POG members toiling away below him in their depersonalized, collarless tunics, like Marxist worker bees maintaining their strange community. What was it about the People's Order of Gabriel? Every time he thought he'd got the bogus establishment sussed out, another bolt of craziness came hurtling out of the blue.

CHAPTER 28

Jessica climbed into the Winnebago carrying a grande Starbucks and a canvas tote. Her pixie cut was mucky blonde with lime green highlights.

Virgo said, 'You changed the color of your hair.' Mr. Observant.

She pulled a laptop out of her bag and opened it up on the RV dining table. 'I got fed up of pink, and you said it was no good for conducting covert surveillance.'

'Whereas now it's perfect.'

'Stop whining and watch this.' She fired the computer up and selected a file. 'This is the first one. See what you think.'

Virgo leaned forward. A familiar scene began to unfold. A guy dressed all in white grinned into the camera. Pointed to the red cross on his chest and gave a thumbs-up. Then his hand disappeared, and when it came back into shot, it was holding a black pistol with a sound suppressor fitted to the muzzle. That was a first. None of the others had appeared to care about noise, but then those other addresses had probably been chosen because there were no neighbors nearby.

The next difference was the door itself. It was a grand

entrance up a couple of steps and with a tiled porch above it. Ornate oak balustrades either side and a brass name plaque that said *Winthrop Lodge*. The guy rang the bell. Nobody answered. He looked around, unsure what to do. Rang it again. Then again. It was all different to the other videos.

Finally, the door opened, and the differences grew even greater. It was a man who answered the door. Late seventies with wisps of white hair and a cane in his right hand, which he was using to support himself. Immediately, his mouth fell open in shock, and he tried to close the door. No lingering or studied look of confusion. No hands up in front of the face.

Next thing, the back of his head flew off. Pieces of skull and scalp. No neat hole appeared in the forehead, just a hint of blackness in one of the eye sockets where the bullet had entered. The cane hit the floor first. Then the body.

Jessica said, 'Dead enough for you?'

'I've seen worse, but yes. That's no stunt.' Virgo's mind was already trying to work out the quickest method of locating Winthrop Lodge. FBI's data explorer system or open-source search options available on the internet. Either-or. 'You mentioned another?'

Silence while Jessica drank a gallon of filter coffee and snapped the lid back on her cup. Then she dabbed her mouth with a tissue and said, 'This next one's wrong on so many levels.' She selected another file and shook her head.

The screen fuzzed up. It cleared to reveal a kid in freeze-frame. Not much more than eighteen with a mousey rice-bowl haircut and the rash some boys get when they first start wet shaving. Maybe he was a late developer. He had an overbite and a thousand-yard stare. White tux and pants with a red crucifix on a chain around his neck. No hat.

Jessica selected the *play* arrow, and the horror unfolded. The kid reached inside the tux and pulled out a revolver that looked like a classic Smith and Wesson Model 29. He held it at arm's length in one shaky hand and posed for the camera. Look at me, Dirty Harry. Then he strolled down a long driveway that was bordered on either side by flowerbeds and neat-trimmed miniature rose gardens. He seemed to be trying to boost his confidence by putting some swagger into his step.

Like the last video, the house looked big and well maintained. Double doors. Ionian columns holding a pitched roof above the entrance. The kid rang the bell. Again, nobody answered, and he rang again. Then banged on the door with the stock of the revolver until a light went on in the hallway inside. The door didn't open, and words were exchanged, but the sound was muffled. Then the door opened, but only a fraction.

The kid wasn't taking any chances. He kicked the door wide open to reveal his target. An old woman. Eighties or older, her back and shoulders hunched by age. Frail. A touch of lipstick and salon-set hair to show she still made an effort. Somebody's grandmother. She looked like she'd just seen the devil.

Bang. No silencer. The kid put the slug from a magnum cartridge in her chest. She dropped like a rag doll. The kid hadn't finished. He crossed the threshold, stood over her body and said something else. Maybe, *are you feeling lucky, punk?* Then put another bullet in her chest. A toy poodle wearing a pink bow was running around and around in circles, going mad. The kid turned, nodded and showed his overbite grin to the camera to acknowledge mission accomplished. Big man.

Jessica said, 'If he had killed that dog, I would have hunted that son of a bitch down myself and ripped his fucking head off.'

'Killing the old dear is okay?'

'No, just different.'

'Don't you think the kids committing these atrocities are

victims as well? In all those other fakes, the person firing the gun didn't know it was a setup. The intent to kill was the same.'

'Victims? No, they knew what they were doing.'

Virgo smiled. 'You remind me of my old captain in the Army.'

'Attractive divorcee? Forty but looks younger? Likes cocktails and romantic fiction?'

'He didn't have a sympathetic bone in his body.'

'Hey.' Jessica snapped the laptop shut. 'Why don't you come over for dinner tonight? I'll cook something nice.'

Virgo was interested, but smelled a rat. 'Is this about smooching me into being a business partner?'

'You're so cynical.'

'Blame it on the fact most people always act in their own best interests.'

'Joey really likes you.'

'No, he doesn't.' Virgo realized dinner had strings attached and wasn't sure he wanted to get tangled up in them. 'I think he's mistakenly impressed because I've killed real people, not just those on a Nintendo.'

'Please yourself.' Jessica looked deflated. She closed her eyes as though counting to ten, and when she opened them, the zest and gusto were back. 'Hey, come on, let's roll.'

'Two minutes.' Virgo kicked himself for flunking the dinner invitation. He pulled his cell out. Googled Winthrop Lodge, California, and scrolled. Only three hits down was an item in an online publication called the *Monterey County Chronicle*. He opened it up.

> *Detectives from Carmel Police Department are today investigating the death of retired businessman and local benefactor William Berg, whose body was found by gardening staff arriving for work at his home, Winthrop Lodge, in the*

Laurelwood area of the city. It is believed Mr. Berg died from a gunshot injury, and police are working on a number of theories, including that this was a home invasion that went wrong and ended in tragedy. Neighbors said that the widower, who lived alone, was an active member of the community and well known for his support of several mental health charities. No members of the family were available for comment.

Virgo checked the date of publication. Six months ago. He passed the phone to Jessica. 'Why this old guy?'

She read the article. 'He doesn't look like a sinner who needed saving by an avenging angel.'

'Exactly.' Virgo knew there must be a reason why William Berg had been selected, because Dr. Daniel Nelson was mad, but he wasn't stupid. The answer was inside the compound of the People's Order of Gabriel, out on the road past La Esperanza. Beyond hope.

CHAPTER 29

Jessica sat alone in the Beetle. Top down with SoCal Sound on the radio. Parked in pine shade some thirty yards from the entrance gates to the Templar Sanctorum. She opened another envelope and pulled out an invoice. The monthly rent was due again on the premises of Artemis Associates. She threw it with the rest on the passenger seat. More than ever, it was clear the only thing that could save the business was getting hold of Casey Bender and delivering the mixed-up girl in person back to her mother. That was the big payday.

She stared again at the gateway, willing Casey to walk out. Skip, cycle, jog, ride naked on a horse or anything just to put an appearance in. Nothing moved. Apart from the air shimmering up in a midday haze.

She opened the last of the mail that she'd collected at the office on her way up to meet Virgo and saw it was a bank statement. Not much income from the detective agency and zero child-support payment again from the turd who had once been her husband. Last time, she'd made a complaint to the LAPD Internal Affairs Group and requested it be automatically deducted from his pay, but they'd said it was a matter for the family court. It was all bullshit and bureaucracy.

Joey was already dropping hints about going to San Diego with his friends next spring break, and that wouldn't be cheap. Before that, there was his birthday and Christmas. What could she do? The bottom line of the bank statement showed a balance of two hundred and sixty-eight dollars. Maybe she should drive to Vegas and put it all on the spin of a wheel. Not much of a way to decide important life choices, but at the moment it looked more promising than getting hold of Casey Bender.

Whoa. Wait. Movement down the blacktop. A vehicle approaching from the direction of La Esperanza. She used her binoculars and saw it was the black GMC Sierra flagged as being used by John Rinker. She brought up the camera on her cell phone and waited until the pickup was starting to turn into the POG compound before taking three quick snaps. Once she'd got Casey back to her mother, she'd send Detective Malone the photographs, but not before. The last thing she wanted was anything that could scupper the one thing that could save her business. Two minutes later, the GMC Sierra's hood appeared between the wrought-iron gates, and it thundered away back down the highway. Pick up or drop off? Whatever it was, it hadn't taken long.

Jessica groped around in the bag for her Reese's. Excitement over. It was time to relax, and she needed sugar. The orange foil wasn't off the first peanut butter cup when there was more movement. A car exiting the compound. She grabbed the binoculars and saw it was a Tesla. Two guys in the front and a female in the back. *Wait a minute. Really? Fuck Las Vegas and roulette.* It was Casey Bender in the flesh and as clear as day.

The Tesla shot silently towards town, and after leaving a

suitable gap, Jessica doof-doofed after it. Nothing silly. She kept calm and drove at a safe distance. If the driver in front picked up he was being tailed, he could lose her in no time. They started the descent into town, past the riding school and a windmill built by settlers to pump water from a well on their farm. Houses appeared. Picket fences. Then the bijou stores, and before long they were in the main square of La Esperanza, where the Tesla parked in a row of bays marked *Permit Holders Only.*

Jessica drove past and abandoned the Beetle round the first corner. Then she ran across the road into the park that filled the town square, just in time to see Casey enter one of the stores that lined the far side. She used the thick tree trunks as cover to make her way closer without being observed. Past a row of garbage containers and a couple of bronze statues, then around the gazebo-style bandstand until she could see the name of the establishment Casey had entered. *OMG.* The sign said *Sandra's Bridal Couture.*

The driver was still in the Tesla. No sign of the other guy. He must have gone into the store with Casey. Jessica waited and weighed up what her best opportunity of executing a kidnap in broad daylight might look like. Inside the store or on the way back to the car? It depended on where the minders were, and whether she could engineer some way of speaking to the girl in private. Big ask. But then the guy who was inside the store came out and just mooched about on the sidewalk. Some men don't like wedding dresses.

To avoid walking past the Tesla, Jessica took a detour and approached Sandra's Bridal Couture from the opposite direction. She stopped outside the window of a nearby store and pretended to browse a display of hand-carved ornaments until the mooching guy wasn't looking, and *three, two, one, go, go, go…* She was in.

A woman sat at a desk wearing a lot of makeup said, 'Have you got an appointment?'

Jessica said, 'Sorry. Have I come into the doctor's office by mistake?' She looked around the store. It was small. No sign of Casey. There were a couple of doors that were closed.

'I'm Sandra, and this is my bridal boutique, but I'm afraid all my consultants are busy.' Sandra's tone was a little sharp.

Jessica guessed you could count the number of her consultants on one finger, but smiled anyway and said, 'Mind if I take a look around?'

'Do you have a date fixed?'

'For what?' Jessica didn't like the way Sandra looked her up and down.

'The wedding.'

'No.'

'May I suggest you make an appointment when you have a date, and we will be delighted to work with you to fulfil your dreams and make your special day the best it can possibly be.' Sandra held out a card.

'Stuff marriage. I'm not making the same mistake again.' Jessica opened the nearest of the two doors and walked through. It was empty. Just a storeroom of boxes and material.

She came back out, and Sandra stood up. 'Excuse me, madam. What do you think you're doing?'

Jessica ignored her and went through the second door. It was a large, mirrored fitting room with two cream leather sofas, a drinks cabinet and ice buckets for fizz. Casey Bender stood in the middle of the floor in just her bra and panties while a woman ran a tape measure down her leg.

Jessica said, 'Get dressed. You're coming with me.'

Casey's face went red. Anger not embarrassment. 'Get out. I can't believe my mother's still paying you to spy on me.'

'Wait a minute. Tell me you're not marrying him. Chief

scumbag.' Jessica noticed the two stick-angel tattoos on Casey's arm.

'I said get out. Leave me alone.'

'Listen. There's something important I need to tell you, which I guarantee will make you change your mind.' Jessica turned and smiled politely at the assistant. 'It's a private matter.'

The woman looked terrified. Like she'd accidentally stumbled onto the set of a tempestuous TV drama. She scuttled out.

Jessica closed the door. 'You didn't kill anyone. It was all a setup. That video in Dr. Dan's loyalty library is just to stop you leaving.'

The color evaporated from Casey's face. 'I don't believe you.'

'Come on, get dressed. I'll show you.'

'You're lying.'

'I promise you I'm not.'

'The same as Mr. Virgo promised not to tell another person about it.'

Jessica puffed her cheeks out in frustration. 'We're trying to help you before someone else gets killed. Look what happened to Jake Dearman.' She saw something flicker in Casey's eyes and tried to capitalize on it. 'You know it was wrong. They beat him to death and then tried to frame an innocent man for his murder. What frigging book of the Bible is that one from?'

The door flew open, and one of the minders bowled in. Before Jessica could react, he punched her in the stomach and gripped her in a headlock. Then dragged her out and into the storeroom next door. She ran a heel down his shin and tried to smack him in the balls, but he yanked her around and pinned her up against the wall. He flat-handed her across the face and said, 'Stay away from the girl.'

Jessica was dizzy and felt sick. Cheek on fire. She could smell his deodorant and sulfur breath. He had a square face, hair buzzed at the sides, longer on top, and wore a red polo shirt. The same stick-angel tattoos on his arm, but three not two. She said, 'Do you like hitting women?'

Sounds of commotion came from the store. Sandra's voice shouting something about the police. The guy turned to leave, then changed his mind and came back, leading with his right fist. Jessica saw it coming and snapped her head sideways, but it still caught her in the mouth.

'Hey,' she shouted after him, the metallic tang of blood on her tongue, 'tell Dr. Dan to go fuck himself.'

CHAPTER 30

It took Virgo less than ten minutes to find three more items of open-source material relating to the death of William Berg. The first was an obituary posted by a local funeral home. Short and sweet. Next was a feature that paid tribute to his contribution to the community of Carmel. How he was a self-made man who had built his significant wealth from combining a successful jewelry business with shrewd investment, and played golf at Pebble Beach. Married late in life. Retired after the death of his wife and devoted himself to charitable work, specifically supporting those with mental illness.

The final article was a concise follow-up piece to the initial report in the *Monterey County Chronicle*. It said police had made no arrests and were still appealing for anyone with information to come forward. No property had been stolen in the attack, and the motive was unclear. Virgo had been expecting to find something about William Berg's involvement with the church or some kind of religious institution, but there was no mention. Nothing to make him a potential target for the warped warriors of the People's Order of

Gabriel, but there was no way it could have been a freak, random killing. What was he missing?

There was still the second victim to identify. The old lady blown away by the kid with a revolver. Maybe there was a link between the two or some common feature in their personal backgrounds that would indicate why they were chosen. Virgo debated with himself whether to make the call. It had been over a year since he'd left the FBI in disgrace, and none of his ex-colleagues had reached out to him. Likewise, he'd never tried to contact them, partly because he was *persona non grata* and it would have put them in an awkward position, and partly because he thought they didn't like him much. There was one exception.

He paced up and down the confines of the RV. Agonized and procrastinated. Then he picked up his cell and called the exception. Her name was Betty, and she worked at the J. Edgar Hoover Building in Washington, DC. A relic from the William H. Webster era, she terrified the kids who worked there today, and her bosses, in equal measure. But she loved Virgo. Or used to. She'd been his designated analyst on an operation that ran for six months into a gang of commercial extortionists. A hackneyed classic. Injecting shit into pouches of baby food on supermarket shelves and blackmailing the manufacturers. Except on this occasion, it had been liquid ketamine and posted on TikTok and X back in the days when it was a blue bird. Thanks to work by Betty, Virgo had nailed them at a Kroger's in Illinois.

He held his breath as he was put through. It had been a long time. People change. 'Hi, it's Eddie.'

'You still owe me dinner at the Waldorf.' The voice was gruff. Semi-threatening. Same old Betty.

'You got the roses though, right?' Virgo had come to accept that many of his relationships were based on material transactions and that he was the party doing the financial lifting.

'I was sorry to hear about your wife.'

'Thank you.'

'And that other business.'

Virgo smiled. Nice use of words. *That other business.* No mention of the homicide conviction and stretch in the slammer. 'I was ready for a fresh start.'

'So, what are you doing now that needs me to grant you a favor?'

'Can't I just call and have a little catch-up? See how you're doing?' He laughed.

'Wait a minute.' There were some clunking sounds on the line. Then Betty's gravel voice came back on. 'Sorry, just had to wipe some bullshit off the receiver. I think it came clean through from your end.'

'Okay, I'm after identifying an old lady who was killed in her own home. Probably California. Probably in the last twelve months. Probably nothing stolen from the scene. Two bullets to the chest.'

'Piece of cake,' said Betty, 'but give me some time. I need to make sure I don't leave a digital footprint that could come back and kick me in my sixty-five-year-old ass. I know, I don't look it.' She hung up. Brusque to the end.

Virgo opened the fridge. Three tins of Canada Dry, a pint of milk and a bottle of Gatorade. No food. There was meat in the freezer, but he needed something fast. He had a lot going on, and while Jessica was staking out the Templar Sanctorum, the top of his to-do list was finding where John Rinker hung out. Maybe conduct a recon of the place and try to glean what kind of criminal network he commanded. Or just front him up and ask why some of his guys wanted to give Virgo a ride in the back of a Transit.

There was a can of Spam in the cupboard and a packet of

instant noodles. An inspired combination. He was firing up the gas hob when he saw a police cruiser pull into the parking lot. It made a beeline straight for the RV. Change of plan. It looked like the gangbangers had filed a complaint after all, which was a shame because he'd taken the top off the luncheon meat. He turned off the gas ring and went out to say *hi*. No point waiting for the knock.

It was a different pair of uniforms this time. Already out of their Chevrolet blue and two, they looked more hospitable than the previous couple, but appearances can be deceptive. The smaller of the two, who looked ex-military, took out a notepad, and the taller one, who had a walrus mustache, said, 'Sorry to trouble you, sir, but can you account for your movements this morning, please?'

Virgo said, 'What's this about?'

'We've got an ongoing situation and are following all possible lines of enquiry to achieve a solution.'

'What kind of situation?'

The two cops looked at each other like they didn't know how much they could divulge. The one with the notebook wore a name plate above his right pocket, *Officer T. Clifford*. He said, 'We've got an officer missing on duty. No GPS.'

Virgo ensured his face remained impassive. Didn't want to show the slightest relief that he wasn't being hauled in for the shotgun business. 'They're probably having a sneaky beer somewhere or on a tryst with a secret lover.'

The tall guy's name plate said *Officer B. Meisner*. His walrus lip didn't twitch. 'We don't think so.'

'Okay, sorry for the inappropriate attempt at humor.' Virgo spread his arms. 'Why me?'

'We believe you were one of the last people to speak to Detective Malone.'

Virgo had a bad feeling. Cops didn't press the panic button and start searching for a colleague unless the situation looked potentially dire and ominous. If something had happened to Malone, he didn't want to be fingered for it. 'Yes, I called him early. Maybe nine thirty.'

Officer Clifford wrote something down and said, 'In connection with what exactly?'

'I wanted to let him know that a group of men had attacked me.' It was an edited version of the full story. Virgo didn't want to lie.

Officer Clifford's eyes kept flicking away from Virgo's face and to his arms. 'Why did you think that was something Ben Malone needed to know?'

'The goons that jumped me were part of John Rinker's crew, and I know he is a person of interest to the detective.'

Meisner said, 'You don't seem to have a lot of injuries for a guy on his own who was attacked by a gang.'

Before Virgo could answer, Clifford said, 'Show my colleague your arm.'

Virgo knew what the officer was getting at. He held his right forearm out. The one with the tattoo of a two-handed sword and the inscription *Veritas Omnia Vincula Vincit*.

Clifford said, 'There's your answer, Benny. Mr. Virgo was US special forces.'

Virgo said, 'Which regiment did you serve in?'

'I was a Ranger.' Clifford's spine went even straighter. Chest out.

Meisner looked unimpressed. Then again, he could have been grinning like mad behind the walrus mustache and nobody would have known. He twitched it now at the tattoo. 'What do the fancy words mean?'

Virgo said, 'Truth conquers all.' It was The Activity's motto, which he'd lived by and had faith in, but now more than ever he needed it to come good. There was something evil happening here, based on falsehood and illusion, and he was worried Detective Ben Malone was its latest victim. Had he got too close to the source of the nitazene, or had he found out what had happened to Jake Dearman? Who was the confidential informant he had been going to meet, and had he walked into a trap?

Officers Clifford and Meisner climbed back in their Chevrolet, and Virgo watched them head off to continue their search for the missing detective. The fat lady hadn't started to sing, so it might turn out to be a false alarm. A mistake or misunderstanding they could laugh about in years to come, but he didn't think so. He hoped he was wrong, but his gut told him that this was just the start and there was more to come. The old sixth sense. In Syria, Afghanistan and Colombia, he'd had the same feeling just before something major erupted out of nowhere. Truth conquers all, but sometimes there are casualties.

CHAPTER 31

Jessica moved the bag of ice away from her mouth. 'I always wanted bigger lips.'

'What did he look like?' Virgo passed her a towel and bent down to get more ice from the RV freezer cabinet.

'Wide jaw that made his face into a box shape and three of those angels on his arm.' She gave him a sideways glance as she dabbed her face in the mirror. 'Don't think about getting all macho and going into the compound after him. I'm all right.'

'I might bump into him in a dark alley, and he could accidentally fall on my fist.'

'Luckily for him, I'd left my bag in the car.'

'Is it like Joey's just-in-case bag? Pepper spray and prophylactics?'

'He told you about that, did he? The little shit.'

'He's over six feet.'

'The big shit. What did I say? He likes you.'

Virgo crushed some fresh ice in a polythene sandwich bag and swapped it for the part-melted one. 'He thinks you're an embarrassing mother who's trying to make sure he never gets laid.'

Jessica slapped a hand to her cheek. 'Don't make me laugh. My gum'll start bleeding again.'

That was the last of the ice. When it had gone to mainly water, they sat at the table in the RV kitchen, and Virgo made some coffee. He showed her the three articles on his phone that he'd found relating to the death of William Berg and filled her in on the latest visit from La Esperanza police department. It didn't do much to lift the mood.

Jessica sat there with a white face, and Virgo could tell she wasn't taking it all in. A punch in the mouth sends the body into shock, and it reacts by restricting the flow of blood to the brain. It takes time for the body to realize it's no longer under attack and switch itself back on in safe operating mode. He watched her shaking her head and tearing a tissue into a million tiny paper shavings. Then gradually, he realized it wasn't shock. It was pure anger.

He said, 'What's the matter?'

'I told her about the video, and she still doesn't want to leave the fucking place. I mean, how is that possible?'

'She's got an idea in her head.'

'Big fucking deal.'

'People think that the most resilient parasite in the world must be some kind of bug or a virus, but it's actually a brain worm. An idea. One that burrows into the cerebrum and makes itself at home. There's no point trying to budge it with logic or facts. The ultimate parasite.'

'Thanks, but it doesn't help my bank balance.' Jessica picked her compact mirror up again and squinted into it. 'I need to go and see Mrs. Bender. Keep her sweet. Sound her out about investing a few more dollars to secure the return of her daughter.'

Virgo was uneasy about Jessica's predisposition to treat

her client as a cash cow, nor did he want to be overly judgmental. He didn't have a family to support, and he'd never had to work in the private sector. He'd always had a government pay check, so he drove them in the RV.

It had been parked under the canopy of a big-leaf maple, and his habitation battery needed juice, either solar from the roof panel or from the alternator when the engine was running. You never know when you might need more ice. The highway from Atascadero was as clear as well-polished crystal, and in no time they saw the three defunct smokestacks of Morro Bay's old power plant and swung south on State Route 1.

When they arrived, it appeared Mrs. Margaret Bender had company. There were two cars in the limestone-chipped parking lot, but still enough room for fifty more. Jessica climbed down from the passenger seat and said, 'Let me handle this on my own.'

Virgo didn't argue. He spun his seat one hundred and eighty degrees and put his feet up. Pulled out his phone and called the number that Detective Malone had tucked under his wiper arm, just on the off chance that there was an innocent explanation for his disappearance and he was now back in contact. It tripped to a recorded greeting. *Please leave a message.* There didn't seem much point adding to a virtual mailbox that was probably already full of frantic dispatches from colleagues and maybe members of the family. Was Ben Malone's body going to turn up at the side of the road in the early hours of the morning the same as Jake Dearman's had?

Forget it. Virgo closed his eyes and slowed his breathing down to try to catch some rest. Turned on the radio like he always did to take the edge off the noise in his damaged left ear. Little Stevie was singing 'Superstition,' and every now and then there was a plip from the fan in the RV roof as its blades met a bug that had got through the mesh grille. He hummed along and tried to ignore the acrid smell from the chemical toilet that was mixing with the stale odor of drains coming up the sink plughole. The glamorous life of the open road. It's not all barbecues and gazing at star-filled skies.

Like a dog that returns instinctively to its own vomit, he couldn't stop himself going back to the one thought. What if Malone really was one of the good guys? It's hard to believe when you see the crap on TV and listen to the news, but there are still some decent cops, and he could be one of them. Maybe Virgo should have levelled with him and told him everything he knew about the People's Order of Gabriel, including the time he saw Sergeant Chambers paying a visit. Was it now too late?

Sleep wouldn't come. It hovered seductively, showing brief glimpses of herself and egging him on before turning her back and leaving him wide awake. It was at that point that another thought occurred to him.

Virgo was spinning the seat back to the front when Jessica climbed back in. He saw her face and said, 'Never play poker.'

Jessica said, 'Stupid woman.'

'Let me guess. Mrs. Bender no longer wishes to retain the services of Artemis Associates.'

'She's got a personal trainer and a therapist in there because she's turned over a new leaf and thinks the only way to get Casey back is to make herself a better person.'

'Good for her. Maybe she's right.'

'Shut up.' Jessica jumped down his throat. 'I preferred her when she was hammered all the time.'

Virgo started up the diesel engine and coaxed the Winnebago around the parking lot and back onto the long driveway. 'How good's your memory?'

'Short- or long-term?' She still looked angry.

'Yesterday, Detective Malone took us around the boonies

and backends of nowhere because he didn't want to be seen talking to me, which made me think – what if he had a meeting with a confidential informant? Where would he take them, or where would he arrange to meet them?'

'Somewhere remote that he's familiar with.'

'Exactly. I think we need to try and retrace the route he took us.'

'Okay, what are we waiting for?'

Virgo smiled to himself as he swung the RV round and back onto the tree-lined driveway. Jessica McGann never seemed to stay angry or down for long. She always bounced back quickly, which was something he liked about her. No sulking or prolonged bouts of grouchiness. It reminded him of Crystal. The times he'd been late home because a kidnap or extortion had come in and she'd prepared a beautiful meal for two that had to go in the freezer. She never complained. Only once he forgot to call, and that dinner went in the waste disposal, but she didn't stay cross for any length of time or ever mention it again. He was the other extreme. He could hold a grudge in perpetuity. Maybe it's right what they say about opposites.

Back on the highway, Jessica said, 'It's no good. I'm going to have to shut my business down.'

Virgo glanced across to the passenger seat. She was drawn and fretful, and he realized perhaps he'd been wrong this time about her bouncing back. She'd just been putting on a brave face.

CHAPTER 32

Casey sat in her room, reading the Bible. It wasn't the New International Version or the New American Standard. It was the People's Order of Gabriel Revised Edition, which contained most of the complete books within the Old and New Testaments, but with some omissions and redactions. Her childhood had been too occupied by tennis to leave space for Sunday school or religious education, but in the past few months she'd become well acquainted with the scriptures. This version also contained an addendum of prophesies written by Dr. Daniel Nelson. Her future husband.

It still felt unreal to think she would soon be married. She'd not seen Dr. Dan since the proposal, and the only communications she'd had were nonspecific and reluctant updates from the apostles, who clearly felt some kind of enmity towards her. Either they resented her because of the trouble her mother had caused, or they were simply jealous that someone else was the beneficiary of the prophet's attentions. Of course, there was a third possibility, which she didn't like to dwell on: Jake Dearman. Did they know how she felt?

She looked at the white dress hung up on the wardrobe door. A simple and plain garment, which she'd chosen on purpose to represent the frugal ideals of the People's Order. It was a pity the fitting had been ruined by her mother's interference and had to be completed back at the Templar Sanctorum. That would have cost the Order extra expense. All because her mother was manipulative and selfish. It was almost worth getting married just to imagine the look on her face when she found out.

Things were moving so fast. Could she stop it now even if she wanted to? Did she want to? She went back to the Bible. Ephesians 5:22. *Wives be submissive to your husbands as unto the Lord. For the husband is the head of the wife, just as Christ is head and savior of the church, which is His body.* Did she want to submit herself completely to another person, even if he was Dr. Daniel Nelson? She wasn't sure.

There was a knock on the door, and Myra came in, all of a fluster. 'I can't believe what just happened.'

Casey put a bookmark in the Bible and said nothing. A story was about to come flooding out, and she just had to sit back and let it wash over her. Whatever it was, she was pleased Myra was happy again. When Casey had told her about Dr. Dan's proposal, there had been a definite frostiness. Again, it could have been the sin of envy or genuine disappointment that she would be losing her new friend so soon.

There was only a single study chair in each room, so Myra sat on the bed. She said, 'I was working in the field when I was summoned to see James, the son of Alpheus. Guess what?'

Casey fabricated a smile. 'You were awarded a merit? That's great.'

'Better. Way better.'

'Two merits?'

'Keep going.' Myra couldn't contain herself. 'I've got my baptism.'

'Really?' Casey was surprised. She herself had been a model pupil, and it had taken much longer.

'Tomorrow. Can you believe it?'

Casey was having difficulty accepting it. Myra was enthusiastic and devoted, but her manual work and scripture study needed improvement. She hoped the forced smile on her face didn't give away what she really thought. 'Congratulations.'

'I've got to select my outfit in the morning.'

A thought materialized in Casey's head. What if Myra was getting special treatment now because she was *her* friend? Future wife of the prophet. Would her new status impact on other aspects of life with the Order, as she bathed within the reflected glory of Dr. Dan? Might she be able to influence the direction of the movement of the POG and be the catalyst that pushed it to do more good work in the field of social justice? Appealing though the idea was, she filed it away and said, 'It will be a day that changes your life forever.'

Myra giggled with nerves. 'What's it like?'

'I'm not at liberty to say. We all take a vow not to disclose the details of the ceremony.'

Myra leaned forward, eager to collude in a little subversion of the rules. 'Come on, just give me a clue.'

Casey felt uncomfortable. A knot twisted and turned in her bowels. She was sure that the madwoman with fluorescent green highlights was lying about the baptism videos being fake. It was clearly what her mother had paid her to do. And yet there was something about her own baptism that still seemed strange. She had not consciously pulled the trigger, but there had been a shot, and the man had died. The only plausible explanation was that she had been in such a state of hyperactive and frenzied exaltation that she didn't know what she was doing. Her actions were being directed by a supernatural power that is possessed only by Him.

'Come on, pleeease…' Myra was persistent.

'You will be taken before Dr. Dan, and he will bless you and explain how you shall make your commitment.' Casey saw her friend about to launch into another plea, and stuck out the palm of her hand. 'No, that's it. That's all I can say.'

Myra pouted a little in disappointment, but it didn't last long. She jumped up, all bubbly and wide-eyed, and glanced at the wedding dress hung on the wardrobe door. 'Sure you don't want a bridesmaid?'

Casey shook her head. She wasn't even sure she wanted to get married. 'Thanks, but I want to keep it simple.'

'Hey, don't look so worried. You're gonna smash it.' Myra bent down, gave her a little hug and skipped out of the room.

As soon as the door was closed, Casey got down onto her knees and began to pray. She asked for forgiveness and guidance, but she couldn't feel anything coming back to give her succor and direction. It was if her connection was lost. Time was running out, yet despite all the fears and conflicting emotions building up inside her, she knew there was only one thing she could do. Keep the faith.

CHAPTER 33

The baroque, Germanic castle looked like it might house a Disney princess, as it commanded the hillside in the late afternoon sun. As soon as he saw its turrets and spires, Virgo knew they were still on the right route. Some of the hairpins were steep and narrow, and the only way he could get the RV around was to swing out onto the opposite side of the road. No problem so long as a tractor didn't come steaming around the bend from the opposite direction.

He recognized the next turn coming up and cut right, down through the orchards, and onto the wider two-lane highway that ran down one side of a turquoise lake. On the previous occasion, there'd been a couple of red-tailed hawks drifting on an ocean breeze that had sailed in from the Pacific, but this time the sky was clear. Just a group of shoveler ducks dabbling about on the shoreline.

Jessica was the first to spot the Honda. It was fifty yards down a dirt track: one of the fire roads that ran off into the forest. Its green paintwork made it blend into the pines and fescue. Virgo pulled over, and they made their way towards the vehicle on foot through the conifers so as not to contaminate any tire marks or footprints on the track itself. Inside the canopy of the forest, it was quiet. Just the sound of their feet and the occasional snatch of song from a siskin or warbler.

Detective Ben Malone was in the driver's seat. There was an entry wound to the back of his head, and what was left of his face was slumped forward onto the steering wheel. No need to check for a pulse. Virgo tried to figure out the angle of the bullet's trajectory to determine if it had been fired from the back seat or from someone stood outside, but it was unclear. It could have been either.

What was clear was that Malone hadn't been alone in the car. The front passenger seat was soaked in blood, and there was evidence of pooling in the footwell. Smears all over the internal trim of the door and the glove compartment. But no body. There was a slender possibility that whoever's blood it was, they had been badly injured and got away alive. However, the obvious conclusion was that the passenger had been killed and their body removed.

It was tempting to go looking for clues to support this hypothesis in the immediate vicinity, but that was somebody else's job. They carefully retraced their steps through the pine and fescue back to the highway, and once inside the RV, Virgo called La Esperanza police department and asked for a message to be passed on to Officer Clifford. He gave the location of the Honda and, when asked who was calling, said, 'Just tell him it's his friend from The Activity.'

He wondered whether he'd done the right thing calling it in and if it might result in him getting dragged in for questioning, but deep down he still believed in the system. He'd been part of it. There aren't many innocent guys in prison because the evidential threshold to prove guilt is high. He had no motive to kill Malone, and he could account for his movements all day. If that bonehead Chambers tried to pin anything on him, he'd make sure it was the last stunt the useless sergeant tried to pull as a serving officer.

They drove in silence back toward town. The vineyards didn't seem as lush all of a sudden and the sky not quite so holiday-brochure blue. Some kid's daddy was not coming home from work. It happens every day somewhere, but it still knocks you sideways and makes you promise yourself to live for the moment. Virgo felt it. He'd been stuck in the past or just ticking the days off as they went by. He'd forgotten what it was like to feel glad to be alive. Maybe it was finally time to change.

Dropping down into the outskirts, Jessica's phone rang. She answered it with a bad-tempered, 'Yes?' Then pulled a notepad and pencil out of her bag and started to scribble. Once or twice she huffed and grunted before saying, 'Yes, you go fuck yourself too.' Call ended.

Virgo said, 'Friend of yours?'

'No, it was the turd.' Jessica curled her lip. 'My ex, Joey's father.'

'Nice to see you keep in touch with each other.'

'Okay, here's the thing.' Jessica started to nibble the end of the pencil. 'When I saw those angels on Casey's arm, I remembered something. When I was on the force, every time we processed a prisoner, we had to do photographs and fingerprints and fill in the descriptive form.'

'Same in the Bureau.'

'That form was a real pain in the ass. You had to record ethnicity, height, weight, hair and eye color and identifying features such as scars or tattoos so they could all be recorded in the database.'

'For identification and intelligence.'

'Exactly.' Jessica picked a splinter out of her teeth. 'So for intelligence purposes, I just had a search done of the database to see if anyone had been arrested with a stick-figure angel on their arm.'

'You got your ex-husband to do that for you?'

'Yeah, well, if he paid his child support on time, I'd have nothing to blackmail him with. The point is, we got a hit.'

Virgo shook his head and laughed. Jessica's resourcefulness would be a loss to the world of private investigation if Artemis Associates did not survive its current financial difficulties.

She looked at her notes. 'Guy called Ricky Coody. He was arrested six weeks ago for stealing packed meat and razor blades at a 7-Eleven. Got a community sentence because he's in a program for addicts.'

It was still a long shot, Virgo knew. The angel tattoo on this guy's arm might be some kind of massive design with feathery wings or a touching tribute to an old flame called Patty. Cops are notoriously bad at accurately recording mundane but important information like that. But there was an outside chance that here was the exception to the rule: the only member of the People's Order of Gabriel to have escaped its iron shackles. There was only one way to find out.

He said, 'Did the turd have an address for Ricky Coody?'

CHAPTER 34

The James Dean Memorial Junction lies twenty miles from La Esperanza at the intersection of Highways 46 and 41, classified as being located in the township of Cholame, but in reality it's bang in the middle of nowhere. On September 30, 1955, the star of *Rebel Without a Cause* died instantly when his Porsche 550 Spyder, called Little Bastard, crashed head-on with another vehicle. Immortalized at the age of twenty-four. Forever young.

Dr. Daniel Nelson walked along the fence that had been turned into a shrine. Someone had left a garland of roses in the shape of a heart that had withered and died, and there were battered photographs, a white T-shirt streaked with dust and a dozen or more packs of Marlboro: original cowboy reds, not the crappy Lights. A little farther down the blacktop was the official memorial, a simple, engraved steel band wrapped around a tree and a couple of benches. Not the grandest of commemorative features for such an icon.

There was a time when Nelson had imagined his own epitaph would be something on a much bigger scale. Perhaps a museum of his work or even a bespoke mausoleum where followers of his teachings could stand in line for hours to pay respects to the remains of his mortal body. The legend. Those days were gone, and now he'd settle for something like the one in front of him.

He stared out across the hills and wondered how long he had left. It was the beginning of the end. He knew it. Still, no regrets. He'd flown too close to the sun and must pay the price. What he didn't want to do was end his days like Hitler, in a bunker waiting for the enemy to arrive at the gate and then at the last possible moment take a tablet or blow his brains out. A coward's death.

No. Daniel Nelson had contingencies. One of them was to go back to being plain Brian Salt and lead an anonymous life of comfort in the Florida Keys, but he didn't fancy that. Not his style. The other plans were more dynamic. Of course, he could stay to the bitter end and bluff it out. He'd always been a risk-taker, but the problem was, the threats to his position were not just external. There'd been rumblings of disquiet within the POG, and the more ruthless his method of quashing them, the greater the chance it could boil over into outright insubordination and rebellion.

He got back into the rear seat of his chauffeur-driven limousine and popped one of his special pills that made the situation seem not so important. Half a mile down the road, they pulled into the parking lot of a small café, with the engine running and the air-con maxed out. Cars flew by, taking people from Fresno and Bakersfield to the coast, and after a while one of them slowed down and pulled into the parking lot.

John Rinker got into the back of the limousine and said, 'What are we doing out here in this shithole?'

'It's for your own protection.' Nelson buzzed his window down halfway. A stench of body odor had just accosted his nostrils. 'I don't think you should visit the Templar Sanctorum again in case it's being watched.'

'Has another kid died? What did I tell you about taking a dump on your own doorstep?'

'No, another kid has not died.' Nelson tried to keep his tone reasonable. There was a casual disrespect in Rinker's attitude that got his hackles up. 'A police detective was arranging to apply for a drugs warrant to search the property of the People's Order of Gabriel, and I had to order executive action be taken to ensure the eventuality was avoided.'

'What? Speak fucking English.'

'The detective will not be executing any more warrants.'

'What?' Beneath the brim of his cap and the cowl of his hood, Rinker screwed up his face. 'You killed a fucking cop? What did you think you were doing?'

'Saving our collective backsides. You know the scale of the operation within the compound, and you know that even with twenty-four hours' notice, we couldn't have got the place clean.'

'I thought you said you had them in your fucking pocket?'

'Did you get rid of the ex-FBI guy?'

'Not yet.'

Nelson took a deep breath and chewed on the inside of his cheek, trying to stay calm. Ending it all seemed attractive when faced with this moron. 'This is not the time for recriminations or apportioning blame, faultless though I am. What I've done at the very least is buy us some time, and of course, it is possible that nothing at all will come of it.'

'Brian, you're a grade A bullshitter. Always were.'

'You were piss-pot poor, and now look at you with a ranch and a collection of Harleys.'

'But I've still stuck to my roots. Not like you.'

'Okay, that's enough.' Nelson cradled his head in his hands. Why wasn't the magic pill kicking in? 'The point is,

I've been thinking for a long time that we ought to have an exit strategy.'

'Such as what?'

'I'm not sure, but when the pressure became too much for Jim Jones in San Francisco, he moved his temple to Guyana.'

'Yeah, Jonestown.' Rinker laughed, and it turned into a guttural hack. He coughed up some mucus and opened the door to spit it out. 'Fucking hilarious.' Pulled the door shut. 'That ended well. How many died?'

'To the ignorant and fatuous it might have seemed like a disaster, but imagine how Jones must have felt. To inspire such loyalty in his followers that nine hundred killed themselves simply because he told them to.'

'Okay, you fuck off somewhere and tell your idiots to drink the Kool-Aid, but I'm stopping here, and I expect compensation.'

Nelson groaned. Patience growing thin. 'For what? We dissolve the partnership and split what we have fifty-fifty.'

'No, that's not how it works when you walk away from a business like this. If you take away the distribution network, it will be a year, maybe two, before it's back to what it was, and in the meantime I've still got people to pay in Texas and Mexico, or I lose the trade and route across the border for good. That's why I need capital.'

'I'm sure we can reach a settlement that is agreeable to both parties.'

'Yeah, and if we can't, you won't need to worry about buying any of that cyanide juice. I'll do it for you. Trust me.' Rinker got out of the car and slammed the door shut with his boot.

The more Nelson thought about it, the more he warmed to the idea of transferring the Order to somewhere remote but temperate, and without the overreaching technocrats that come with a democratically elected government. The brave new world. A classless society based on social equality and justice, where everyone works together to worship the man who built it. They could call it Nelson-boro or Nelson-opolis.

The bumping of the limousine back onto the highway jolted him out of his reverie, and he checked the diary on his phone. Tomorrow was a special day. Dealing with the detective had given him some breathing space, and he had to make the most of it. The most important thing was marrying the Bender girl, because she was the key to making his vision of utopia become a reality. Marry her soon.

CHAPTER 35

The address they'd got for Ricky Coody was in a ramshackle collection of buildings in the south of the county. It had the look of a shantytown, used primarily by migrant farmworkers. Garages had been turned into temporary apartments, trailers filled any patches of spare, barren land, and dogs roamed the streets, sniffing abandoned sacks of garbage. There were a few little kids running around, but other than that it was quiet because the rest of the folk were still in the fields.

Virgo made a quick assessment and inwardly nodded to himself. If you wanted to get away from the People's Order of Gabriel without going to the other side of the world, it was as good a place as any. No major highway, no shopping malls, no passers-by. Of course, it meant that if you needed to score dope, you had to travel some distance to steal beef from a 7-Eleven, but nowhere's perfect. It was better than getting a bullet in the head from some kid in a white suit pretending to be an angel.

The wooden houses didn't have numbers or names, so he and Jessica split up and began knocking on doors. Nobody answered. He peered through some windows, but the rooms were empty apart from mattresses on the floor and clothes hung up on drying racks. Then he saw Jessica talking to a group of kids who were taking turns riding a beat-up bicycle. She reached in her bag and handed something to the tallest kid, who pointed to a trailer that stood on its own near to a pile of tires and tarpaulins that had been strung up on rickety frames to provide shade.

Virgo joined Jessica and said, 'How much did you give the kid?'

'More than his father gets an hour picking fruit.'

They crossed the street, and the sound of drum and bass came to meet them before they reached the trailer. The door was open. It stank of urine and unwashed armpits, and the only person inside was a skeletal woman lying in bed with bruises on her neck where she'd been mainlining straight into the jugular. Glassy eyes like a salmon on Costco's fresh seafood counter and used needles strewn on the floor.

Jessica said, 'Whatever drug program they're on, I don't think it's working.'

Virgo led the way around the back and into a den that was covered by canvas. Three guys and two women, recumbent in shabby beach chairs. A table in the middle with a Bunsen burner, Bowie knife and rubber hose. There was an old-school boombox pumping out the sound, and when Virgo yanked out the power lead, five faces turned to him, and he said, 'Which one of you is Ricky Coody?'

One of the women said, 'Never heard of him,' and the guy nearest said, 'Wrong address, pal.'

The guy sat in the middle had long ginger hair and a braided beard. 'You a cop or something?'

'I'm a something.' Virgo put his palms out shoulder high. 'We just want to talk to him, that's all.'

Ginger beard picked up the fighting knife. 'In that case, you'd better fuck right off. You're trespassing.'

'I would, but it's important.' Virgo looked at the guy in the corner, who hadn't spoken. He was the only one wearing a long-sleeved shirt.

'Last chance.' Ginger beard stood up. 'Or I'll cut you to pieces.'

'Yeah, right.' Virgo walked up to him, grabbed hold of his wrist and twisted it until the knife fell on the floor. Then he turned to the silent guy in the corner. 'You. Roll up your right sleeve and show me your arm.'

The guy didn't hang around to be asked twice. He bolted through a slit in the tarp walls and was gone. Virgo clambered over the camping table and beach chair and went after him, with the cries of ginger beard ringing in his ears and one of the women screaming, 'Leave him alone, you fucking douchebag.'

Jessica had doubled back around the trailer and was already heading after Ricky Coody by the time Virgo burst into the fresh air. He relaxed and fell into a gentle jog. No point working up a sweat when the guy you're chasing is a skaghead whose lungs are going to implode in fifty yards. Half a mile later, Coody was still galloping along an avenue through a field of almond trees, showing no signs of collapse, and Jessica had given up trying to run in block-heel slingbacks. Virgo crunched after him across the almond hulls and shells and cursed under his panting breath. Maybe Coody had been in training to outrun the store's detectives the next time he went to the 7-Eleven.

At the end of the almond orchard, Coody skipped a fence and cut across the corner of a giant ploughed field with huge harvesting machines kicking up clouds of dust. Virgo saw he was aiming for the adjacent field, which was covered in polytunnels and would give him plenty of places to hide. Back in special warfare training, Virgo could do twelve miles in two hours, rucking forty-five pounds on his shoulders, but that had been a while ago. He was about to switch the afterburners on when the junkie's legs gave way, and he went down in a heap next to a gully at the edge of the plot.

'Don't take me back.' Coody was already crying.

'I'm not here to take you back to the People's Order of Gabriel.' Virgo held out a hand to pull him up.

Coody hesitated. 'What do you want?'

'I just want to talk.'

'Seriously. I'd rather die than go back.'

'Nobody's taking you back.'

Coody clasped Virgo's hand and allowed himself to be pulled up. 'But that's what you want to talk about, right? Once he was on his feet, he rolled his right sleeve up and held out his arm. There was a big pad of gauze taped to his forearm, and he peeled it back to show an angry red mess of scar tissue and burnt, ulcerated flesh. 'I couldn't afford to go to one of those tattoo-removal clinics, so I did it myself. Held it against the bar of an electric stove until I passed out.'

'Anything to erase the memory?'

'I just wanted to get rid of that fucking angel.'

'Because of how you earned it?'

'The baptism?' Ricky Coody laughed. 'No, that was bullshit. One of the apostles told me it was all a bit of theater to snare us into obedience. They're all in on it, you know, the apostles and Nelson.'

'That's what I want to talk to you about. I'm going to take them all down.' Virgo looked at the gauze patch and saw that it was oozing with putrid yellow and black stains. 'Come on. We should get a medic to look at that wound of yours.'

They walked back slowly in the shade of the almond trees.

Every now and then Coody stopped and said, 'You really going to take Nelson down?' And made a weird laugh that sounded like two roosters fighting. In between making the chicken noises, he told Virgo how he'd never done drugs before joining the People's Order of Gabriel. Not even toked a joint. Then one day, after his confirmation, he was sent to work in the POG factory.

The apostles called it the processing plant, where the body of Christ was made, because it was in a secure unit at the back of the church. A pharmaceutical setup where they pressed powder into pills and heat-sealed them into blister packs. It was a good number. Operatives had to wear paper suits and face masks, but it was better than working the hothouses or fields.

Then he had an accident carrying some cartons into the basement and fell down the stairs, damaging one of the vertebrae in his neck. After that, recurring pain became part of his life until another guy working in there gave him a strip of the pills and told him how to take them. Soon after that, he was hooked. Security checks on leaving at the end of a shift were random and not thorough. It was easy enough to clench a strip between your butt cheeks and still walk out in a normal way.

It became clear that a few of the factory workers were doing the same thing. There was a black market within the compound with some of those who did other jobs buying pills with valuables or sexual favors. Everything was good until somebody got greedy. There were rumors that one of the guys was dealing outside of the Order. A guy called Jake. After that, it all changed. Regular stock checks, routine body searches and weekly piss samples for drug testing. That was when he knew he had to leave. The unquenchable desire for chemical pain relief had become an integral part of his being, and he couldn't survive without it.

Virgo drove the RV with Jessica in the front passenger seat and Ricky Coody hunched over the dining table on one of the unbelted benches. Heading north on the 101 for the Sierra Vista Medical Center in San Luis Obispo, he saw road signs for places upstate: Big Sur, Salinas, Monterey. It flipped a memory switch in his mind, and he turned back over his shoulder. 'I don't suppose you've ever heard of an old guy called William Berg who lived in Carmel?'

Coody scratched the top of his head with both sets of fingernails, as though he might have lice. 'No. Why should I?'

'No reason.' Virgo shrugged. Worth a punt. Traffic was starting to thicken up as the office day came to an end and commuters made their way home. He switched the radio to a local news channel, expecting there might be a report on the shooting of a police officer in the hills near La Esperanza, but it was all about a man who'd been diving for lobsters and got scooped up in the mouth of a humpback whale, then spat back out. Great story, but let down by the fact the guy's name wasn't Jonah.

Jessica checked the time on her cell phone and said, 'Does this thing go any faster? I ought to get home for Joey.'

Virgo pressed his right boot to the floor, and the speedo needle crept from fifty-five to fifty-six. The stream of vehicles overtaking in the outside lane didn't decrease any, and it felt like he was driving through molasses. Nobody spoke. Time slowed down, and he found his thoughts drifting off to when, as a young man, he'd ridden in military convoys across never-ending barren landscapes in another part of the world. Gone to fight the foreign man for Uncle Sam.

A mile out of Pismo Beach, Ricky Coody shouted up from the back, 'I know a Nancy Berg. She's from Carmel.'

'What?' Virgo blinked himself out of his reverie. 'How do you know Nancy Berg?'

'She's in the sect.'

'What sect?' Virgo knew the answer before his mouth had finished the second word.

Ricky Coody shouted, 'The People's Order of fucking Gabriel. How many sects do you think I've been in, man?'

CHAPTER 36

The medical center had a multilevel parking garage with a height restriction too low to allow entry to Virgo's RV. He skirted past it and pulled round onto the access road for the main entrance, which was busy with people leaving the building. Maybe the end of visiting hours or a shift changeover. Every time he saw or caught the iodine scent of a hospital, it catapulted him back to when he met Crystal. It seemed so long ago.

As soon as he pulled up, Ricky Coody threw himself to the floor and shouted, 'Not here. Keep going.'

Virgo looked down the sidewalk to see what had prompted the reaction. The only thing it could have been was a group of four ugly mothers in biker gear, all just lighting up as they left the main doors. He thought one of them looked familiar. 'What's the problem?'

Coody said, 'Don't let them see me.'

'Thirty seconds and they'll be gone.' Virgo waited with the engine ticking over, driver's window down. 'Do you owe them money?'

'No.' Coody crawled under the table so even someone

peering in from outside couldn't see him. 'They're the delivery crew. The fucking powder guys.'

Virgo watched them get closer in his door mirror, and as they drew alongside the open window, he turned his head and looked directly at them. All four slowed down and stared back. A mixture of hatred and menace emanated from their ink-covered faces. He recognized one of them as the driver of the Transit who had tried to abduct him. Maybe they'd just been to visit the guy Virgo had filled with shotgun pellets. They were Rinker's crew. That explained the black GMC Sierra's visits to the People's Order. They were delivering powder to be pressed into pills and distributed.

When they'd passed by, he said, 'It's okay, Ricky. You can come out now.'

Coody didn't move. 'If they see me, they'll tell the apostles.'

'Relax, they've gone.'

'They'll find me and kill me or, worse still, take me back to the living hell.'

'Trust me.' Virgo did a one-eighty in his seat to face the diner. 'After tomorrow the People's Order of Gabriel won't exist.'

Jessica made a big sigh to express her impatience. 'Come on. Stop overpromising, and let's move. I need to go and feed my son.'

It took ten full minutes to coax Ricky Coody out of his hiding place. No time for hanging around in the emergency department, so Virgo gave him fifty bucks for the cab fare back to shantytown and made him swear not to spend it on heroin. It wasn't the most convincing vow he'd heard, but he'd realized a long time ago that there's little point in blaming yourself for the actions of addicts. They'll always find a way to get what they need, and the only person who can truly help them is the one in the mirror they don't want to look in.

As soon as Coody was out of the vehicle, Virgo circled back towards the highway and said, 'What are the chances that Nancy Berg is William Berg's daughter?'

'Both from Carmel.' Jessica slipped on the big, oblong Dolce and Gabannas. 'Could be a coincidence.'

'Do you think?'

'No.'

'Me neither,' said Virgo. 'One of them a member of the People's Order of Gabriel and the other murdered by them. The only thing is why a real killing when all but one of the other baptisms were staged?'

Jessica turned and frowned. 'It's obvious, isn't it?'

'Not to me.'

'Follow the money.'

'You mean, who stood to benefit from William Berg's death?'

Jessica nodded her neon green pixie cut. 'He was a wealthy guy, and those newspaper articles said he was a widower.'

'They also said he was a major philanthropist, so maybe he left his estate to charity.'

'Or it could have all gone to Nancy.'

'And then straight into the coffers of the People's Order of Gabriel. My bet is that Dr. Dan sweet-talked her into donating all her worldly goods to his empire in return for eternal salvation.'

'Don't you think Nancy might have put two and two together when her father was shot on the doorstep? Realized it was a POG baptism?'

'Maybe, but don't forget the MO was a little different, and there were no witnesses to say that the shooter was dressed all in white. We know that now because we watched the video.'

'There's one other possibility.'

'Nancy didn't know how her father had been killed?'

'Exactly. The kids in the POG are totally estranged from their families. I mean totally. It took me weeks to find that Casey was in there, because she'd severed all ties with her mother and didn't want to be found.'

Virgo nodded. 'It's all part of Dr. Dan's plan. Turn kids against their parents, and he cuts off their main support mechanism, which makes them easier to control. He becomes their family.'

Jessica said, 'Prison's too good for him.'

Virgo turned left onto Foothill Boulevard and saw the motorcycle pull out a block away and fall in behind him four cars back. That's the problem with driving a motorhome: you're an easy target to spot. He kept checking the mirror, and sure enough, a second bike appeared and fell in beside his buddy. No doubt the mothers from the hospital, who'd recognized him. They certainly weren't a couple of motorcycle outriders come to escort him safely to his destination.

There'd been four of them outside the medical center, but Virgo could see no sign of the other two. That meant they were probably up ahead somewhere and in radio contact with the pair behind. Once he'd committed to a direction of travel, they'd co-ordinate an attack on him somewhere down the road. Maybe call up more personnel and more firepower and engineer an ambush like they had on the previous occasion. But that wasn't going to happen this time, because Virgo was going to decide where the battlefield was and fight on his own terms.

He took another left and pulled into a Starbucks. 'Why don't you get yourself a coffee and wait here. I'll be back before you finish it.'

Jessica took her sunglasses off, and one eyebrow dipped in suspicion. 'What for?' Then she craned her neck out the passenger window and saw the bikes pulled over at the side of the curb twenty yards back. She reached down into the footwell and came up with the Walther from her bag. 'Let's go. I'll ride shotgun.'

'Please yourself.' Virgo swung back onto the highway and onto a road that ran under the state route. A little farther on, he saw a sign for a country park and turned off down a narrow track that was covered in pine straw. The bikes followed, making no secret now of their presence or malicious intent. Up ahead, the park opened out into a series of areas and activities. Lawns and picnic tables. Volleyball and horseshoe pits. A block of restrooms and an adventure-style playground with lots of benches and barbecue spots.

Not busy, but a smattering of folk enjoying the facilities and the last remains of the afternoon sun, so Virgo carried on towards the far end of the park that disappeared into the forest. He had to stop when he reached the creek that marked the boundary, and he spun the RV around to face the oncoming enemy. Showdown. The motorcycles stopped the width of a football pitch away, and two smoke-tinted visors pointed back straight at him.

Jessica said, 'What are they waiting for?'

'Possibly reinforcements. There's only two of them.' Virgo climbed through the gap between the driver and passenger seats and into the back of the motorhome. 'I'm going to get ours.' He got busy with a screwdriver and removed the internal panel.

When Jessica saw the Glock, she said, 'I might report you to the police. A felon with a firearm is punishable with ten years.'

'It's not for me, it's for you in case you need a backup.

Lock the doors.' Virgo passed her the gun grip first and jumped out of the RV.

He didn't have a plan, more like a few options that were fluid in his head and adaptable. The guys on the bikes looked like the sort who liked their combat operations in a concrete jungle not a real one. That meant luring them into the trees and out of their comfort zone. He walked around the nose of the RV and then made sure they could see him as he ran around the back and across a footbridge over the creek into the forest. What they didn't see was him grab the four-foot steel rod he used for winding out the sun canopy on the Winnebago roof.

The engines of the motorcycles growled as the throttles were twisted open. Virgo couldn't see them hurtling towards the forest because he'd doubled back, slid down the bank of the creek and belly-crawled under the bridge. But he could hear them getting louder, and he prepared himself. As is often the case, timing was key. He assumed a crouching position and took three controlled breaths to focus his senses.

Then it was all about sound and anticipation. As soon as he heard the front wheel of the lead bike make contact with the first plank of wood on the bridge, he was moving. *Rat-tat-tat-tat-tat-tat.* The staccato noise of the tires as they rattled machine-gun-like above provided the perfect cue. He shot up just as the leading motorbike reached the end of the bridge, and swung the steel rod around to meet it. Bang.

Virgo had been aiming for the chest to give the best chance of a hit, but he was a little high. The rod made contact with the rider's neck and flipped him into a back somersault. The bike zoomed on. Today's lesson: never accelerate into danger because energy equals mass multiplied by speed, and your velocity will therefore count against you in the equation. On this occasion, the rider was fortunate not to be decapitated, though the trauma to the windpipe might prove fatal.

What was disappointing was that the first guy had been going so fast, he'd opened up a gap on his pal, who now had time to stop his bike before he ploughed into the body blocking the bridge. Virgo stared at him across the creek. The guy's body language betrayed uncertainty. He took his gloves off and pulled a gun out of his leather jacket. Still, he didn't move. The gun was for self-defense, not pursuit and attack.

Virgo realized what was happening. It was a containment ploy. The Harley cavalry were on their way, and this guy was happy to wait for backup rather than go on a solo mission. Five seconds later, the distant buzz of engines grew into a roar as two more motorcycles appeared and flew down the length of the park. All that was missing was somebody waving a flag and a band playing the 'William Tell Overture.'

No point hanging around. Virgo scrambled up the steep bank into the forest and, as soon as he was out of sight, made his way off at a tangent to the left, where he waited behind a close-knit group of sycamores. It was a long time since he'd trained for jungle warfare. Everybody in the Army hated it. Communication is always a problem. One tree looks the same as another tree. It's dark. Camouflage works. It's easier to be a defender than an attacker, and hit-and-run guerrilla strikes are easy. That's why the most important thing as a fighting unit is to stick together as close as possible. He was banking on the bikers not knowing this.

The V-twin engines went quiet, and soon the only noise was the faraway murmur of the interstate and some squirrels or birds up in the branches. Motorcycle boots are not made to glide silently over the debris of a forest floor, and after a while Virgo heard a pair maybe twenty yards away across the hillside. He held his breath and listened hard. Blanked out the whistle in his left ear and breathed a soft sigh of relief. One pair of boots. The fighting unit had fanned out and opened themselves up to getting picked off.

Still not an easy task. Stealth is important when attacking an opponent who is armed, and although his desert boots had crepe rubber soles, they still snapped twigs thanks to the weight bearing down inside them. That's why distraction had to be an integral factor. He waited. Then he squatted and slowly pushed his head out beyond the leaves of a sapling. The guy was ten paces away, heading up the slope. No crash helmet. Shaved head. A gun in his right hand.

Ideally, Virgo wanted him no more than five paces away, but that wasn't going to happen. OODA time. Observe, orient, decide, act. The guy looked uncomfortable with the environment and was moving slowly due to his heavy build and full motorcycle leathers. Virgo could wait longer to see if the guy made a second pass nearer his position. This might be the best opportunity. Okay, decision made.

There was a two-foot length of rotten wood covered in fungus by his feet. He picked it up and sent it cartwheeling through the trees back down the slope. The biker froze. Then he changed direction and took a step to follow the noise. Virgo was already right behind him. The biker seemed to sense something and turned. The steel rod came round with a swing speed of seventy miles per hour and made contact just below the left earlobe. There was a crack and then a cacophony of crunches and rustling as the unconscious body hit the detritus of the forest floor.

Before the sound died down, Virgo was already gone. Hit and move. Back up onto the higher ground, he dropped down behind a clump of sagebrush and waited.

There was a shout. 'Is that you, Taz?…Taz?…Taz, where are you?'

Then another voice. 'Shut the fuck up, Jacko.'

Virgo could tell the remaining two were still some distance apart. Some people never learn. He waited. Then he waited some more until he heard the motorcycle boots.

Second time round it was like stealing candy from a very small and inattentive child. Jacko blundered straight past him and then looked shocked when he saw the winding rod of a sun canopy arcing into his left temple. Two down. Hit and move.

There wasn't to be a third. Soon after Jacko was put to sleep, he heard the sound of boots running and sliding down the hill and then the V-twin engine cough and roar away. Virgo allowed himself to laugh and get intoxicated on the sweet pine-scented air. He'd not felt this good in a long time. All those years as a negotiator in the Bureau, he'd spent his days sitting in an office or having to talk nice to the nastiest creatures ever to crawl out of a womb, when what he'd really wanted to do was administer a little instant justice. This is what he'd missed.

CHAPTER 37

The Panda Express was busy with workers picking up boxes of orange chicken and Wagyu beef dumplings before heading home to the suburbs. Virgo parked on the street outside the entrance that led up to Artemis Associates. Jessica sighed and said, 'I'm going to miss this place.'

'You're really going to quit?'

'I can't afford to keep it going.'

'Where will you do yoga?'

Jessica laughed. 'I felt such an idiot when you walked in and I was doing the downward dog.'

'It was a headstand.'

'I can't remember because it was so embarrassing.'

'You were so embarrassed you took your leotard off.'

'I was trying to make out that I wasn't embarrassed and overcompensating as usual. It's what I do.'

Virgo said nothing. He didn't want to intrude because she appeared deep in thought as she stared at the building. It was more than bricks and mortar. Good times and bad. Success and failure. Dreams that didn't quite play out in the cold light of reality. Life. The rollercoaster ride that takes you up and down and can make you feel excited and sick at the same time.

When they walked into the Shakespeare, Jessica seemed determined to shake off her wistful cloak. She went straight up to the brass rail. 'Martini, bartender, please, and make it large.'

Max creased his forehead. 'Special occasion?'

'Yeah, I resigned.'

'From your own company?'

'Shut up and put some decent music on.'

Virgo chose a West Coast IPA that was on the pump, and they took a booth in the corner.

Jessica took a big drink and stared at the olive on her cocktail stick as she twirled it round. 'If I'm honest, I feel a bit scared.'

'About the future?'

She nodded. 'How did you feel when you had to leave the Army?'

'I didn't have to leave. They would have found me a role, but it wouldn't have been combat operations.'

'Okay, you chose to leave, but you must have been worried about what you were going to do?'

'I didn't have time. I met Crystal, and the days flew by. She got a job in Washington, and I just applied for the FBI because I wanted to be near her.'

'Sounds like true love.'

'It was.' Virgo smiled. 'Still is.'

SOME MOTOWN GROOVES came hustling and do-wapping out of the speakers. Smokey and the Miracles seconding that emotion, followed by Martha and the Vandellas dancing in the street. Jessica's glass was empty before Levi Stubbs began 'Bernadette,' and she ordered the same jumbo martini again. Told Max to get one for himself.

'Do you know what?' She dumped the fresh olive with the first uneaten one in a saucer. 'You were right about Joey. I need to stop treating him like a little kid and show that I have faith in him.'

'He's a smart kid.'

'What did you say to him last night?'

'Make your bed. Stand up straight. Always say please and thank you.' Virgo rubbed the stubble on his chin. 'I can't remember exactly, but that sort of thing. The little habits that show respect for yourself and others.'

Jessica gazed into her cocktail as though it were a crystal ball. 'If we have to move back to LA, he's going to need to be resilient.'

'You know I really don't want the rest of that ten grand from you. Any of it.'

'Thanks, but it would only be prolonging the pain. If Artemis Associates were a horse, the veterinarian would have already been round to put a captive bolt in its brain and turn it into pet food or glue.'

'What will you do in LA?'

'Same type of work, but for one of the big agencies. There's more folk down there doing the horizontal tango with someone they shouldn't than up here in wine country.'

'Don't you think trying to snare unfaithful husbands is a waste of your God-given talents?'

'Of course it's a waste, but God doesn't pay the bills. Catching cheating bastards does.'

'The wages of sin.'

'And it's not just the husbands who like to play away from home, although in my personal case it was.'

'Whatever happens, you're better off without him.'

'Fourteen years ago. I bet the girl he left me for looks old now.'

'They still together?'

'Last I heard, but we never meet. Joey's not seen his father since he went. I think that was my fault.' A lump appeared in Jessica's throat, and it looked like she didn't want to dwell on the past any more. She washed the lump away with a torrent of martini and said, 'What about you? What are you going to do after tomorrow?'

'I think I'm ready for a change.'

'No more serving breakfast to the homeless guys?'

'I got the RV to travel and never made it more than eighty miles up the coast.'

'And I thought you were running away from something, but you were stuck?'

'I guess.' Virgo hadn't thought too much about it. In some ways, prison had been easy for him because he didn't have to make conscious decisions. It was all regimented: roll call, breakfast, work, lunch, roll call, classroom, dinner, final roll call, then lockdown and lights out. Rinse and repeat. Each day since his release it had become a little easier to force himself to face the day ahead without Crystal and get on with the practicalities of life. Muscle memory.

Max brought over another round of drinks and some potato chips. A few more couples drifted in off the sidewalk, and a group of Chinese tourists laden with bags, going for a world record in the number of selfie-shots in one evening. At one point, two college kids came in and then slunk out when their ID was declared fake.

There were five uneaten olives in the saucer when Jessica said, 'What happened back there in the country park with those motorbike goons?'

'They were fish out of water. It was no big deal.'

'Aren't you worried Rinker will try and track you down?'

'Nope.'

'Is there a basis for your confidence, or are you just showing off?'

'Bit of both.' Virgo smiled. 'The truth is, this is the first time I've felt alive for a long time.'

'Be a shame to die now, then.'

'A shame but not a tragedy.'

The playlist changed again. The distinctive seven-note intro riff to 'Mr. Brightside' rang out, and Jessica said, 'Hey, thanks for coming to my leaving party.'

'Been a pleasure.'

She stood up and laughed. 'Do you want to dance?'

'I can't dance, sorry.'

She put her hands on her hips. 'Okay, how am I supposed to tempt you into kissing me if you won't dance?'

'I beg your pardon?'

'Forget it; stay there.' Jessica came around to his side of the booth and squeezed in. She put both arms around his shoulders and kissed him on the mouth.

Virgo kissed her back. It felt good. But then...

'Aargh.' Jessica pulled her head away, and a hand shot to her mouth. 'Sorry, it's the split lip. Gone again.'

Virgo couldn't speak. He was still wondering what just happened.

'Okay then.' She patted her lip. 'This is where I'm supposed to say I'm sorry, I don't know what came over me, and you say something like let's pretend it never took place and don't mention it again.'

'Why spoil it like that?'

'Because I don't like to get my hopes up in case they get dashed.'

'No pleasure, no pain?'

'Exactly, I'm emotionally flat-lining into my forties. It's easier.'

Virgo stood up and took her by the hand. 'Come on. I lied about not being able to dance.'

CHAPTER 38

Casey stared into the bathroom mirror. Did she look like someone who'd lain awake all night crying and rubbing their eyes? *Tick.* Someone who was scared? *Tick.* Someone whose doubts were now so deeply etched in their face that they might have become permanent scars, there to serve as ever-present reminders of this day? *Tick.* She bent forward and cupped cold water from the sink onto her red and blotchy skin, toweled it and took another trepidatious look. *Shit.* No better. What was she going to do?

The wedding breakfast was in seventeen minutes' time. A relaxed, low-key event they'd said. Just her and a few specially selected guests enjoying a light meal with the bridegroom in his private residence before moving on to the church for morning prayers. The same church where, at two o'clock in the afternoon, a celebrant would ask her the dreaded question, and her mouth would seize up as the words she uttered turned to dust on her lips.

Maybe she could feign illness and secure a postponement. It wouldn't be difficult given her appearance. Dr. Dan was mercurial and might transfer his intentions onto another woman in the meantime before the rearranged date, but what if he didn't? What if by virtue of his powers he could instantly see that she was being deceitful in an attempt to renege on the acceptance of his proposal? No, she didn't think playacting was the answer. There was still time for divine intervention, and if that did not come to pass, then it was simply meant to be. Kismet. She would be married.

She dressed, and at precisely 07:50 there was a knock on the door, and Sister Helena appeared. She was one of the older women in the Order and had been assigned to act as Casey's maid for the day.

Sister Helena saw Casey's face and said, 'Second thoughts?'

'No, I'm okay. Let's go.'

'Don't worry. You're not the first to get cold feet.'

'I'm fine. Honestly.'

'Please yourself. I'm here to do whatever you ask.'

They were driven in a golf cart across the lake and through the gates of the mansion. Once inside, Sister Helena was ushered into a side room, and Casey was shown through into Dr. Dan's office, where the great man himself sat alone behind his desk.

He stood up. 'Blessings on this joyful day. Come and sit with me a while.'

Casey glanced up. She was finding it difficult to look him square in the eye, but when she did, she saw he had a wide smile and was radiating warmth. If he'd noticed anything untoward in her face, he didn't betray it.

Dr. Dan was in one of his hyperactive moods, like when he preached at the front of a congregation. He couldn't keep still. He sashayed around the desk and pulled another chair up. An even bigger smile. 'Are you full of wonder and anticipation for the day ahead, the same as me?'

Casey said, 'Marriage is a gift from God, and I want to honor His will.'

'Oh, you shall. Truly. You look beautiful, and I cannot wait until we are joined as one in the eternal bond.' He sashayed back behind his desk.

Casey sat down and looked at her feet. Beautiful? That was a lie, albeit white and well-intentioned.

At that moment, there was a knock on the door, and a secretary came in. She looked nervous. 'Excuse me, sir. There's a delegation of apostles who want to meet with you as a matter of urgency.'

'What do you mean a delegation?' A switch had been thrown, and Dr. Dan's smile was off.

'Five apostles, led by James, the son of Alpheus.'

'What fresh hell is this?' Dr. Dan consulted his MacBook. 'Diary them in at nine o'clock for thirty minutes. No longer. I've got a busy schedule today.'

'As you wish, sir.' The secretary backed out and softly closed the door.

'Where were we?' Ping. Dr. Dan's thirty-two-tooth light show was back on. He opened a top drawer in his desk and pulled out a sheaf of papers. 'If you'd be so good, I'd like you to sign this document before we enjoy our wedding breakfast together. Three places that are marked in pencil with a cross, and can you time and date each one as well. Praise be to the Lord.'

Casey picked up the document as it was pushed across the leather-topped desk. 'What is it?'

'Think of it as a prenup with God.'

She skimmed a couple of paragraphs. 'It says that I agree to give all my possessions to the People's Order of Gabriel.'

'That's what marrying into the church entails. It means renouncing material goods and devoting yourself to the Lord.'

Casey didn't think of herself as someone remotely interested in the trappings of wealth, but she didn't like signing official-looking documents either. She wavered. 'May I read it first?'

'We really haven't got time.' Dr. Dan didn't look pleased. He puffed out his cheeks and shook his head, as though he couldn't believe the impertinence of the question.

There was a knock on the door, and the nervous secretary came in again.

Dr. Dan shouted, 'What is it now?'

'It's Sergeant Chambers in the lobby to see you, sir. I told him you're busy, but he's insistent. He said it was important.'

'The man's an idiot. What can be so important that he ventures to disturb a groom on his wedding day?'

'Well…' The secretary glanced towards Casey as though she didn't want to explain in the presence of a third party.

'Spit it out.' Dr. Dan's voice was full of repressed energy, as though he might explode. 'We're all family here.'

'The police have found a body, and he says it's one of our members. They need someone to make an official identification.'

'Good grief.' Dr. Dan's shock looked a little forced. 'Show Sergeant Chambers into the boardroom.' He turned to Casey with a smile that was now more brittle. 'Excuse me. This shouldn't take long.' Then he disappeared through a side door into an adjoining room.

Casey sat alone and stared at the document. Should she sign it like a good wife-to-be? How had she allowed herself to get railroaded into such an uncomfortable situation when her time within the Order had once been the happiest of her life? She flicked through the sheets of paper. Every now and then details jumped out from the page and made her catch her breath: the exact address of her mother's property, a list of investments, trust funds, fixed assets such as vehicles.

She couldn't grasp the context and meaning of what she was seeing and turned back to the very first paragraph of the document to start reading again with more attention. The words and sentences were in the peculiarly meticulous but mangled version of the English language that only legal practitioners use. Each line was a challenge. She was on the third one when raised voices came through from the boardroom next door.

It made her lose her train of thought, and she went back to the beginning, but the shouts came again. It was hopeless. She went over to the door and listened. At first it was difficult to differentiate between who was doing the shouting and what they were saying, then she pressed her ear against the door like a genuine, de facto eavesdropper, and that was when she heard the voices of two men who sounded bitter, panic-stricken and guilty.

Dr. Dan said, 'Don't fucking come here and threaten me with your bullshit rules and procedures.'

Chambers said, 'It's not my fault you fucked up.'

'I was assured the body would not be found.'

'That won't stop the investigation crawling all over this place.'

'He was a member of the Order, that's all. A poor victim of today's violent society.'

'You're fucking deluded.' Chambers made a cynical laugh. 'As soon as they make the link with the blood in Malone's car, they'll be here.'

'Then stop them making the link.'

'Not possible.'

'Stall them. Give me some time.'

'Why should I, when I warned you what would happen?'

'You know why.'

Chambers made no answer.

Dr. Dan shouted, 'Now, go on. Fuck off and do whatever you need to do.'

Casey hurried back to her chair by the desk. Heart hammering faster than the pistons of a steam engine. She closed her eyes and said a prayer of thanks to the Lord. She'd wanted a signal, and *bam*, here it was. A powerful one.

The side door opened, and Dr. Dan breezed in with a renewed and cheeky smile, as though he'd just had to deal with a recalcitrant toddler. 'Sorry about that. I promise every day of our married life won't be as manic as this morning.'

Casey swallowed hard and braced herself. 'I've changed my mind. I don't want to get married.'

'Nonsense. You're just tired.' The grin didn't slip.

'No. I was unsure, but now I've realized that my future service to God must be as a single woman.'

Dr. Dan flipped and palm-slammed the desk. 'You promised. There's no going back.'

'As with Saul on the road to Damascus, the scales fell from my eyes, and I have seen the truth.'

'How dare you quote scripture to me.' He grabbed the prenup and a pen. Held them under her nose. 'Sign the damned forms and go and ready yourself to be married. Nobody defies the prophet.'

Casey thought back to when she played tennis. Sometimes older or bigger opponents would try to bully and intimidate her, but she'd developed her own way of dealing with it. A shield that came up in the form of a mask of serene indifference. She pulled it up now. 'No, nein, non, nâo. How many languages does the prophet want my refusal in?'

'There is no choice. We will be married this afternoon, and unfortunately you will have to spend the intervening hours in a detention cell.' He walked round the desk, pressed a button and spoke into a microphone. 'Send in the divine guards.'

CHAPTER 39

Virgo woke in instalments. A series of states of consciousness between the dark, deep world of Morpheus and the bright land of the living, and as he moved through each successive one, he became increasingly aware of the intense pain that throbbed inside his head. *Shit.* Someone had clamped his brain in a vise and ratcheted it up so tight that it was going to explode. The only good thing was it blanked out the constant screech in his left ear. A bonus, but not worth the pain.

He rolled out of bed and padded, eyes closed, to the RV bathroom. When was the last time he'd had a hangover? So long ago, he couldn't remember. He'd never been a big drinker, but last night something had loosened his long-standing inhibitions and led him into a heady upward spiral of intoxication and unaccustomed joie de vivre. That something was called Jessica McGann. The problem was, what goes shooting up must come crashing down. He turned the shower on cold and stepped in.

Ten minutes later, a trio of Tylenol were easing their way into his bloodstream, and some kind of bird was marching backwards and forwards on the roof of the Winnebago wearing hobnailed boots. Metal on metal. *Clang, clang, clang.* Gradually he raised the blinds to let the light in and launch a vicious attack on both retinas. *Zap.* Big yellow ball in a clear blue sky. Great day to try to rescue someone who doesn't want rescuing from a compound of zealots, whilst at the same time feeling as flat as twice-stepped-in dogshit.

The parking lot of the Veterans' Memorial Hall was quiet. A sprinkling of early-bird tourists and no sign of John Rinker's headbangers seeking him out for violent retribution. They knew where he'd be if they wanted him, but he wasn't going into hiding. However, it had been a bad idea to Uber it back to the RV last night when he was in no fit state to defend himself. That was why he never drank to excess: bad decisions make for bad reaction times and co-ordination, and bad outcomes.

There had been a guy in his Army unit called Tyrone who swore that the only hangover cure was raw eggs, tomato juice and Angostura bitters. The only ingredient he had was the eggs, and he didn't feel confident about keeping them down without cooking, so he was firing up the gas hob when he saw a police cruiser peel off the La Esperanza high street and drive towards him. He waited and watched it approach. Single crewed.

Virgo opened his habitation door, jumped down and said, 'If you've come to move me on, don't worry, this is my last day.'

Officer Clifford stepped out of his patrol car. 'I don't suppose you know anything about three ugly mothers who got taken into Sierra Vista Medical Center yesterday?'

'Should I?'

'A member of the public saw a motorhome driving away.'

'Did they get a number?'

'I don't believe they did.'

'Too bad.' Virgo massaged his temples. 'This migraine has been playing havoc with my memory.'

The compact former Ranger still took pride in his appearance. He flicked some lint off the badge on his sleeve. 'They're known associates of John Rinker.'

'I've never met Mr. Rinker.'

'He's an animal.'

'I don't know what I've done to upset the guy, apart from defend myself.'

'Stay away from him. He's bad news.' Officer Clifford looked around the parking lot, as though checking nobody was in earshot. 'That's what I've come to warn you about. Listen, nobody's going to arrest you for nearly killing those guys in the woods, but do yourself a favor and quit now while you're ahead.'

Virgo shrugged. 'I don't do the Q word.'

'I didn't think you would, but I felt it my duty to come and tell you. Have a good day.' Officer Clifford climbed back in the cruiser. 'Hey, thanks for the call about Ben Malone's body. How did you know where to look?'

'Detective Malone took me on a tour of those little hill roads because he didn't want to be seen with me, and I figured he might do the same with a confidential informant.'

'You think he was meeting a CI?'

'He wouldn't confirm or deny it, but yes, I do, and judging by the amount of blood in the passenger seat, my guess is whoever it was is not going to be giving any more information to the police. Ever.'

'Mmm...that might make sense.' Clifford tapped his fingers on the open car door. 'What with the body having a gunshot wound and all.'

'The body?'

'First light this morning, an angler at Lake Mateos saw something floating in the reeds. Turns out it was a white male, late twenties, with three of those matchstick angel tattoos.'

'The People's Order of Gabriel.'

'And no balls.'

Virgo thought he'd misheard. 'No what?'

'Balls.' Clifford shook his head at the weirdness of what he was saying. 'They took the body to prepare for autopsy and saw that the testicles had been removed.'

'Okay, let me guess. They were in his mouth or up his ass.' Virgo had studied the meaning of various forms of post-mortem mutilation at Quantico.

'Neither. They'd been removed relatively recently, but the damage to the scrotum had been surgically stitched.'

'You should close that Templar Sanctorum place down. It's an evil, barbaric institution that gets a free pass because they hide behind God's name.'

'Sergeant Chambers is there now, finding out what the hell happened to the ball-less guy.'

'Maybe you should send somebody else instead of Chambers.'

'Remember the Army? Well, there's a rank structure in the police too.' Officer Clifford closed the cruiser door. 'Take care of yourself.'

Virgo washed the scrambled eggs down with a gallon of black coffee and wondered whether he should have told Officer Clifford about the nitazene-pill-production factory at the back of Dr. Dan's church. The officer seemed solid and straight. The problem was, his junior status made it difficult for him to bypass Chambers and get the resources necessary to mount a serious operation against the People's Order of Gabriel. The best bet was the DEA, and as soon as he'd made sure Casey was safe, he'd be on their hotline.

While he was washing the pots, Betty called from the J. Edgar Hoover Building with a name for the old woman who'd been shot on her doorstep by the kid who thought he was Dirty Harry. She was called Caroline Hemp and was eighty-three years old when she was murdered at her home in Carson City, Nevada, a little over a year ago. Two .44 rounds to the chest and no other signs of disturbance inside the house or property stolen. The case was unsolved. At the end of the call, Betty growled and said that when he took her for dinner to the Waldorf, she now expected champagne as well. Moët. No substitutes.

Virgo turned to Detective Google for further information. She was more polite and less expensive. There was a smattering of coverage in local online publications, with the most useful being a piece in the *Tahoe Advertiser*. Caroline Hemp was a widow who lived alone apart from the ex-thoroughbred racehorses she'd rehomed on her estate. Husband Eric was from a wealthy mining family and had died from natural causes twelve months to the day before his wife. Caroline Hemp was an active member of the church and avid supporter of local charities. She was survived by her only child, Ruby.

What were the chances Ruby Hemp was now a member of the People's Order of Gabriel, the same as Nancy Berg? There could be no other connection between the two shooting cases, apart from the fact that both victims were rich and gave money to charity. Maybe Dr. Dan didn't like cash going to provide racehorses with a nice retirement when it could be diverted into his pocket with some bullshit about baptism and shoving a Smith and Wesson into a kid's hand.

There was a flash of scarlet, a doof-doof-doof, and the old Beetle pulled up alongside. Jessica climbed in and took her sunglasses off to get a better look at the patient. 'How's the head?'

'Still on the neck.' Virgo screwed his eyes up. 'How come you look daisy fresh?'

'Practice.' The sunglasses went back on. 'What's the plan?'

'I thought you'd packed the business in.'

'I have, and as I said to Joey this morning, this is a brand-new chapter in our lives. Goodbye Mother Hen, hello laid-back Cool Mom. This trip today is purely pleasure.'

'It might get messy.'

Jessica pointed to her shoulder bag with a neon green fingernail. 'It's okay. I've finished work but kept the gun.' Then she leant in the doorway with one hand on her hip. 'Hey, about last night. Do you want to do it again sometime?'

'Consume a fatal quantity of alcohol?'

'The other bit. You know, hanging out and having fun.'

Virgo didn't know if he was really ready to take the next step. Yesterday, something had made him want to seize each precious second of time he had on the planet and fill them with those things that can turn a mundane existence into stuff on an IMAX screen: laughter, action, wonder, friendship and the feeling of invincibility. Now was the morning after the night before, and he was back to focusing on tasks to get him through the day, but then he thought about what Crystal would have wanted him to do, and said, 'Sure. I'd like that.' No sooner were the words out of his mouth, he felt a rush of guilt and started to think of ways of disappearing as soon as this was over. His head hurt, and he didn't know what he wanted.

CHAPTER 40

Problem. How do you convince a bride-to-be that she's making a terrible mistake when she's been mentally conditioned into accepting her future husband and refuses to listen to reason or logic? And how do you first locate her when she is hidden away in the depths of an extensive compound that is heavily protected by loyal followers of said future husband, who would happily sacrifice themselves in his defense?

It was something Virgo was kicking around in his Tylenol-filled brain as he sat in the passenger seat of the Beetle and gazed across the blacktop at the entrance of the Templar Sanctorum thirty yards back down the highway towards La Esperanza. There was no chance of fighting his way in when he didn't know where Casey would be, or how he could get her out if she didn't want to leave. Neither did he have the necessary time to just keep waiting until the next time she came out of the property. It might be days.

Jessica opened a bag of sugar-free Pep-O-Mints and held it out. 'How long are we going to give it?'

'Until they realize that we're keeping them under surveillance, which won't be long, thanks to your hi-vis hair.'

She snatched the bag away before he had a chance to take a mint and pulled something out of her bag. It was a floppy, cotton hat with a World Wildlife Fund logo. 'Ten bucks on Amazon, and I've got an instant disguise, and I get to save an elephant. Bargain.'

'I'm still thinking through the options.'

'We've been sat here forty minutes.'

'Blame the IPA and yourself for buying it for me.'

Jessica sucked on a mint for a while, then said, 'Why don't you go and negotiate like I hired you to do in the first place?'

'The last official case I worked as an FBI negotiator, the kidnappers killed the hostage.'

'Okay, not ideal, but you didn't mess up every time, right?'

'I didn't say it was my fault.' Virgo heard a tinkle in the back of his mind. It was the sound of the penny dropping. When Jessica had first persuaded him to visit the Templar Sanctorum to try to secure Casey's release, he was completely ignorant about Dr. Daniel Nelson and the People's Order of Gabriel. Now he knew all about their skeletons in the closet, and that gave him something to negotiate with. Two parties can only agree a deal if they both have something to offer the other side. He shook himself and said, 'You're right. I should just walk in and horse-trade.'

Jessica nearly choked on the Pep-O-Mint. 'Really? I was joking.'

He pulled his phone out, keyed in a message and tapped *send*. 'That's the name and number of the guy to call if anything happens to me.'

Jessica's cell buzzed, and she unlocked the screen. 'Brad Hooper? Is he a cop or in the Bureau?'

'No, he's an Army vet with two prosthetic lower legs, but if anyone kills me, he'll track them down and even the score.'

'On his own?'

'Him and his illegal collection of weaponry.'

Jessica gave him a gentle smile. 'Good luck.'

He smiled back. 'In the Army, we never said good luck or goodbye, just see you soon.'

'Okay. See you soon.'

The wrought-iron gates of the Templar Sanctorum were wide open, but beyond them, the barrier was down to prevent vehicles entering without permission. There was a pedestrian walkway alongside and a white, wooden sentry booth, which housed the guard who controlled the entrance. The first time Virgo had visited, the booth had been empty, but now there was a uniform inside and two more guards patrolling up and down behind the barrier. Security had been beefed up. It looked like the People's Order of Gabriel was expecting trouble. Maybe he was the trouble.

As he walked towards the booth, he saw that the parking lot was full of the minibus fleet, each with their purple POG livery and quasi-heraldic shield. No evangelists out today spreading the word up and down the coast, delivering their packages and bringing in the tax-exempt donations from their many believers and new converts to the faith. Perhaps the Order was scaling back business in anticipation of extra scrutiny, or they were just taking a rest. Saving souls must be exhausting.

The guard was out of the booth before he got there. 'What do you want?'

Virgo ignored the abrupt tone and kept his voice polite. 'I've come to speak to the man who calls himself Dr. Daniel Nelson.'

'The prophet?' The guard looked mildly amused and shook his head. 'I'm afraid that won't be possible.'

'Could you call his secretary and tell them that Mr. Virgo is here to see him.'

'I know who you are, and you need to leave. Now.'

'Not until I've spoken to the chief scamster.' Virgo saw the other two guards had noticed the altercation and were coming over to provide backup.

'Last chance, pal. Turn around and walk away.'

Virgo didn't move. 'The body of one of your apostles was found this morning with his balls cut off. Call Nelson and tell him I'm going to email the story to every media agency in the county. They love shit like that.'

The guard thought about it. 'No.'

'Do you want to be the one who gets the blame for a media circus setting up camp here? What's your name?'

The guard disappeared into the booth and came out a little while later looking chastened. 'Wait here. Someone's coming.'

Someone was four guys dressed in baggy, black cotton suits in a long-wheelbase resort-transportation vehicle that looked like a stretch golf cart with solar panels on the roof. Virgo climbed in the vacant middle seat and was driven through the compound. They passed the main mission-style edifice, and he glanced through the arches into the quadrangle for any signs of activity, but saw nothing. There was nobody walking around or tending to the lawns and flowerbeds, and when they passed the accommodation blocks, he thought he saw faces looking out from some of the windows. It was like a storm was coming and the hatches had been battened down.

The resort-transportation vehicle bumped along the railway-sleeper bridge over the lake and pulled up outside the mansion house. The four ninjas jumped down and formed a cluster to usher him in. There were three other vehicles parked on the gravel forecourt: a plain white box van, a purple people carrier and a limo. The roller shutter of the box van was open, and inside was half full of packing cases.

When they went through the main double doors and into a corridor, they passed a room that had a dozen or more workstations, but half of them were empty. There were still six operators sat at computers, wearing telephone headsets, but there were also two guys unplugging equipment and rolling up cables. Scaling back or shutting down? Virgo wasn't sure, but something was going on at the People's Order of Gabriel. He could sense the tension and unease in the air.

The ninjas marched him through a couple more anterooms and then into what looked like a committee or boardroom. It was oak-paneled with an oval oak table and thirteen chairs. A water machine. Crystal glasses engraved with the crest of the People's Order and the walls covered in plaques emblazoned with the sage words of the great prophet, Dr. Daniel Nelson.

Virgo read a few.

True faith means keeping nothing back in the locker.

Being part of the Order means excusing the inexcusable, just as God forgives the unforgivable in us.

Our future is not to do extraordinary acts in the honor of God, but to perform the ordinary things in an extraordinary way.

The rest were similar. Shameless BS. The kind of thing the great prophet could have got from a fortune cookie or copy and pasted off the net.

Ten minutes later, Virgo was still waiting. The ninjas looked nervous but didn't speak a word. Virgo began to size them up in case Dr. Dan never appeared and he had to fight his way out, or the negotiations ended in acrimony and violence. They were all in their twenties and appeared in physically good shape. No waifs or butterballs. One had scar tissue around an eyebrow as though he might have done some boxing in a previous life, and another had evidence of having had multiple ear-piercings, like he could have come from a rough neighborhood. The other two looked like overgrown choirboys. Individually, it was a quartet that wouldn't present a problem, but together might prove difficult to take out.

Just when Virgo had reread the Dr. Dan quote plaques for the tenth time and was ready to rip them off the walls, a side door opened, and in waltzed the great man, waving a piece of paper in his hand.

Virgo said, 'It's rude to keep visitors waiting.'

'Really? Even when the delay is due to a wedding service?' Dr. Dan pranced over and thrust out the piece of paper. 'You're too late.'

Virgo saw it. *Marriage Certificate.* Signed by Dr. Daniel Nelson and Casey Bender, plus the officiant and a witness. What had she done?

CHAPTER 41

A year before the US was officially engaged in fighting the so-called Islamic State, Virgo was already out in Syria, operating undercover and recruiting human intelligence sources. They worked in male-female pairs to reduce suspicion and always as a married couple because the local culture was more receptive to that status rather than relationships where men and women simply live together. His undercover wife was called Stephanie.

The operation was due to run for three months, and they had a running joke that as soon as it was over, they would get a pretend divorce to end their pretend marriage. Stephanie used to quote all the other short-lived marriages: Eddie Murphy and Tracey Edmonds, Carmen Electra and Dennis Rodman, and Britney Spears and Jason Alexander, who lasted fifty-five hours before filing annulment papers. Virgo and Stephanie never got their pretend divorce because seven weeks into the operation, a suicide bomber killed her and nine others in the lobby of the Grand Eastern Hotel in Aleppo.

The thing was, Virgo knew marriages can be brought to an

end with speed if required. He took a step towards Daniel Nelson, stared down into the smaller man's face and said, 'I know about it all. The powder deliveries. The pill press. The trafficking network. The whole enchilada.'

Nelson grinned, but it wasn't enough to hide the glint of surprised dismay in his eyes. 'You are possessed by an evil spirit, and I shall pray that the Lord has mercy when the day of reckoning comes upon us.'

'Release the girl, and I'll give you twenty-four hours to finish packing up and leave before the DEA tears this place to pieces.'

'My work here has barely begun. What makes you think I'm leaving?'

'I can smell it. The ship's going down, and King Rat is the first to flee.'

'That is a lie.' Nelson was shaken. 'And if I let you take my wife away, there is no guarantee you would not go straight to some law enforcement agency and tell them your totally fallacious and defamatory allegations about this fine institution.'

'Let her go; keep me here.'

For a moment, Nelson looked interested; then his face lit up with rage. 'You've made a serious mistake. Casey will never leave me.'

'You mean because of the loyalty library?' Virgo tapped his nose. 'I know about that too and how you tricked the faithful into thinking they'd shot and killed someone. But it was all fakery and sleight of hand, the same as the rest of this place.'

Up until that point, Nelson had stood his ground, almost on tiptoes staring back. Now he shrank. His knees gave out, and he used the oval table to stop himself falling down. Clawed his way along to a large oak and leather swivel chair and slumped into it. 'What else do you know?'

'I told you. I know everything.'

'Lying lips are an abomination to the Lord.'

Virgo laughed. 'I'll tell you what. Full marks for keeping it up. The method acting. They said De Niro stayed in character all six months it took to film *Taxi Driver*, but you're next level.'

'Have you finished?'

'I'm just warming up,' said Virgo. 'Why don't you tell me about Nancy Berg and how she's getting on deciding what to do with her inheritance?'

Nelson's right hand disappeared under the oval, oak committee desk, and when it came back, it was holding a Sig Sauer 9mm. 'There's no such person as Nancy Berg. I think you mean Nancy Nelson.'

Wham. A realization crashed into the frontal lobe of Virgo's brain, like a runaway train hitting the buffers. Why the hell had it not occurred to him before when he discovered that Casey was to be married? He took a step towards the barrel pointing at his chest and said, 'You married Nancy Berg and killed her father to get the inheritance, and now you're going to kill Margaret Bender.'

'I'm not going to kill anybody.' The sanctimonious smile was back on Nelson's face. He stood up and did a little jig to show there was nothing wrong with his legs. 'Somebody might, but not me.'

'What about the daughter of Caroline Hemp from Carson City, Nevada? Is she one of the harem?'

'Ruby? Nelson's eyes glazed over for a moment, as though seeing the image of a memory. 'She was my first, but God Almighty took her from me to be his servant in Heaven.'

'She's dead? You're a sick bastard.' Virgo gritted his teeth and took another step towards the gun.

'Don't be stupid, or I'll shoot you here and now. Four witnesses will swear it was self-defense.'

Virgo was clean out of negotiating options. He'd been banking on Nelson accepting a trade-off: Casey in exchange for the opportunity for him to disappear before a DEA raid. What he'd not factored in was that Casey was a vital part of Nelson's future plans and could never be let free. She was his personal goldmine. The Bender wealth was not going into the coffers of the People's Order of Gabriel, even if that did exist separate to Nelson's own pocket.

He glanced over his shoulder at the four ninjas guarding the door and then back to Nelson. 'You'd best shoot me, then, because those boy scouts aren't going to stop me leaving.'

'My pleasure.' Nelson narrowed his eyes. 'Tell me first, who else knows?'

'Just me.'

'I don't believe you.'

'Tough. Why don't you ask your pal the Big Guy upstairs?'

'Add blasphemy to your sins and repent quick because you've not got long. The fires of hell await.'

Virgo stared into Nelson's still-slitted eyes. 'The God I believe in judges people on their true character. Maybe it's you who should start getting worried.'

'You blackmailed your way in here today by threatening to go to the media. Who told you about Bartholomew?'

'You expect me to say? You're a sad, deluded piece of shit.'

Nelson threw his head back and laughed. The laugh of a maniac beyond the boundary of social norms. 'I know someone who will make you talk. By the time I'm taking prayers this lunchtime, you will be pleading to be dispatched into the kingdom of Hades.'

'See you there. I'll be waiting.'

'Seize him, guards.' Nelson wheeled away and motioned to them with his arm in a theatrical flourish. 'Take him to the detention cells.'

Virgo allowed the four guards to surround him and two to grab hold of his arms. Nelson still had the Sig, and a knot of bodies provided some protection. He waited until they'd bundled him to the far end of the boardroom and were about to leave via the main door. Then, this was it. Time to make a move. Three, two, one, zero. He yanked his right arm towards him so that the guy holding on to it was swung around. Thud. The top of Virgo's forehead smashed deep into nose gristle. The guard went down.

The guy on his left arm panicked. He should have held tight to help his colleagues. He didn't. He let go. It allowed Virgo to open up a yard of space between them. That made the difference. It gave the punch extra kinetic energy. Power. The fist connected with the guard's mandible like a club hammer. Drove it upwards into the maxilla. Teeth shattered. Another one down and out. Neutralized.

Combat profiling? Intuition? Call it what you will, Virgo ducked instinctively as a baton swung from behind him in a horizontal arc. The guard holding it didn't have the split-second time he needed to regain his balance before Virgo's boot buried itself in his neck. The guy gurgled. His eyes bulged, and he crumpled into a heap.

That left one. The boxer. Last man standing. Only member of the quartet who knew that fighting is about good defense as well as attack. He'd backed off and was blocking the door. On the balls of his feet. Southpaw fists. Virgo didn't have time for the Queensberry Rules. He snatched up the baton that number three had just tried to decapitate him with, and jabbed it straight between the boxer's defenses into his mouth. Then like a Japanese Kendo master, delivered angled blows to the ribs and head in quick succession. *Bang, bang.* The end. Roll credits.

Daniel Nelson was armed and somewhere in the room. No time to look. Virgo dived through the doorway and burst into the hallway. That was as far as he got. Six apostles in the red outfits stood in a semicircle. Each one had a Colt AR-15 semi-automatic rifle. All the barrels were pointing in his direction. *Shit*. He'd been in some crazy places, but this was the craziest.

CHAPTER 42

The detention cells were off the main quad. Down some stairs and along an underground passage lit by industrial bulkhead lights. Damp stone walls. Virgo was marched along it at rifle-point, wrists cable-tied behind his back. Three apostles in front, three behind. Nobody was taking any chances. When they reached the end of the passage, the leading apostle used a proximity card on a lanyard round his neck to spring the lock on a thick steel door.

It opened up into a reception area with a desk and benches. Lockers for property. A board for keys. It was like a miniature prison. The smell of cleaning fluid scratched the back of Virgo's throat and brought the memories of Eagle Valley State Penitentiary gushing back. The place where he'd done his bit for race relations by breaking the legs of the leader of the Aryan Brotherhood and inserting a plastic spork into the windpipe of number two in command. Happy days.

They passed a kitchenette and a jailer office and through another steel door to the cell area. There were just four of them. Basic holding pens separated by metal bars, with concrete bunks and a toilet in the corner where the rest of the world could see you doing what nature made you do. Only one of the pens was occupied, and Virgo was taken aback when he saw the tenant was Casey Bender.

He waited until the apostles had locked him in the pen diagonally opposite and left the room before he said, 'What the hell are you doing here?'

Casey tried her best to pull a weak smile. 'You were right. I feel so foolish.'

'Never mind who was right or wrong. Why aren't you with your new husband?'

'I changed my mind and said no to him.'

'Really?' Virgo sat on the concrete bench and ran the nylon tie up and down the edge. He didn't want to break it yet. Just create a weak spot. 'Dr. Dan just showed me a marriage certificate with your name on it. Signed, sealed, delivered.'

'What? It wasn't my signature.'

'Maybe he's a good forger as well as con artist.'

'He wanted me to sign some kind of prenup as well, but I refused.'

'Good, because I think he had something bad planned for your mother. Something to hasten your inheritance.'

Casey's mouth dropped open. 'You think he was going to kill her?'

'Daniel Nelson married two other members of the People's Order of Gabriel. Nancy Berg and Ruby Hemp. Both from wealthy families. Both only children. Both with only one living parent until—'

'Stop it. Don't tell me.'

'Someone in a white suit turned up on their doorstep with a gun.'

'No...'

'How did you explain it to me? To atone for their sins, the

avenging angel has to shed their blood and so save their soul from eternal damnation?'

Casey stood and marched back and forth in her cell. Distraught and shaking her head. Wishing it weren't true. 'You said that it was all fake. You said the baptisms were just an elaborate hoax to make us think we'd killed someone.'

'They were. All apart from two, and now he's planning another.'

'Oh, my God.' Casey stopped pacing. Her face, which had been red and blotchy, turned white. 'What have I done?'

'It's okay, we've still got time.'

'What if he's forged my signature on the prenup as well? My mother?' Casey began to sob. 'Oh, my God. Forgive me.'

'No doubt Nelson will have put your signature on the prenup too, but his time's running out. By tomorrow this place will be swarming with the law.'

'But it's today.'

'What?'

'Myra's baptism.'

'Are you sure?'

'Positive.'

'Okay, now I see the problem.' Virgo stopped chafing the cable tie and tried to think of something encouraging to say. It was typical Nelson. The sick bastard would get an extra kick from getting Casey's friend to pull the trigger on her mother and release the inheritance. A double whammy.

Casey used a sleeve to wipe her nose. 'Did you see a purple minivan on your way in?'

'There was a Chrysler Pacifica parked outside Nelson's residence.'

'That's the angel transport. It's waiting for Myra. She will go and receive Dr. Dan's personal blessing, and he will explain the initiation ritual and what she must do.'

'Does nobody ever say no, fuck you?'

'Never. They're too in awe. Blinded by the brightness of his presence. Just like I was.'

Virgo wasn't so sure it was all down to charisma. The kids were already mixed up and vulnerable. That was why they were there in the Order. Same as the followers of Manson. What Nelson was good at was creating the illusion of authority and ramping up the social pressure to conform. Normalizing the shocking. Turning the outrageous into routine and getting everyone to conform because they were scared to be different.

There were no windows in the cell area. No way of judging the time from the sun's position in the sky, and the apostles had taken his phone, along with his belt and wallet. He guessed it was a little shy of noon. In all the kill videos he'd watched with Jessica, both fake and real, the shootings had always taken place in the evening. Darkness and light. It was all about the symbolism. A white-clad savior striding through the black night to smite the sinner. But what about Margaret Bender? Nelson was in a rush. What were the chances he'd be happy to wait until sunset? Probably slimmer than the hair on a gnat's asshole. Myra was probably with Nelson right now, receiving her orders.

Casey had stopped crying. A look of stoic determination had chiseled itself into her face and made it ten years older. 'We need to warn my mother.'

'Agreed.' Virgo went back to chafing the nylon cable tie.

'When I was in Dr. Dan's office, I heard him arguing with Sergeant Chambers. A body had been found. I think it was one of the apostles.'

'This morning at Lake Mateos. The corpse had three of your angel tattoos.'

'I think it was Bartholomew.'

'It shouldn't be difficult to identify him, given his distinguishing features or lack of them.'

'What do you mean?'

'Nothing. How does this help us warn your mother?'

'There's been rumors for a while that some of the apostles aren't happy with Dr. Dan. It's gotten worse in the last couple of days, and now I think there's a split in the ranks.'

'Some things never change. Schisms, sects and people taking sides.'

'While Dr. Dan was trying to get me to sign the prenup, a delegation of five apostles turned up, demanding to see him. They've had enough. I think they might help us.'

Math was not Virgo's strongest subject, but he knew that had been an even split until Bartholomew got caught talking to Detective Malone, and then it became six versus five. Interesting. Nice to know, but no help getting him out from behind the iron bars. The six who were still loyal to Nelson had been armed with semi-automatic Colt rifles, which did seem strange. Overkill for one prisoner. Maybe they were already getting the heavy stuff to hand in anticipation of something else. A bit of internecine warfare. Or maybe a show of strength and loyalty to ward off any potential rebels thinking about having a go.

There was a metallic thump as three magnetic deadbolts retracted, and the door opened. Virgo glanced backwards under his right armpit to check what impact the chafing had achieved on the cable tie. Zero. A big fat one. His heart took a dive, and he got to his feet. The same six apostles marched in and unlocked his pen. Pointed the barrels of the AR-15s at him and motioned that he should leave.

Virgo walked into the midst of them and hesitated. 'Any of you guys called Judas?'

A thickset kid with a low brow said, 'I'm Judas.'

Virgo smiled at him. 'Fancy thirty pieces of silver to let me go?'

'Move it, wise-ass.' Judas jabbed a carbine into his left kidney.

They left as they'd entered. Three red-suited apostles, the prisoner, then the other apostles. Virgo took a deep breath. Shoulders back. Chest out. If he was being marched out into a yard and put up against a wall in front of a firing squad, he wanted to go with his head held high. No regrets. Proud of who he was and what he'd done. Even the bad bits. Just before the steel door closed behind them, he heard Casey's voice shout, 'Let him go. It's my fault he's here. Punish me.'

Virgo hoped he would see Casey again. There had been times over the past few days when she'd been infuriatingly stubborn and he'd wanted to grab her by the shoulders and shake some sense into her. She'd been naïve and selfish in relation to her mother. But in the final analysis, she was a victim, who had shown immense inner strength. She was honest and brave. Yes, he hoped he'd see her again, but he didn't think it was likely. Sometimes, happy endings only happen in fairy tales.

CHAPTER 43

Outside, the brilliance of the day hurt his eyes. He squinted. Breathed the air and walked towards destiny. It wasn't a wall riddled with bullet holes. It was a black Transit van. The same one that had stuck its nose into the rear of his RV. One of Rinker's. Three goons stood next to the open cargo door. Looking tough. Tattooed faces and snarls. One with an over-and-under Remington, the other two with handguns.

Virgo stopped. He didn't fancy getting in the back of the van. He could remember what was in there. Chainsaw. Rope. A can of diesel. No doubt a whole load of dried blood where he'd pumped a group of pellets into one of the gangbangers. Nobody moved. Both the apostles and Rinker's crew just stood and looked at each other, like they'd not got their handover protocol worked out in advance.

Then three of the apostles charged and pushed him onto the ground. Began kicking him. Nothing he could do except absorb the impacts. No way of protecting his head. The cable ties dug into his flesh as he tried to snap free of them. No chance. A few of the kicks hurt. One did some damage to his left shoulder. He tensed all his muscles. Rolled this way and that. After a while the pain became less, and he knew he was approaching the danger zone, but that was when it stopped.

Slowly, he got to his feet. The apostles went back into their group, out of breath and pleased with themselves. The Rinker gang were laughing. He made a snap assessment of his condition. Cracked rib, torn shoulder ligament, deep and surface bruising, mild concussion. He'd had worse. Much worse. Back in the day, he would have thought nothing of it and been first out of his rack the next morning, doing more push-ups and faster interval sprints than anyone else in the platoon. But that was then. If there was to be a tomorrow, his body would be sore. If…

'Hey, Virgo.'

Virgo looked up.

It was Judas. He smiled. 'Not such a wise-ass now, huh?'

The other five apostles smiled.

Virgo looked each of them in the eye. 'Any of you guys seen Bartholomew's balls? I hear he lost them.'

They stopped smiling.

Two of the Rinker crew grabbed Virgo by the arms and pushed him into the back of the van. A sack was put over his head. Tied with rope. Something hard struck him on the left cheekbone. Probably the butt of the Remington. It knocked him off his knees. Two of them rolled him onto his stomach. Then a boot slammed down on the back of his neck and stayed there.

The van moved off. It turned right out of the compound onto the main highway and then left about a mile down the road. Virgo tried to use gravitational forces to keep track of which way the vehicle kept turning. Right, then left. Then left again. Not easy with the boot still on the back of his neck and his face pressed down onto the corrugated metal floor of the van. At some point the sack over his head had been used to carry engine parts, and the smell of burnt oil clogged up his sinuses.

Transits are not the quietest vans. This one was rear-wheel drive and turbocharged, which made it worse. In addition, the inside walls of the cargo area were not boarded out, so there was nothing to absorb the engine and road noise. All this frustrated him because he was straining to hear every word the guys in the van uttered. He wanted to pick up everything. Nicknames. Accents. Voice tone. Pronunciation. Peculiarities of speech. Whatever might subsequently help him in identifying them, because there was one thing he was certain of. If he lived, he would find and kill them.

He reckoned they'd traveled seven or eight miles, largely uphill, when the vehicle took a left turn and began to drive over bumpy ground. Maybe a rutted track. Maybe a fire road with potholes or a private driveway that had not been well maintained. Less than a mile later, the Transit swung around to the right and came to a stop. Engine off. Virgo heard the cargo door slide open. Fresh mountain air. The boot pressing down on the back of his neck was removed, and he was dragged out of the van. Marched into a building and made to sit down.

The cable ties on his wrists were cut, but before he could stretch his arms and get the blood flow going again, they were restrained, and something hard with sharp edges cut into his flesh. The guys were laughing. Talking about where they were going to go that night. A bar called Tiffany's and then a motel on the West Side Freeway to meet up with some hookers, who provided a variety of services at very reasonable rates. Virgo took it all in. The chances of him still being alive at sunset were looking slim, but he liked to be prepared for every eventuality. Particularly if it involved the opportunity of settling a few scores with those who'd treated him badly, and spoiling their fun.

When the sack was taken off his head, Virgo saw he was in some kind of barn. Wood. Oak beams. A row of vehicles covered by dust sheets. Drums of gasoline or oil. Hydraulic ramp. Welding gear. The three guys who'd transported him there in the van were walking away towards double doors at the far end, looking like they were still planning their evening of booze and cheap sex.

But they hadn't left Virgo on his own. Two yards in front of him was an ugly motherfucker he'd never seen before, who shouted, 'Boss, he's ready for you.'

Something cut into Virgo's wrist. He looked down. Steel shackles. One either side, clamping them to the flat, wide wooden arms of a sturdy chair. He instinctively flexed to test the strength of the fastenings, but there was nothing doing. The metal was thick and the bolts heavy duty. All that happened was they dug deeper into his flesh and jammed up against his radius and ulna bones. There were no restraints on his ankles, but that was no use unless somebody unlocked the shackles on his wrists.

The only person in a position to do that was the mother in front of him. Virgo could see the key on a chain fastened to one of the belt loops on his jeans. He wore a white vest to show off his big, tanned muscles, and the end of his nose was turned up snoutlike to give him the look of a pig. There was a knife in his right hand that he was sharpening with a whetstone, which Virgo guessed was for show. Part of the psychological buildup to the big event. A tactic used the world over to soften subjects up prior to hostile interrogation. From police stations in uncivilized countries and war zones, to backstreet joints in the piss-poor area of any major city.

There was a small drywall office inside the barn. The door opened, and a man walked out. Rinker. Black vest. Black cap. Black hood pulled up over the top. Long pointed nose and a thin face with eyes sunk so deep they were in the back of his head. He swaggered over as though he'd got all the time in the world. Stopped to check the pressure on the front tire of a Harley that was on its stand by a tall, red tool cabinet. Just building the suspense. Enjoying it. Virgo saw he was carrying a small plastic box. The type used in the military to hold a first aid kit. Tourniquet, chest seals, surgical razor, wipes, gloves, combat gauze. He guessed Rinker's box contained something intended to hurt rather than heal.

Pigface set the knife and whetstone down on a camping table, satisfied the blade was up to the job. Then he folded his tree-trunk arms and smiled. Virgo smiled back. He'd only ever been properly tortured once in his life, and that had been by his own side. Special forces selection. Nothing could be worse than that. Forty-eight hours without sleep. Naked. Fastened to a wall in a position that made it impossible for his limbs to relax. Disoriented by white noise. Then subjected to hostile interrogation, which had been specially tailored to him. Threats to his family. Peanut butter, which he hated. His personal Room 101.

Rinker sauntered up and spat in Virgo's face. 'You put four of my guys in the hospital.'

Virgo felt a globule of saliva snake around his brow and drop into his eye. 'That was self-defense.'

Rinker passed the first aid box to pigface to hold, and said, 'Defend this.' Then he punched Virgo square in the mouth.

Virgo stared back and said nothing.

Rinker said, 'Who else knows about the drugs?'

Back in the Bureau's Crisis Negotiation Unit, they had a saying for when a situation was so dire and hopeless that there was no possible means of recovery. *Negotiate your way out of that one.* Virgo said it to himself now. The only feasible option available at the moment if he wanted to stay alive was to talk. Talk fast. He said, 'I know Dr. Dan's fucked it up.'

Rinker looked interested. 'Meaning what?'

'He went too far with his mind games and physical abuse. Turned one of his own apostles into a police grass.'

'That's been taken care of.'

'Has it? I just left the compound, and half his loyal troops aren't so loyal anymore. Ten bucks says it all kicks off today.'

If Rinker was concerned, he hid it well. 'Nelson's a fucking lunatic, but he knows how to control people.'

'Like dressing them up as angels and making them think they've killed someone?'

'I know all about that. In our line of work, it's good to have an insurance policy that stops people switching allegiance or going solo.'

'The problem is, it only works with the foot soldiers. All the apostles are in on the scam.'

'Shut up. That's enough bullshit.' Rinker was getting edgy.

Virgo said, 'Did you know not all the shootings were fake?' He saw from Rinker's reaction that it came as news to him. 'Nelson has got a habit of marrying members of the Order who have just inherited a lot of money. Parents shot on the doorstep. My guess is that money doesn't go into the business, but it attracts a lot of police activity. Not something you want.'

Rinker gave up trying to hide his annoyance. He turned to pigface. 'What did I tell you? Nelson's become a fucking liability.'

Virgo saw an opportunity. 'Nelson is carrying out another one as we speak. A van is on its way to kill a woman called Margaret Bender, whose daughter he married this morning. The other two murders were miles away, but this one's local. He's taking you for a mug, and that's not all. He knows the house of cards is about to come crashing down, and he's already packing his bags. He's going to disappear with your share of everything.'

Rinker's pinched face grew even sharper. 'Where does she live, this Bender woman?'

'I don't know the address, but I can take you there.'

'Nice try,' said Rinker. 'But you're going nowhere.' He sloped to the far end of the barn where the double doors were open, and disappeared.

Virgo swallowed the bitter taste of resignation. It had been worth a shot. Negotiation failed. What next? Nothing sprang to mind because he'd run out of options. Maybe he should have tried something back at the Templar Sanctorum, but it's not easy when there's six guys with AR-15s. Still. It would have been better than this. Maybe his hindsight was through rose-tinted spectacles.

From outside came the sound of the Transit engine firing up and rear wheels churning some dirt. Rinker came back in, moving now with a sense of purpose. The show of nonchalance gone. He came up to the chair and said, 'Have you ever been subjected to physical violence by someone wanting information from you?'

'Let's say it's not my first rodeo.'

'I guessed as much, and I don't want blood all over the floor of my unit.' Rinker took the square plastic box from pigface. 'That's why I'm going to let chemicals do the work. Much cleaner and more effective.'

Rinker took a strip of pills from his pocket and a small Ziploc bag from the box. He emptied the pills into the bag. Took the knife from pigface and used the butt of the handle to crush them into powder. Emptied the powder into a phial of liquid and shook it until it dissolved. Took a hypodermic syringe and pulled the plunger to suck up the solution. 'No need to heat this. Uncooked will increase the risk of infection, but it really doesn't matter in your case, does it?'

Virgo tried not to look at the needle. He didn't like them.

'It's okay, I've got a strong immune system. The only thing I'm allergic to is assholes like you.'

'Come on. You'll be my best friend when this juice gets into your bloodstream.'

'I doubt it.'

'Let's find out.' Rinker rammed the needle into the top of Virgo's bicep and emptied the contents. 'You've got thirty minutes left to live. Tops. Your breathing will slow down and then stop.'

'Do I have to spend half an hour looking at you two ugly bastards?'

'Why don't you tell us who else knows about our network, and then we can leave you in peace to enjoy your final moments?'

'Because truth serums have been debunked. Sodium thiopental or whatever shit you just put in my arm won't work.'

Rinker dropped the needle into a used-sharp container. 'Those were all barbiturates. This is nitazene. It will put you to sleep more quickly, and in that twilight zone of semiconsciousness just before your brain shuts down, you won't even know who I am, and you will talk.'

Virgo started to feel it. The rush. That feeling heroin addicts crave as morphine finds its way into the nervous system to work its magic. His mouth went dry. Skin all over his body began to glow with the euphoric heat. Someone had attached lead weights to his legs and pumped his head full of helium. He felt his mind drifting away and fought it. Tried to shout to himself. *Come on, fight, fight...*

He forced himself to focus on the two creatures stood in front of him. Smiles on their faces as they watched him die. He hoped his eyes gave them the message. Fuck you and the horse you rode in on. Then he switched off. He didn't want to spend a fraction of a second more on their pathetic existence.

He thought only about Crystal. The day he met her. How he felt when they moved in together. The first time he saw her in a ballgown and she took his breath away. So many happy nights and precious memories of a love that would remain for eternity even when both of them had gone. He felt himself drifting and didn't try to fight it...

CHAPTER 44

BANG. Virgo was back. Startled. A flash of black crossed his line of sight as Rinker dived behind a stack of oil drums. Pigface was laid out on the floor. Dead or dying. A red circle on his white vest growing in circumference. Silence. He scanned the barn for any sign of movement. Nothing. He tried to free his arms again, but they were heavy and made no impression on the shackles. Adrenalin had rebooted his system, but already he could feel his breathing starting to slow down again.

There was a roar. The sound of the Harley's engine filled the barn. Virgo's eyelids defied gravity, and he saw Rinker tear out through the roller-shutter door on the motorbike. He wasn't hanging around. Still nothing moved. Virgo fought to stay awake. It wasn't easy. His opponent in this particular fight was a wondrous feeling of pleasure that his body had never experienced before. He was about to submit to it when he saw one of the dust sheets move and Jessica McGann step out and run towards him.

She saw the keys on pigface's belt and pulled them off. Began to unlock the shackles.

Virgo said, 'Too late…Overdosing on nitazene…Casey locked up…Kill mother…'

Jessica said, 'I'm not leaving you.'

'Please…'

'No.' She removed both steel restraints and grabbed hold of his hands. 'Come on. Move it. Quick.'

Virgo stood up. Woozy. His feet wouldn't do what his brain told them. 'Wasting time…save Casey…'

'I've got Joey's Naxolone in the car. Come on. Quit messing around.'

'Can't…I'm going…'

Jessica draped his left arm around her shoulders and guided him towards the open door. His body wasn't his. His head spun. He was on another planet, part of a different solar system, in another galaxy. He managed three steps and collapsed. Jessica couldn't hold his weight. She cushioned the fall as best she could and said, 'Stay with me. Do you hear? I won't be long.' She started to leave, then stopped and slapped him across the face. Hard. 'Hey, I said stay with me.' Through his half-closed eyes he watched her go and went to sleep.

He woke and gagged. Something in his mouth. Jammed into the back of his throat. Jessica knelt over him and said, 'Breathe normally.'

It was magic. One minute out for the count. Next minute, *POOF*, back in the game. He looked at his hands and feet and wiggled them. They were his again. He slowly stood up and waited. Nothing happened. His head didn't go into a tailspin. His knees didn't turn to Jell-O. There wasn't a ninety-ton weight pressing down on his chest.

Jessica put the Naxolene inhaler back in the black canvas flight bag and said, 'It's something to do with the opioid receptors in the brain. This stuff cleans them straight up. It's like putting a tablet in the dishwasher and hitting the super-express cycle.'

Virgo felt better, but there was still fog clouding his thought process. He took a few deep breaths and tried to reassure himself of what was happening. Be certain that his short-term memory had not confused reality with drug-induced hallucination or psychosis. Recap. Nelson had forged a marriage certificate and probably a prenup. Casey was in prison. Her friend Myra was all set to shoot her mother. The baptism. Trigger the inheritance that would soften the blow for Nelson losing his empire. Fund him to set up somewhere else. Was any of that imagined? No. Unfortunately not. What was the priority? Margaret Bender.

He pulled the sheets off the line of vehicles. Five trucks. A nice selection so the same plate didn't register with the authorities too often when Rinker was crossing the border into Mexico and back into Texas. The gear lying around the barn suggested that the drugs were carried in secret metal compartments. Welded underneath the chassis. Covered with Waxoyl or some other underbody seal, and then removed with an angle grinder when safely back at base. Pure powder. Ready to go and be mixed with caffeine or lidocaine and pressed into pills at the back of Nelson's church.

All the pickups were ready to roll. Keys in ignition, gas in the tank. None of them were standard models. They'd all got major horsepower under the hood in case speed was necessary to evade law enforcement or fellow bandits. Virgo walked down the side of a Ram TRX that could top 100 mph in ten seconds thanks to its Hellcat engine, climbed in the passenger seat and said, 'You drive. I'm still coming out of la-la land.'

Then he called Margaret Bender and told her to sit tight. Under no circumstances answer the door. Lock it and secure all the windows. He tried not to panic her because the last thing he wanted was her running around outside, presenting an easy target. It was unlikely that Myra and her apostle chaperones would break in. They hadn't done on previous occasions, but things had changed. Nelson was desperate. He knew he'd reached the tipping point.

Traffic was light. Jessica made the Hellcat scream down Highway 41. Sideways round some of the blind bends. Flat out on the straights. Nearly wiped out a group of tourists road-tripping on Electra Glides. Neither of them spoke. It was a time for total concentration, and they knew that anything they said would sound hollow or be a forced displacement activity. The fact was, they were behind the curve, and the chances of them reaching their destination before an avenging angel were slim.

Virgo closed his eyes and focused on getting his mind and body back together. He needed them to be the well-oiled machine they used to be. When he opened them again, the driveway to the Bender estate appeared on the right, and the Ram TRX flicked its back end out and barreled down it. The tarmac road cut through a plantation of giant sequoias and redwoods. A little over halfway along, he heard a sound he thought he recognized and shouted, 'Stop.'

When he buzzed the window down, he was sure. Gunfire. Small arms. Jessica pointed to the Walther in a pouch under her left shoulder and passed him the Glock 19, then set off again. Cruising this time, not over-revving the engine. Before they reached the limestone-chip parking lot, he saw two vans. The POG's purple Chrysler and the black Transit from Rinker's ranch. The gang boss must have found out Margaret Bender's address and sent his goons to intercept.

It looked like they'd failed. There was a body lying in the doorway. Two more face-down on the gravel – an apostle in red, the other a gangbanger in black denim. The gunfire had stopped. All the doors of both vans were wide open, but there was no one to be seen. Tumbleweed. Those still alive had taken cover. There was no shortage of concealment options around the frontage of the mansion. Marble statues. Exotic plants. Stone benches. A low, red-brick wall around a rectangular rose garden.

Jessica nosed the pickup into the parking lot. *POP*. A bullet shattered the windshield. Virgo was already out the passenger door by the time the second one hit. He skirted round the back of the vehicle and away into the trees. The damage to the Ram gave him a rough trajectory for where the bullets had been fired from. If the attackers were ex-forces, they'd shoot and move, but he was banking on them never having worn a proper uniform. Just either the collarless tunic of the People's Order or the black jeans and jacket of a street gang.

The rounds had come from the direction of a small outbuilding beyond the far corner of the house. A timber storage unit for garden equipment or small utility vehicles. Virgo ducked his way through the trees until the mansion itself provided cover. Then he ran behind it, past the tennis courts that Casey had grown up on and past an aqua blue swimming pool. To the rear corner of the house. Halt. He pressed his back to the stucco wall and controlled his breathing. Took a moment to assess his condition. Now the nitazene had been neutralized, he ached all over. The kicking he'd taken at the Templar Sanctorum had been comprehensive. So what? Sixty percent of a Green Beret is better than the whole of most other fighting units, and this time he had a gun in his hand.

As soon as he burst out into the open, he heard the pop-pop of Jessica's Walther start up to provide him cover. *Go, go, go*. He had thirty yards to make before he reached the outbuilding. Ten still to go, and a figure jumped out. One of the goons. And it was the one with the Remington. That was a problem. A moving target is difficult to hit with a handgun, but a 12-bore cartridge blasts its shot across a wide radius. And the guy had a lot of cartridges slung across his chest in a bandolier like a Mexican revolutionary. Virgo dived forward. The muzzle of the Remington flashed. The hairs on the back of his neck felt the air move. Then came the bang. He fired back.

The goon had lowered the two barrels after the recoil and was pulling the trigger again when he died. A nine-mil hole in the cranium. Just above his left eye and close to where a cobweb tattoo ran down half his face. Virgo lay on his belly and waited to see if another target presented itself. Nothing appeared. He heard the sound of boots running across stone chippings. Then the slam of a door. An engine started. He got to his feet in time to see the Chrysler Pacifica belonging to the People's Order career around the edge of the parking lot, spraying up gravel, and disappear towards the highway. Someone had seen an opportunity to escape and grabbed it.

It looked like the stand-off was over. Two seconds later, another goon broke cover from behind a granite water feature and jogged over to the abandoned Transit. Instead of jumping in the driver's seat, he disappeared into the cargo area and came out with a stubby-barreled assault rifle.

Virgo grabbed hold of the Remington that the guy with the cobweb face had dropped. Helped himself to a handful of cartridges from the bandolier. Buckshot. Nine pellets of 8.4mm in each shell. The choice of the US Army for combat operations, though they prefer to fire them from pump-action Mossbergs. He closed the action on the gun. Rolled it over and slid four rounds into the magazine tube. Released the action and he was ready to go.

The goon had the carbine on his hip, ready to let rip. As soon as he saw Virgo, he thought better of it and ran behind the Transit. One of the first things Virgo had learnt when he left The Activity and trained to be an FBI agent was the difference between an army and a civilian vehicle. A US armored car is made from military-grade steel – MIL 12560 – whereas civilian vehicles are one millimeter of standard steel. The only safe place to take refuge from a bullet is behind the engine block or the brake discs. Not easy if you're six three and somewhere north of two hundred pounds in weight.

Whoever the goon was from Rinker's team, he'd seen too many movies. Virgo simply walked towards the Transit and pumped three rounds. Center. Then ten degrees left and ten right. Enough spread to cover the target zone and a little extra for good measure. When he walked around the back of the van, the guy was lying on his back. Three wounds to the chest. Two in the gut. One in the left thigh. Game over.

Virgo helped himself to the weapon. It wasn't an assault rifle. It was a Ruger semi-auto. To be an assault rifle, a gun needs to be selective. Semi or fully automatic and burst mode. The Ruger was just semi-automatic. One trigger pull per shot. Still, it was an opportunity not to be passed over. At this rate he'd soon have more firepower than a small European country. That gave him an idea.

Jessica ran over. 'Are you okay?'

'Never better.' Virgo went through the dead guy's pockets. 'What about you? How's retirement?'

'So-so. Kind of boring.'

Virgo dumped the goon's personal effects on the ground. Wallet. Disposable lighter. Pocketknife. Rolling papers. Cell phone with a locked screen. He wasn't sure what he was looking for. Something that might suggest where Rinker had gone. There was no Harley here on the Bender estate or any sign of a dark hooded figure.

They walked over towards the front door of the mansion. It was clear that the female body lying outside was not Margaret Bender. It was dressed all in white. When they got there, Virgo gently rolled her onto her back. Myra. Dead on her own special day. It was hard to feel sorry for someone who not long ago had been intending to end the life of an innocent person, but Virgo tried his best. She was just a kid. Tricked into a fool's errand and not equipped to deal with Rinker's gang or anybody else who had a firearm. He called Mrs. Bender and told her it was safe to come out.

While they waited, Jessica said, 'What are we going to do about Casey?'

'Only thing we can do,' said Virgo. 'A thunder run.'

'Meaning?'

'In the Army, the term *thunder run* has two meanings. It's either a bar crawl or an unexpected incursion deep into enemy territory.'

Jessica put a green fingernail to her lips. 'I guess we're not doing the bar crawl?'

CHAPTER 45

Casey knelt at the side of the bunk and prayed. In silence. Just in case the megalomaniac had installed hidden listening devices. It was the kind of outlandish thing he'd do. Try to tap in to other people's innermost thoughts. Play God. Once she'd thought his reckless approach to the staid traditions of conventional religion was a shaft of celestial light. Exciting. A brightness to blow away the fusty rituals and injustices of the past. Literally, a ray of hope. Now she knew the truth. And it hurt.

How long had it been? Her knees were tender from the rough-textured resin floor of the cell. Her stomach had cramps from not having eaten all day, and her mouth was parched. She scolded herself. Jesus fasted for forty days in the wilderness, and it was churlish of her to complain after only a few meagre hours. Faith would sustain her. There was nothing she could do physically about the fate of her mother. That was in the hands of the Lord. All she could do was keep praying. *Dear Heavenly Father…*

A metallic snap. The door to the cell area opened. The apostle known as James marched in with four of the divine guard. It wasn't a welfare visit. There was no tray of food or even a plastic cup of water. Her heart sank. That meant it was something to do with Nelson and the sham marriage. What if he wanted to consummate it? The blood froze in her veins, and she began to shake. No. Not while she had the strength to fight. Death was a preferable destination, and on her way there, she'd inflict what injury she could on his pathetic body.

One of the guards opened the cell door, and James said, 'The prophet requests your presence.'

Casey remained on her knees. 'I don't want to see him.'

James said, 'You talk like someone who's got a choice in the matter.'

'I have.' Casey lay rigid on her back. Arms at her sides. 'I can walk freely, or you can drag me kicking and screaming. I choose the latter, thank you.'

'Suit yourself, precious. You always were halfway up your own asshole.' James nodded to the four guards, and they went in the cell and took hold of her.

In the event, Casey did not kick or scream. She let them pick her up and carry her out of the detention area because she wanted to conserve every last ounce of energy in case that creep tried to touch her. They carried her along the underground corridor and up into the main quad. Then through an archway on the opposite side and towards the ceremonial chamber. She'd never been inside it before. No one had. Only the apostles. It had the reputation as a place of punishment beatings and playground politics.

The door opened, and they carried her in. Nelson was standing on a raised dais behind a large instrument console. The four divine guards set her down and left the room. James went and stood with the other apostles. That made five of them, and the one known as Simon had a bandage wrapped around his head that wasn't quite enough to stop a trickle of blood leaving his hairline. There was dirt on his tunic, like he'd been rolling on the ground. All of these men, the prophet's most trusted apostles, looked agitated and eager to be anywhere apart from there. Verging on panic.

Nelson was his slick-as-oil self. He smiled wide. Pushed a button, and the walls filled floor to ceiling with videos of him in action. Delivering his teachings in a full range of oratory styles. Calm and considered. Wild and dramatic. Angry. Meek. Avuncular. Fire and brimstone. The human chameleon. Soft classical background music began to play, and the man himself stepped down from his raised platform and skipped towards her in tight pants and Cuban heels.

Casey flinched. 'Stay away from me.'

He chuckled. 'That's no way to speak to your husband on our wedding day.'

'Go fuck yourself.' She closed her eyes. 'Forgive me, Lord.' When she opened them, she saw six rifles stood against the wall and a basket full of handguns. They were too far away. No chance of getting there past the apostles.

'Have you forgotten what holy scripture says about the role of a wife?'

'Being submissive?'

'Yes, and the rest.'

'Try to touch me and I'll gouge your designer eyes out.'

Nelson laughed and pulled some folded paper from his pocket. Opened it out into an A3 sheet and held it up. *Certificate of Marriage.*

Casey said, 'I never signed that.'

'Relax.' Nelson went back in his pocket and produced a lighter. A plain chrome Zippo. 'This marriage is hereby annulled. On account of your apostasy.'

'I still believe in the Lord. It's just you who I now know to be false.'

Nelson flipped the Zippo lid and thumbed the wheel. A

golden flame appeared. He lit one corner of the certificate and held it up. Watched it burn. 'Ashes to ashes…'

Casey had a bad feeling, Something about the demented look on his face. 'Why are you doing this?' Then she realized. Something had changed. There was nothing to be gained from the marriage for him. She smiled. 'They didn't kill my mother, did they?'

Nelson held on to the burning paper until the flames were licking his fingers, then dropped the last corner and stubbed it out with his stack heel. 'Myra turned out to be a big disappointment.'

'Excuse me, sir. I am compelled to speak.' It was the apostle known as Simon. 'It wasn't Myra's fault. The men who work for Mr. Rinker attacked us. None of us are safe here anymore. Including you, the great prophet. We should leave now. Before the other apostles and the rest of the Order turn against us.'

Nelson raised his right hand. 'Patience, my son. Our work here is nearly done. There remains one task for which I need a volunteer.'

The apostles looked at each other. None of them moved.

The music coming from hidden speakers was Wagner. 'Ride of the Valkyries.' Nelson began to march up and down. 'Jesus died to atone for our sins. But sometimes His blood is not enough for the evil we have done. There needs to be an additional sacrifice, and today Sister Myra failed in her mission to spill the Bender blood. Fortunately, we have another sinner from the same family in our midst today.'

'What?' Casey felt faint. Short of breath. 'You're not seriously talking about killing me?'

Nelson ignored her. A feral zeal in his eyes. He stopped in front of the apostles. 'Do I have a volunteer?'

CHAPTER 46

The helicopter was a Sikorsky S-76. It landed two miles northeast of La Esperanza on the site of an abandoned stone quarry. It kicked up a little dust, but the ground here was now mainly plates of bedrock, crisscrossed in the cracks with ryegrass. Virgo watched the door open and a familiar figure climb out, stoop beneath the rotor blades and come towards him on elbow crutches, rucksack on his back. Heavy.

The new arrival had titanium lower legs, and when he reached the pickup, Virgo gave him a man-hug, then turned to Jessica and said, 'Meet Brad Hooper.'

She waited for the blade noise of the chopper to die down as it rose back up and banked away towards the Pacific. 'Some entrance. I'm impressed.'

'My other vehicle's a Learjet.' Hooper slung the rucksack onto the bed of the truck and unfastened the clips.

'He's kidding.' Virgo held the crutches while the bag was emptied. 'What have we got?'

Hooper lined up six grenades. 'I wasn't exactly sure what

you had in mind. So I brought a selection. Fragmentation. Concussion. Smoke. Two of each.'

Virgo said, 'I'm thinking of a thunder run.'

'You mean a penetration maneuver into enemy territory without prior reconnaissance, intended to exploit the element of surprise and seize whatever tactical opportunities present themselves once inside?' Hooper whistled. 'How many hostiles?'

'Five or six equipped with Armalites and maybe twenty other guards, weaponry unknown.'

Hooper laughed. 'And two of us?'

Jessica said, 'Three.'

Hooper turned and glared at her.

Virgo said, 'Don't argue, Brad. She's okay for an ex-cop.'

'Says the ex-con.' Jessica pulled a tight smile and pointed to the grenades. 'I don't suppose you've got a Federal Explosives License for those things?'

Hooper said, 'Once a cop, always a cop.'

Virgo said, 'Brad's a dealer. He trades in a very specialized area of the market.'

'Munitions are my thing.' Hooper gestured to his prosthetics. 'They blew my legs off, so I reckoned they owe me a living. I buy and sell. Some of it legit from soldiers with approved bring-back papers, some not. The guy in the Sikorsky who dropped me off is one of my best customers.' Hooper reached inside the rucksack and pulled out two short-barreled Sig Spears. 'He lent me these.'

'Put them back in the bag, Brad.' Virgo sighed and shook his head. 'I just want to get Casey out of there, not machine-gun to death a bunch of misguided kids.'

'What about if we just take them as backup?'

'No.'

'Please yourself.'

'And no frag grenades. We only need the stun and smoke.'

'Shit.' Hooper began to reload the rucksack. 'You don't like to make it easy for yourself, do you?'

They traveled in the pickup down the valley to La Esperanza. Hooper drove. Virgo rode shotgun. Jessica chewed gum in the back seat and stared out the side window. Virgo turned to ask her if she was alright, but saw the faraway look in her eyes and decided to leave her to her own thoughts. Maybe she was worried about Joey and what he would do with himself if anything happened to her. Bullets don't discriminate between a parent and a childless adult. What could he do? He knew there was no point trying to talk her out of being part of the team.

How long ago was it that he'd broken the guy's arm in the office of Artemis Associates? It was half a week, but felt like half a lifetime. He smiled to himself. What had she called him? A moron? He had only been trying to help, but she had too much stubborn self-respect to let him. Now her business was gone, and the future was uncertain. He wished there was something he could do to make things work out for her. She deserved it. But sometimes there's an unfairness in the world that punishes hard work and enterprise, and rewards bullshit and luck.

Traffic was backing up in the main square. Late afternoon and some of the artisan stores had closed. Tourists and locals were transiting to where their evening lay ahead of them. Home. Restaurants. A bar. Hotel suites or inns and vacation rentals. In the park, stalls were being assembled for the night market, and already the air was thick with the smell of charcoal. Cases of wine lined up on trestle tables. Jars of wildflower honey and baskets full of cookies. Another day in paradise drawing to a close.

They made it around the square and began to climb the

road out towards the Templar Sanctorum. Virgo's brain went into flashback mode again. This time it was nearly twelve years ago. Brad Hooper was driving, just as now, but Virgo was in the back. They'd just left Hamdan military airport and were on the highway toward Abu Kabal in Syria. Something was different. There were no little kids begging for candies or older ones chasing cigarettes. It was a sign that should have been heeded. Because that was when the IED blew the Special Operations Vehicle into the ditch. The sergeant in the front seat lost his life. Brad Hooper his feet. And for what? The world was no safer.

Virgo blinked his way back into the present. The three-domed bell tower of the People's Order of Gabriel was visible through the trees on the left. They were closing in on the gateway to the compound. Time for the thunder run. Five hundred yards. Four. Three. Two. One. Hooper didn't slow down. He threw the RAM TRX across the highway and into the entrance. Straight at the barrier. Two guards slack-jawed it, then dived out of the way. *Crunch.* The front of the pickup snapped the red and white pole as if it were an Italian breadstick.

A siren sounded. The vehicle roared through an avenue of oaks and into the central lawned area made up of concentric circles from which paths radiated. To the left, the accommodation blocks. Ahead, the lake and Nelson's residence. To the right, the main mission building. Hooper drove onto the grass, and the chunky all-terrain tires cut up the turf and sent clumps flying in their wake. Then he slewed the Ram through one-eighty degrees and said, 'Okay. I'll wait here. But if you're not back in five minutes, the Sig Spear comes out of the rucksack.'

Virgo jumped out of the pickup, four grenades on his belt, the Glock in his hand. Jessica joined him. No sooner had their feet hit the ground, the fire doors of the accommodation blocks burst open, and a stream of people started to leave. Some with cases. Others carrying nothing but grips and purses. A few ran, but most speed-walked with a fierce determination on their face, as though they were late for a train or cutting in line for Super Bowl tickets.

A guard, dressed in black pants and tunic, tried to block the route, but was bundled over and beaten. The two guards who'd dived out of the Ram's way at the barrier came racing in, saw what was happening and stopped in their tracks. Threw down their batons and merged into the flow of members hightailing it out of the place. Authority had broken down. It was a phenomenon Virgo had witnessed in other parts of the world when tin-pot regimes collapsed, and was generally something to be welcomed, except for one thing. It was always the most dangerous phase in the process of change.

Beyond the lake, a plume of smoke spiraled into the sky and was carried away on a Santa Ana towards the ocean. Nelson's private residence. It had been torched, and it wouldn't take the late-summer wind long to whip it up into a destructive inferno. Where was Casey? Still in the detention cells under the main mission building, or had he taken her back to his mansion?

Two utility vehicles came haring over the bridge. Ignored the circular pathways and cut straight across the flowerbeds. Virgo watched them drive straight towards him, and soon registered their red uniforms. He had the Glock ready, but there was something about the party approaching that told him they weren't a threat. No firearms visible. No attempt to protect themselves. No electric impulses running down the length of his spine that always came when he sensed that someone might be a suicide bomber.

The two carts pulled up, carrying a mixture of apostles and guards. They all jumped out, and one of the guys dressed in red said, 'We don't care if you want to kill him or arrest him. We want to help.'

Virgo said, 'Where's Casey Bender?'

The guy saw Virgo glancing towards the smoke. 'It's okay, she's not in there. Everyone who's left is in the mission.'

'Who are you?'

'I was the apostle Matthew, but my real name is Troy.'

'Okay, Troy.' Virgo gestured to the main building. 'What have we got in there?'

'Apart from Nelson? Maybe five apostles and a dozen guards who are still loyal. But they've got control of the armory.'

'What about the rest of the guards and members of the Order?' Virgo nodded to the stream of people leaving the accommodation blocks.

Troy gave a bitter laugh. 'We told everyone about the baptisms. How they were all set up. The loyalty library was just a clever control job.'

'They saw the light. Hallelujah.' Virgo pointed his gun at the mission building. 'Is there another way in there apart from through that archway?'

'There's a back door into the church and depository where the safe is. Only Nelson and John Rinker have a key.'

'If it's a way in, it's also a way out.' Virgo turned to Jessica. 'You cover it.'

She gave him a suspicious look. 'What are you going to do?'

'I'll take the main archway.'

'Whoa.' Troy shook his head. 'There's walled balconies all around the quad. It's real fortified. As soon as you go in there, you'll be a sitting duck.'

Virgo smiled. 'Sometimes you've got to take a risk. It's

God's way of making you appreciate the mundane bits of life.'

'Go through that arch, you can thank Him personally because you'll be dead,' said Troy. 'Of course, that's assuming your soul ascends to Heaven and doesn't go the other way.'

CHAPTER 47

Casey stared at the five apostles, and not one of them could look her in the eye. They were jittery. Sweating. Each focused on saving their own skin and scared they'd made the wrong decision in sticking with the leader and founding father of the People's Order of Gabriel. Was it too late? Occasionally, a couple of them glanced at one another, checking for any sign of a mutiny, but none of them wanted to be the first and take the lead in case nobody else followed. There would be violence and bloodshed. No one fancied becoming a martyr.

Nelson went behind the console and came back with a knife. Huge black blade with a serrated edge curving up into a point. Rambo special. He laid it flat across both upturned palms, like he was presenting a tray of consecrated bread and wine for holy communion, and held it out before the apostles. This time he shouted. 'The prophet wants a volunteer. I shall not ask again.'

Nobody moved. Silence apart from Wagner's opera. The Valkyries still escorting the souls of fallen heroes to Valhalla.

Casey closed her eyes and prayed. Held her breath.

Wished it had all been a dream or a play within a play where the characters take off their wicked masks to reveal it was just a piece of light-hearted metadrama. She wished that the apostles might realize that their time was up. The hours they'd spent competing with each other to be the one with the brownest nose had been for nothing. Maybe they might feel some humility. Regret treating people below them in the organization as though they were genetically inferior.

Still nobody spoke. Casey dared not open her eyes. Maybe the sight of the ugly black steel knife had turned their stomachs. It was one thing to shoot a bullet, another to stick a blade into someone's vital organs or cut their throat. And these were guys who hadn't even fired a bullet. All they'd done was stand behind idiots like her and film them shooting a gun. Real heroes. Maybe they'd spend the rest of their days terrified of a knock on their own front door. It would be poetic justice.

The wait was torture. All she could see was the last thing she'd been looking at when she'd closed her eyes. The outline image of Daniel Nelson imprinted on the back of her eyelids, like a cheap Turin shroud. All she could smell was the burnt remnants of her own marriage certificate on the floor and fear – her own and that of the apostles. And that was when she heard the four words that signaled the end of her life on earth. 'I will do it.'

Casey opened her eyes. Please, no. Be a mistake. Please, no…

It was the apostle known as Simon. 'I will do it.' He stepped forward. 'It was my duty to supervise the baptism of Sister Myra, and I was weak. Now I am strong again.'

'Thank you, my son.' Nelson pulled an exultant smile and proffered the knife. 'It is a noble thing you do.' Then when Simon had taken the weapon from his hands, he threw his arms up in the air and addressed the others. 'Rejoice. The

Lord has chosen one of you to be his avenging angel. To deliver unto Him the blood sacrifice. Rejoice, rejoice, rejoice…'

The fear in Casey's chest melted away. She looked at Nelson trying to turn the others into cheerleaders for her own murder and could take no more. She ran at him and punched him on the nose. Threw an arm round his neck and yanked out a clump of hair. He was only an inch taller than her, but stronger. He dropped a shoulder and shook her off onto the floor. She jumped straight back up and went at him again. This time flinging her fists wildly at his face. Not really connecting. The energy seeped out of her muscles, and then it was over.

She was on her back. Four apostles had grabbed her, and now they each had a limb. Pinning her down. She was out of breath. Spent. A figure stood over her, silhouetted against the lights in the ceiling of the chamber. Simon. He dropped to his knees, both hands on the handle of the black knife. Then he raised it above his head. The point directly above Casey's chest.

Nelson shouted, 'Not here. On the altar. Take her to the church.'

Casey closed her eyes again and prayed once more. Then it happened. *BANG. BANG. BANG.* The ground shook. The whole building vibrated. It was like World War III had just started in a sleepy wine-growing valley of Central California. Or the Lord had sent a bolt of lightning.

CHAPTER 48

The guards on the balcony fired down into the smoke-filled quad, but the M84 grenade had done its job. Caused them to become temporarily disoriented by the deafening noise and the eight megacandela explosion of light. Flash blindness. When they regained their senses, the two smoke grenades had turned the central courtyard area below into a swirling sea of fog. The bullets they fired into it were wasted because Virgo was already up on the balcony.

Top of the steps, the first guard had his back to him. Leant over the balustrade, staring down into the smoke. An easy target. Virgo darted up behind him in a crouch. Grabbed his ankles and lifted him over the edge. The drop was only twenty feet, but it was enough. By the time of impact, momentum would have flipped the body over to land on its back. Severe spinal or head injury.

The dull noise was enough to divert more gunfire down into the quad. The smoke grenades were white phosphorus, not the normal solid-filler ones. They were designed to provide instantaneous concealment, but their duration was less. Virgo knew he didn't have long. Ten yards to his right came the *pop-pop* of firearm discharge. Short barrel. Standard caliber.

The problem with concealment in a combat situation is it works both ways. The thick luminous smoke and heat from the phosphorus had now risen to balcony level. Virgo had to approach an unseen enemy. He moved quick. Silent. Homed in on the *pop-pop*. Out of the murk, a black figure loomed into view and swung a handgun around in his direction. Too late. Virgo's shoulder drove into the guard's ribcage and sent him flying backwards off his feet into a huge ornamental vase. The guy's lungs fought for air. Winded. Virgo had the opportunity to finish the guard off with a bullet but chose to put him to sleep with a vascular neck clamp.

When he stood back up, the smoke was starting to clear. Maybe he should have used a slug on the last guard instead of wasting valuable seconds. He heard shouts. Risked a tentative look over the balustrade. There were figures in the haze below. Casey. Four red-suited apostles carrying her, as she bucked and spat. Nelson leading the way. No doubt where they were heading. The church.

Plink. A round took a chunk of stucco out of the wall three feet behind Virgo's head. Visibility was returning to normal. The bullet had come from a guard on the balcony on the other side of the quad. Directly opposite. Three more of the black ninjas, all armed. Virgo returned fire. Using the polished marble balustrade to rest the barrel of the Glock. The guard who'd fired was only twenty-five yards away. One bullet and he was dead.

The three other guards started to run. Virgo watched and waited. He expected them to make a left and left again. Get onto his side of the quad and use their numerical advantage in a shoot-out. They didn't. The three black figures disappeared down the stairwell and out into the quadrangle. Then ran straight through the arch and away.

They'd had enough. Virgo had encountered soldiers with poor motivation before. It was down to bad leadership, poor training, no discipline and low team morale. In this instance, it also looked like the whole People's Order had lost faith in the cause. The king had got no clothes on. The only question was, why had it taken so long for them to notice?

He moved quickly to the church end of the quadrangle. Looking for a staircase to take him down. Nothing. He tried a couple of doors with huge iron handles. Locked. Then the next one turned, the door opened, and he stepped into a world of celestial light and soft choral music. He was in the church. High up in a roof gallery looking down the full length of the nave to where the massive cross towered over the altar. But then a feeling of dismay punched him in the guts. Was he too late?

Nelson was in the pulpit. Head back and arms wide open, in a show of thanks to the heavens. Before him in the chancel, four apostles knelt with their heads bowed. Armalite rifles slung around onto their backs. A fifth apostle stood in front of the altar, gripping some kind of oversized commando knife in both hands. The blade was raised above his head, as if waiting for a signal. Laid out on the ornate oak altar was Casey Bender. Wrists and ankles bound. Not moving. Resigned to her fate.

Virgo shouted, 'Hey. You with the knife. Is this what you signed up for?'

The kid turned and looked up. The rest of the apostles jumped to their feet and scrabbled to get their semi-automatics back in position. Nelson looked like he'd seen a ghost or maybe Beelzebub himself.

'Is it?' Virgo removed the primary and secondary pull rings from the last grenade on his belt. 'Let me tell you something. She's not a sacrificial lamb, and that fucking clown in the pulpit is not the son of God. It's over. The end. Judgment Day.'

Bullets began to come his way. They hammered into the huge organ pipes at the rear of the gallery. Ricochets rang out. The high notes fizzed; the deep ones resonated throughout the entire edifice. They were just the gentle orchestral prelude for what was to come next. When the M84 exploded in the central aisle, the noise level went off the scale and kept going. By the time the apostles realized that they'd not actually been killed by a nuclear blast, Virgo had climbed down to their level and was behind a row of pews, firing with an accuracy that only comes from experience in combat situations.

First to take a hit was the guy with the knife. It had a nasty-looking blade, but no contest for a 9mm round-nose bullet. Virgo felt no regret. The number one objective of the operation was to preserve the life of Casey. No time to stay still. Fire and move. He scrambled five yards left behind the wooden benches and fired again. Another apostle down. This time he saw Nelson drop down behind the lectern of the pulpit. Maybe it was bulletproof, like the Popemobile after John Paul 11 was shot in Saint Peter's Square. It was tempting to pump a few rounds into it and check the theory, but he'd only got five left in the mag. *Pop, pop, pop.* The AR-15s of the three remaining apostles rang out. The acoustics of the church doing its job.

Virgo returned fire. Two taps. Both wide of their mark. That left three. He scrambled to his right and dived headlong on the polished parquet floor. Slid to where a Doric column supported the vaulted ceiling. Fired twice more. Took cover and waited. He needed to make ground to the front of the church. There was a crash behind him. *Shit.* The main doors flew open. A group of guys ran in firing weapons. Red and black. Rebel apostles and guards led by Troy. Virgo was in danger of getting caught in the crossfire. He ran to the far edge of the church and down a side aisle.

The noise grew. It had become a firefight to the death. One of the final three loyal apostles went down in a hail of bullets. The other two kept shooting and making their way towards a side door. Virgo saw his chance. Nelson. He ran behind the altar. Charged around the lectern into the pulpit. Left hand joining his right on the handle of the Glock, ready to discharge its one remaining round into the man responsible for this whole fucked-up mess. *No.* Nothing. The pulpit was empty. There didn't seem to be any obvious way out apart from the door at the back of the sanctuary, and he'd not seen it open. Maybe this guy really was a miracle worker.

The body of the apostle who had been about to kill Casey lay at the foot of the altar. Virgo picked up the fallen knife and cut the thick plastic cable ties on her wrists and ankles. The words she mouthed were lost in the cacophony of gunfire. Something in her eyes screamed danger. Virgo spun round. Nelson was there. Bent down, relieving a dead apostle of their semi-automatic. Its lanyard was trapped under the torso of the corpse. He yanked it with surprising strength, and the strap snapped. He brought the barrel up. *Bang.*

Virgo fired first. The Glock's final round hit Nelson square in the chest and threw him backwards. The assault rifle flew out of his hands and skittered across the herringbone tiles to the far end of the chancel. It was over. The madman's reign as the new messiah and leader of the People's Order of Gabriel. Gunfire in the church had become more sporadic, but still a threat. Virgo helped Casey down from the altar. She was in shock. Breathing rapid. Skin blue. Legs not responding.

'Hey.' Virgo heard a shout and turned. Nelson had gone. *What the…* More shouting. The rear door of the sanctuary was open. The one that led to the nitazene factory. Virgo sat Casey down. Then ran into the back room. A hooded figure, gun in one hand, gym bag in the other. Rinker. The door to a large standalone safe was open. Strips of pills strewn all around. Piles of boxes and tea chests. A rotary tablet press on wheels in the middle of the room. No sign of Nelson. There was an outside door wide open, and Rinker ran out.

Virgo went after him. Jessica was out there. It was one of the doors she'd been covering. He got as far as the pill press. Then something hard whacked him in the face. From nowhere. He dropped to his knees. Reeling. Brain flirting with tripping the circuit breaker of consciousness. *No. Not now. Not now. Not…*

Nelson stood over him. A ceremonial mace in his hands. Four feet of steel stave with a bulbous gold head. He swung it again, and the pear-shaped end caught Virgo under the chin and sent him crashing onto his back. Nelson planted one of his heavy platform boots on Virgo's neck and glared down with unbridled hatred. He took the mace back over his shoulder in a two-handed grip for the final coup de grâce. Paused at the top of his backswing. 'You cost me my worldly goods, but you cannot defeat me in battle. I have the Lord on my side.'

Virgo swiped the boot from his throat. 'The Nazis sprayed *Gott Mit Uns* on the sides of their tanks. How did that work out for them?'

Nelson swung the stave. The bulbous end hurtled down. Virgo grabbed Nelson's left foot and twisted it one-eighty degrees. It was at the exact point in a right-handed swing where weight transfers from one foot to the other. Left was now load-bearing. Nelson couldn't adjust his body. The knee ligaments snapped. He yelped. The tip of the mace made contact with fresh air. Now he was on his back.

Virgo rolled on top. Rammed a knee into the pit of Nelson's stomach and ripped open his shirt, which had a neat nine-mil bullet hole. A Kevlar covert vest. No miracle. The prophet had obviously been expecting trouble and had taken precautions.

'Stop.' Pain contorted Nelson's face as he tried to smile. 'We can do a deal. How much do you want?'

'I used to negotiate with murderers for a living, but not anymore.' Virgo punched him in the mouth. Three times. Clubbing right fists. Smile gone.

He dragged Nelson back into the church. The packet of heavy-duty cables ties used to bind up Casey were at the side of the altar. He used a couple to truss him up. Checked on Casey, then went back into the pill factory to see if he could get on Rinker's scent and chase him down.

The outside door was still open. He raced through it into late afternoon shadows. Nothing moved. No sign of Rinker. The rear of the main mission building was set out like a garden of remembrance. Long rectangle of lawn. Fountain at the far end. Two symmetrical lakes in the middle. Pathways all around with benches, ornamental hedges and granite statues. The garden had eight entrances comprised of arched trellises covered in clematis and bougainvillea. Multiple concealment positions.

Maybe one day, it was going to be the People's Order of Gabriel private cemetery. Now it was a maze that required searching. Virgo worked clockwise. Walking fast, not running. Head constantly on the swivel. He'd almost completed the full circuit when he saw something on the flagstones. Blood. Definitely blood. A pool, then sprayed droplets. Jessica? He started to follow it, but the trail cut across grass and became difficult to discern. It seemed to be heading for one of the eight arched trellises, then disappeared.

He was about to go through and see if he could pick it up again when a voice made him stop. 'Help, help...' It was Casey. She was standing by the outside door of the pill factory. Horror written in the lines of her forehead. 'In the church.' She turned back inside.

Virgo went after her. Through the back room where the nitazene powder had been adulterated and pressed into tablet form. Into the sanctuary. There were no gunshots. *Wait. Not again...* Nelson had gone. The spot where he'd left him barely conscious and turkey-tied was empty. Maybe he was some kind of magician. Then he saw Casey's face and followed the direction of her tormented eyes.

The body of Daniel Nelson was high up on the cross. Fastened with cable ties. Neck, arms and ankles. The Kevlar vest that had saved him once rucked up on the left side. The handle of the commando knife stuck out at an angle. Its blade up under the ribcage into the heart. The flesh on the false prophet's face was pulled back in one terminal cry of agony. Taut. Now more jaundiced than tanned. In death, the perfect teeth turning him into the screaming skull from a low-budget horror movie. A fitting end for a counterfeit messiah.

Virgo surveyed the scene of carnage that this one man was responsible for. Twelve or more bodies. Dead or dying. Once all trusted and loyal. What had he done to turn them against each other? Like all dictators, had he morphed into someone willing to do anything to remain in power? Ruthless. Tyrannical. Evil. History is full of examples, and the People's Order was just a microcosm. But the oppressed will rise up. Troy and his band of rebels were just the latest in a line of liberators, though possibly the first to actually crucify their oppressor.

There was no time for schadenfreude. Virgo ran back through the pill factory and picked up the blood trail. It came and went. Out through an archway. Round the side of the mission building. There were contact smears of blood along the stucco wall, as though someone had leant on it to keep upright and aid movement. A larger deposit on a sandstone paver where they'd paused to rest. Around the corner. Under the fronds of a row of young fan palms. Past a reproduction well that had been made to look like a relic, then into a small square of mosaic tiles. And that was where he saw her spreadeagle on the ground. Jessica.

Virgo ran over and made an initial assessment. Gunshot wound upper left chest. Major hemorrhage. Weak pulse. Stage one hypovolemia. Decreased cognitive function. 'You're going to be fine,' he lied.

Jessica opened her eyes. Tried to talk. Her lips moved, but no sound came out.

Virgo said, 'Rinker?'

She made a barely perceptible nod. Closed her eyes.

'Hey.' Virgo took her hand in his. 'My turn. Stay with me. Come on, stay with me.'

Jessica squeezed his hand. A faint increase in pressure that came from an inner strength, and her mouth tried to form a word. This time she managed to produce a breathless whisper. She just said, 'Joey…'

CHAPTER 49

It was pushing six hours since the sun rose over the Sierra Nevada mountains. Virgo scanned the horizon through the Nikon binoculars for any sign of movement. Nothing. The highway and dirt track leading to the ranch were both clear. No matter. He could wait. Patience and resilience were in his genes. Baked in. At some point, John Rinker would appear, and he would be ready to complete the job. Find. Fix. Finish.

When Virgo had applied to join that most secretive of special forces known only as The Activity, he was unsure what qualities he had to offer them. Primarily, they wanted linguists and knob-turners to intercept communications and run foreign intelligence sources. It transpired they were also after soldiers who could operate for days on end without sleep and kill opponents if necessary to achieve the primary objective of the mission. They called it *operational preparation of the battlespace*. It was this skill got him through A and S – assessment and selection.

Training involved parachuting into the middle of a desert with no food. No means of communication. No map.

Covering fifty miles in a day and surviving on strength and initiative. It was all preparation for what was to come: the hours of covert reconnaissance inside enemy territory. When US Navy SEAL Team Six stormed the compound in Pakistan and killed HVT-1 – high-value target number one – Osama Bin Laden, it was because The Activity had paved the way. All yours, glory boys – come and take the credit.

Today's target was not the head of an international terrorist organization. Rinker had no political axe to grind or religious message he wished to spread around the globe. The only reason he did not value the lives of other people was purely personal – money – and he did not seek fame or notoriety. On the contrary, his entire criminal life had been devoted to flying under the radar. He was about to find out that true anonymity does not exist in the age of modern technology. Rinker had moved to a new ranch, but Virgo still knew some knob-turners who could locate the most careful and elusive of fugitives. Phase one – find – had been completed six days ago.

Virgo checked the G-Shock on his wrist. Temperature eighty-three degrees and minimal breeze. It was shaping up to be a perfect day for a kill. He was on a plateau two hundred meters from the property. A renovated farm building surrounded by chaparral. Virgo was in a spider hole he'd dug at three o'clock in the morning. Not so deep as a foxhole. Covered by camouflaged webbing. A person could walk directly by and not spot he was there unless they happened to have help from the nose of a bloodhound or retriever.

In the two weeks since the shoot-out and crucifixion that marked the demise of the People's Order, he'd toyed with the idea of handing Rinker over to the police to deal with. Sergeant Chambers no longer posed a problem. He'd blown his brains out with a service handgun in his bedroom the morning a SWAT team surrounded his house. But life in a prison cell was too good for Rinker. He wouldn't be the first to maintain a drugs importation and distribution business from behinds bars. No, he had to be eliminated.

It was President Ford in 1976 who signed the first executive order banning any employee of the US government from carrying out an assassination, but Virgo was no longer a federal agent, and Rinker was not a politician. This was a war, and on the battlefield the rules are different. Do what the enemy least expects. Surprise is an underestimated tactic and is often the most effective way for a small unit to overcome much larger forces. Rinker was about to get a bolt from the blue.

Virgo rechecked the view through the scope. The gun was a Springfield M25 White Feather. The latest sniper rifle of the US Special Forces and loaned to him by Brad Hooper's Sikorski-owning customer. It had a Krieger carbon-steel barrel and a fiberglass McMillan stock. Fitted with a Leupold tactical scope and ten .308 Winchester rounds in the mag. The most accurate self-loading firearm in the world? Probably. In any case, not an issue at this range. Aim and squeeze the two-stage trigger.

Over the course of the past fourteen days, he'd sat for hours with Joey at Jessica's bedside in the hospital and contemplated how he would kill John Rinker. The obvious method that he kept coming back to was doing to Rinker what Rinker had done to him: Tie him to a chair, inject him with shit and watch him die. Seemed a no-brainer. The other alternative was to beat him to death with his bare hands. More painful for Rinker. More cathartic for Virgo.

But in the end, he dismissed both options. They attributed too much significance to Rinker as a human being. The man was a rodent to be exterminated, the same as any other piece of vermin that spreads disease and destruction. Quick. Painless. Minimum mess. Dispatched without ceremony so that everyday life could continue in a more clean and healthy environment.

Virgo opened the mapping app on his cell to view the current location of the target. Three miles and closing. ETA four minutes, forty seconds. Rinker was astute and surveillance-conscious. He kept the use of his cell to a minimum and switched it off when not in use. But he didn't take out the battery or SIM. The knob-turners could access a phone remotely and plant a virtual bug. That was how Virgo knew that Rinker had set off from Brownsville, Texas, two days ago and spent last night at an address in Phoenix. Tracking and control of the target meant phase two – fix – had been completed.

Just time to take on board a small amount of fuel. Virgo unpeeled and ate a banana. Placed the skin back into his rucksack. When he left the scene, there would be absolutely no trace he'd ever been there. The cops wouldn't bust a gut to find out who'd smoked a major trafficker, but Virgo didn't want to take any risks. He'd already spent sixteen hours in police custody following the shoot-out at the compound. Ultimately, it was Casey's witness statement that had exonerated him, and of course, it helped that the two sets of apostles had been trying to blast each other into the next life.

Troy and two of the other red rebels were still on the run. No doubt stopping off somewhere for laser treatment to remove their angel tattoos because nobody wants to be branded for the rest of their days as a loser who thought that a scumbag like Nelson was the Second Coming. Except Casey. She'd kept the ink on her arm as a reminder that isolation from family and friends can make a person vulnerable to manipulation. Everyone needs support.

ETA one minute, twenty-five seconds. Virgo scanned the highway. Any time now. He saw three vehicles approaching from the south. Pickups in convoy. He watched them come up through the shimmer of the valley air and onto the plateau. Turn left onto the track leading to the ranch. Dust cloud in their wake. If this had been Afghanistan or Syria back in the day, he would have called *strike*, and a Predator drone overhead would have unleashed a Hellfire missile, but today he had to rely on the accuracy of his own hand-eye co-ordination. The stability of his nerves.

Army Sniper School was located at Fort Moore, Georgia. He'd not done the full seven-week course, but had trained with their instructors and knew the key principles that affected bullet trajectory. Distance, windspeed, humidity, temperature and the specific ballistic characteristics of the bullet. They'd all been factored in and the scope adjusted accordingly. All he had to do was aim for the center of the target area.

Virgo settled into position. Slowed his breathing. Used the optical scope on the rifle to watch the vehicles travel the final section of track and pull up in front of the ranch. This was the only point where something could frustrate the goal of the mission. If the pickups parked side by side and the occupants disembarked in a certain order, there was a chance their bodies could shield the target until he was inside the property. It was unlikely. Virgo had calculated that the target would be in the passenger seat of the middle vehicle and had chosen his position on that basis. He watched and waited. Bingo. He was right.

A hooded figure climbed out and looked directly in his direction. The target. They say that terrorist leaders who are about to be taken out by covert special forces always seem to sense at the last second that their time has come and glance towards their nemesis. Maybe Rinker just had a feeling that he was in the crosshairs.

It was the third and final phase of the operation – finish.

No hesitation. Virgo pulled the trigger. Headshot. John Rinker was dead before the recoil of the rifle had dissipated. Another soul gone to plead their case in front of the ultimate arbiter.

Virgo knew the time would come when he had to face his own judgment day. Not everything in life is black and white, and he'd worked his fair share of gray areas. The highest court in the land is your own conscience, and his told him that he'd done the right thing. Whether that counted for anything in the next life, he didn't know. Nobody knows. Scientists can explain everything in the universe except religion and the human heart.

CHAPTER 50

Max yawned and dried a glass. It was the graveyard shift in the Shakespeare craft beer and sports tavern. Monday, a little after 4 p.m. A curly-haired hipster woman in the corner was knitting a fat scarf, and there was an old guy in a window seat who'd fallen asleep with his chin on his chest. The place was really rocking.

Virgo watched Jessica suck a small dash of margarita through a pink flamingo straw. It looked like a real effort. He said, 'You really shouldn't drink while you're still on the meds.'

'Come on. You can't have a celebration without a little booze.'

'What did Margaret Bender offer you?'

'Artemis Associates are now security consultants to the Bender family. Not a full-time role, but she'll pay a monthly retainer, which means I can take on other cases and still have financial security.'

'That's great. You deserve it.'

Virgo tapped the neck of his Bud on the rim of her cocktail

glass. *Cheers*. It was only six hours since he'd collected her from the Sierra Vista Medical Center, and he couldn't help noticing Jessica didn't seem her buoyant and sassy self, even though she'd just had the good news about her business. Certainly not like someone who was out on a celebration. Maybe she was tired. You can't spend five weeks in hospital without some muscle wastage and general fatigue. Then they'd gone straight to the Bender estate for her to finalize her new business contract.

He'd been at Jessica's bedside on the occasions when Casey had visited the hospital, so it wasn't the first time he'd seen her since the demise of the People's Order, but it was good to see her actually back in the family home with her mother. Even playing tennis again, but now strictly for fun. She'd not lost her faith, but it had changed. Softened. She wore it less openly and avoided the subject where possible. It might get tested again when she had to testify as a witness and relive the horrors of what took place within the surreal and sadistic confines of the People's Order of Gabriel, but that was possibly months away.

Jessica leaned forward and put a hand on his. 'I can't thank you enough for keeping an eye on Joey.'

'It was no big deal. He's a good kid.'

'Even so, I owe you.'

'Do you think?' Virgo laughed. 'Where would I be without your one-woman rescue mission in the barn and Joey's inhaler?'

'It was down to you that I took the just-in-case bag off him.'

Virgo took a pull on his beer and shook his head. 'I still can't believe you managed to be inconspicuous and keep that van under surveillance all the way from the compound to Rinker's ranch. After all I said about your hi-vis hair.'

'I've got a confession.' She made a deliberately bashful

pout. 'I made a phone call and got the address from the police intelligence system.'

'Not the turd?'

'How did you guess? At least I'm not reliant on his child-support payments anymore.'

Max came over with a tray of tapas. Bowls of Manchego and olives, with some tomato bread and ham. Nothing too gourmet and on the house, because he was happy that his best cocktail customer was out of the hospital.

Jessica nibbled on a solitary piece of cheese, but couldn't finish it and pushed her plate away. 'The thing is this, I'm so grateful for everything you've done for me.'

Virgo pulled a rueful smile. There was a *but* coming, and he thought he knew what it was going to be. 'I got you shot. Don't thank me.'

'There's not much to do when you're lying day after day in a hospital bed except think about things.'

'Things?'

Jessica put her hand on his again. 'I think it's time for you to move on.'

He'd been expecting it. There'd been something in her demeanor for a few days that foreshadowed the decision. A hint of melancholy and regret. He said, 'You mean leave altogether? Get the hell out of Dodge?'

'I think it's for the best.'

Virgo wasn't sure what he'd been expecting. There was no plan. His intention was to just hang around spending time together, and maybe they'd pick up again where they'd left off the night they danced in this very bar. Play it by ear and hope everything turned out for the best. Perhaps she'd sensed this lack of clarity and resolve in him. It was still too soon after Crystal.

Even though he knew she was right, he said, 'Are you sure?'

'You're not ready to put down roots.'

'All I know is I feel different to how I felt before I met you.'

'That's good, but what you need to do now is finish your travels. Get it out of your system. Take as long as you need until you feel it's right and proper to commit to another relationship. It might be six months. Could be a year or even two. You'll know when the time is right.'

'To come back here?'

Jessica came round and kissed him on the cheek. 'If you want.'

EARLY MORNING, Virgo headed out on the 101 north, all the way through San Jose, Freemont, Oakland and across the Richmond-San Rafael bridge to Santa Rosa. He took it easy. Not pushing the Winnebago's modest horsepower. The sun was setting when he pulled into an RV park on the coast, halfway between San Francisco and Portland, and hooked up to the mains supply.

He spent the evening listening to music and cooking himself a supper of red snapper tacos. Heavy on the cream and cayenne, but it was still light and zesty. Same as the tunes coming out of his Bluetooth speaker. Beach Boys, Train, Goo Goo Dolls, James Brown and Queen. Nothing downbeat. The tacos were accompanied by a Zinfandel left over from his stay in La Esperanza, which was strong but still mellow on the palate.

Midnight, he lay in bed and listened to the waves. Their timeless rhythm not only soothing the noise in his ear but also giving him reassurance for the future. An almost spiritual presence. Sure, bad things had happened in the past, but he wasn't going to be defined by them. Anyone can let themselves be a victim. The choice is yours. He'd chosen to break free from his chains of adversity and rise above the past, but Jessica was right, he still had a way to go. One day, he might go back and thank her personally, but it was unlikely, because the moment had been and gone. His focus now was to get on with his life and stay out of trouble. It was the second part that could be a problem. A man may recreate himself and improve his persona, but a leopard cannot change its spots. It's the spots that keep it alive in a world full of predators and prey.

ABOUT THE AUTHOR

Did you enjoy *Judgement Day*? Please consider leaving a review on Amazon to help other readers discover the book.

———

Growing up, Steve Sheffield always wanted to be a writer and went to university where he managed to gain a bachelor's degree in English Literature. However, due to spending too much money on drink, he was forced to abandon his literary ambitions and get a job in the police, where the pay was more reliable. He became a detective and worked multiple homicide inquiries and investigations into organized crime, while also completing a master's degree in Criminology. The final seven years of his service in the force, he was head of a specialized crime department responsible for intelligence, surveillance, drugs and undercover operations. These days he writes books about a different kind of investigation and justice — quicker, unorthodox, brutal and generally more satisfying. He still spends too much on drink.

ALSO BY STEVE SHEFFIELD

The Eddie Virgo Series

Zero Hour

Judgement Day

Printed in Great Britain
by Amazon